MY PERFECT MARRIAGE

MY PERFECT MARRIAGE

AJ CAMPBELL

bookouture

Published by Bookouture in 2024

An imprint of Storyfire Ltd.
Carmelite House
50 Victoria Embankment
London EC4Y 0DZ

www.bookouture.com

ISBN: 978-1-83525-136-2
eBook ISBN: 978-1-83525-135-5

For Andy.
Every day spent with you is a blessing.

PROLOGUE

10 JUNE, 6 A.M.

Roberta Splinter tiptoes down the stairs to avoid disturbing her family. She yawns, deeply regretting her offer to drive their friends to the airport to catch an early-morning flight. What had she been thinking? She blames the third bottle of red they polished off last week when today was too far away to think about.

She opens the garage doors. The rising sun radiates a rosy glow across the morning sky. Pulling out of the driveway, she turns onto the country lane leading to her friends' house, a journey as familiar as her reflection.

At the T-junction, she slows. Do the brakes feel a little spongey, or is it her imagination? She must get them checked out – another problem to add to her expanding list. Life has become far too busy – too much nonsense to deal with. And far too many bad apples spoiling the barrel.

Roberta turns her music up loud. You can never go wrong with a blast of Bruno Mars. A perfect choice to fully waken the soul on sleepy mornings.

Turning onto Plough Lane, she accelerates through the

gears, skilfully negotiating the dicey bends of the familiar country roads, but she misjudges the tight right-hand bend.

Desperately battling with the steering wheel, she glances at the speedometer, her heart pounding to see the dial pushing past sixty-five miles an hour – way too fast for any country road.

She should've been concentrating more.

But as Roberta's eyes return to the road, an oncoming car, travelling equally as fast, confronts her.

She swerves, careering at speed towards a huge ancient oak tree; the small wooden crosses adorned with faded photographs and dead flowers at its base show where numerous lives have met a fatal end.

The impact reverberates around the cockpit, a chorus of destruction.

Metal buckles. The beige leather of the seats fragments.

The force flings Roberta around, despite the seat belt trying to secure her in place. Amid the confusion, the instinct to keep alive is all-consuming. Panicked, Roberta thinks of her husband, sleeping peacefully in their bed, oblivious to her plight, as she comes to an abrupt halt, gasping for breath.

Her chest tightens, not with pain, but with an overwhelming desire to survive. Disorientated, her mind races. She just needs to breathe and live. Breathe and live. She doesn't want to die. Not now. Not like this.

But as the terror grows, the less she can summon the strength to free herself. Her eyes water, bulging at the sting of smoke. She can't see properly. Her hand twitches as she tries to wipe her eyes.

Fight. Fight. It's a time to fight for her life. Her strength is fading.

But where's the pain? Shouldn't it be excruciating?

She finally concedes, relaxing for a moment as sadness washes over her. Sleep is calling, tempting her like a warm blanket on a chilly night, but intuition vehemently tells her to stay awake.

Her life can't end like this. She still has so much she wants to achieve. Thoughts of her kids, unaware of the horror, make her want to cry.

She wants to say a proper goodbye...

Just in case she never sees them again.

That can't happen. Stay awake. She must stay awake.

But her eyelids are too heavy, the urge to sleep too appealing. A desperate voice inside her shouts in protest. This can't be it. She has dreams to fulfil, places she wants to see, experiences she wants to share...

Monsters she needs to deal with.

The last she sees as her eyelids drop, surrendering to the endless darkness, is the smoke from the engine igniting into a ball of explosive flames.

ONE

21 JUNE

Ashley can't help studying her husband, standing at the patio doors, from where she is unloading the dishwasher.

He's wearing that white polo shirt. The one she bought him for Christmas. It complements his white trainers with the three blue stripes. He runs his hands through his short, dark hair, damp from the shower. Stretching his arms behind his back, he slides his hands into his jeans pockets. That perfectly contoured butt. It makes her want to squeeze it.

'Are you ready to go, darling?' he asks in his husky voice. A voice she has always found so sexy. 'We'll be late.'

Ashley takes a deep breath. The party is one to be endured, in all honesty, even if it is being thrown by one of the people she is closest to in the village. She glances at the oversized kitchen clock hanging in state, commanding an entire wall of the breakfast room. 'We don't need to leave just yet.'

Danny is a stickler for time. He can't be late. Never. In his book, there's never an excuse for lateness. Punctuality is the easiest thing in life to get right.

'Susie should be here any minute,' she says, referring to her sister, who is coming with them.

He stares out of the patio doors into their garden. 'Did you lock up?'

'I think so.' Did she? She can't remember.

'I'll go and check,' he says in a playfully reprimanding tone.

He takes the key from the ceramic pot on the corner table. She loves that pot. They bought it during a holiday to Greece the summer she was pregnant with Elliot, nine years ago. Danny opens the patio doors. Ashley watches him from the kitchen window. His lean frame that hollers efficiency and control strides purposefully along the garden path to their home office, from where they run their marketing company, Blue Banana Studios. A name she has never particularly liked, but it was Danny's idea. 'Fresh and innovative, it suits the vision I have for us. We've got to be imaginative,' he claimed. Ashley had thought a more conservative name would be more appropriate, but he was adamant.

Danny also christened the small light log cabin 'The Hub' when they had it installed because he said that's where it *all* would happen. It would be the engine room of their empire. Ashley was disappointed at first. She thought the name was more suited to the kitchen, the hub and heart of their family life. Not that she said anything. The names grew on her. He designed The Hub himself from scratch, claiming an ergonomic set-up and optimal natural lighting were key.

Through the kitchen window, Ashley sees Danny try the door to The Hub. It opens.

'Ash, you must make sure you lock up.' Danny returns and throws the key in the pot. 'There's been that spate of burglaries in the village. You forget all the time. It's our world out there, darling,' he says, slightly irritated.

She mutters under her breath. 'I thought it was meant to be safer in the country.' Isn't that one of the main reasons they moved to Thyme End? It was definitely one of the many benefits of living in the country he'd sold to her, along with his mum and dad and brother, who all live in the village, being around for Elliot.

As Danny brushes past her, a trail of his aftershave engulfs her senses. The intoxicating blend of smoky sandalwood. She loves that smell. He hasn't changed it since they met seventeen years ago at university when she was an innocent eighteen-year-old starting out in the world. He was two years older and in his final year. But that didn't matter. He stole her heart and has never given it back.

Popping his head around the kitchen door, he calls up the stairs, 'Come on, buddy. We're going to be late. You don't want to miss the ice cream.'

Ashley checks the text her sister sent earlier. 'Susie left over an hour and a half ago,' she calls out. 'She should be here by now. Probably stuck in traffic.'

The family's Rhodesian Ridgeback, Rufus, saunters over to her. Ashley runs the cold water tap and fills the dog bowl, placing it on his mat.

Danny returns to the patio doors and looks out into the garden. 'It's boiling out there. We need to get some suntan cream on Elliot. I'll sort it.' He taps the pane of glass with his fingers. 'I don't know what the builders were thinking when they built this house. That bed has solid rock under it. They must've dumped all their cast-off rubble and covered it with the thinnest layer of earth they thought they could get away with. Sloppy, that's what that is. Lazy and slapdash.'

'I know. So you've said.' Ashley is amused at how precious he has become over the garden since moving there. He always promised it would be one of his projects when they moved to their dream home. From having little or no interest in plants, flowerbeds or garden centres, he is now bordering on obsessive.

'I'm going to break it all up and plant something to give us some privacy. I'm thinking laurels. Or maybe cypress trees. I read somewhere the other day that cypress signifies the end of a major stage in life and the shift into a world of new choices.'

What's that meant to mean?

Before she has time to ask, Danny turns to a knock at the door. Rufus bolts out of the room. 'I must fit that new doorbell. A job for next weekend.' He has been saying that every weekend since they moved. It's been nine months; forty weeks of hearing the same intention. The doorbell hasn't worked since the day they moved in. Another thing the builders cut corners on. 'Cheap crap. You only get what you pay for,' he has said numerous times.

Danny dashes out of the kitchen to the sound of Elliot thundering down the stairs. Ashley closes the dishwasher, picks up her handbag and follows her husband into the hallway.

'Careful. You'll end up going through the front door.' Danny stretches out his arms to rescue their stumbling child. He throws a giggling Elliot into the air, catches him in his arms, and tickles him vigorously.

He is such a good father – when he's not stressed with work.

'Dad. Stop it.' Elliot laughs uncontrollably, struggling to tear himself away from Danny's powerful grip.

Ashley opens the front door, greeting her sister with a big hug. Rufus tries to join the embrace, nuzzling his wet nose between their legs.

'Sorry I'm late. I got stuck behind a tractor.' Susie rolls her big brown eyes. 'Bloody thing wouldn't go past thirty. How do you put up with them? It'd drive me insane.'

Ashley shares the same brown eyes, but that's where the similarity between them ends. With her short black hair cut pixie-style, petite and delicately sculptured nose, and thick natural lips, Susie sure turns heads everywhere she goes. Not that she's aware. Ashley, on the other hand, has a bumpy nose and shoulder-length blonde hair that is currently a faded pink from the latest dye she hasn't had time to reapply.

'Aunty Susie.' Elliot wriggles himself free from Danny and throws himself at Susie. 'Why haven't you been to see us for so long?'

'I've been busy with work,' Susie says, hugging him tightly.

Danny kisses Susie and glances at his watch. 'We need to get going.'

'I've left my handbag in the car,' Susie says. 'I'll just grab it and meet you out there.'

'Shoes.' Danny picks up Elliot from under his armpits and swings him like a pendulum towards the cupboard by the front door.

'Have you got the present, Mum?' Elliot slips his feet into his trainers.

Ashley nods at the large gift bag by the door. 'The balloons are already in the car. I need to pop to the toilet before we go.'

Danny kisses her on the cheek. 'Be quick.'

Elliot dives for the bag. 'I want to hold it.'

'Take that bag as well.' Danny points to the backpack by the front door. 'I put a towel and a change of clothes in it for you.'

Ashley heads to the downstairs cloakroom to check her hair, wishing she shared her husband and son's excitement about the party. She's so tired today. It's been a busy week. Sundays are meant for relaxing: a pause button to recharge with family time and indulge in reading a book, or work on one of the paintings she has on the go. Danny would tell her to put her feet up if he knew how she felt, and take Elliot on his own. She knows he would. But she can't do that to Elliot. He's been looking forward to his best friend Grace's party for months; he hasn't stopped talking about it.

When Ashley emerges from the toilet, Danny grabs the keys off the console. 'Let's go.'

'I'll drive back.'

'We can get a cab home and pick the car up tomorrow,' he says. 'Then you can relax.'

'We'll see.' Ashley isn't in the mood for alcohol. Usually, she's the first in line for a glass of wine and would agree to leave the car, but she's still got some work to do.

Once they are all in the car, Danny starts the engine. He puts a hand on her knee and squeezes it. 'Have we got everything?'

Ashley nods before turning to look out of the passenger window. 'Just go.'

The sooner they get this over with, the sooner she can get back home.

TWO

Danny drives through the village, where a mixture of time-weathered Georgian houses and terraced cottages with front doors that open directly onto the pavement line either side of the road.

They start singing along to the soundtrack from *Mamma Mia!* Normally, Ashley would join in, much to Danny's comical despair, but she can't find it in herself today. After two miles, Danny pulls into a narrow hedged lane and drives a hundred metres or so until they arrive at two brick pillars supporting tall iron gates announcing the entrance to Lucy and Lee Ellis's estate, Pelham House. A garland of pink balloons the size of a small car arches over the gates.

Susie leans her head between the two front seats. 'Are we going to a wedding or a kids' birthday party?'

Ashley laughs. 'You wait until you see the house.'

The car scrunches up the sand-coloured pea shingle road.

'Can you imagine owning a place this big? Four acres it sits on,' Danny says about the vast country house that he sees as a symbol of success. It leaves him awestruck and envious every time they go there.

Not Ashley, though. Money doesn't impress her. She is more attracted to the simple things in life: a non-conformist who isn't enthralled by grandeur.

'One day.' Danny taps her leg. 'One day, we'll own a pad like this.'

Ashley forces a smile at her husband's relentless ambition. His business aspirations have gone into overdrive lately. Even the house they already have is too big in her mind. All she wants is more children. She blames the stress of trying to build the business empire Danny desires on why she hasn't conceived, although he is adamant he wants another child.

It didn't bother her at first. Elliot was a handful, and their cramped London flat was hardly conducive to a growing family. So she stayed on the pill. But when Elliot began nursery, she stopped taking it. Danny was confident she would fall pregnant straight away. But he was wrong. They've had the tests, but all the prodding and probing revealed there was nothing physically wrong with either of them. So stress can only be to blame in her eyes.

Ashley peers at Lucy and Lee's Georgian-style, double-fronted property with its paired chimneys, multi-pane windows and long, paved walkway that leads to the panelled front door.

'What do they do with all those rooms?' Susie pipes up from the back seat. She tickles Elliot. 'I bet they have some great games of hide-and-seek.'

Elliot squeals with delight, craning his neck to gain a better view. 'Wow! Look at those.' He is referring to a line of giant inflatables. 'Look at Grace at the top of that slide, Mum.' He points to a slide on the lawn to the right of the property, which must be at least eight metres high. On the left of it stands an obstacle course with a bunch of kids bouncing and jumping, and on the other, a huge Disney-themed bouncy castle.

Adults are mingling beneath a mammoth marquee at the back of the display, sipping drinks. A converted van serves wood-fired pizza out of a hatch for the kids. Really? When there's a barbecue on offer too? What happened to sausages in a finger bun? It's overly extravagant for a nine-year-old's birthday party. But that's Lucy Ellis's style. She is not a half-measures kind of woman.

Danny drives to the left of the property, where several cars are parked in front of two double cart lodges. One houses Lucy's cutting-edge BMW and Lee's scarlet Porsche. The other is closed off and used as a garage, above which sit their swish offices, from where they run their successful construction business, Tomorrow's Housing Today. They have several offices scattered around the country, but their roots are planted firmly in the village.

Driven businesspeople, Lucy and Lee have embraced modern-day eco-friendly housing developments – building carbon-negative homes that produce more power than is needed to run them – and have made a killing.

Danny and Lucy have known each other since childhood, and she was instrumental in Ashley and Danny's relocation to the village. Lucy has been Ashley's best friend since they moved there, despite Ashley's belief that you should never mix business with pleasure. But Danny insists that his friendship with Lucy and Lee is as solid as the houses they build.

'Park over there,' Ashley says, pointing to a vacant spot on the fringe of the parking area bordering the pea shingle road. 'We can make a quick exit if need be.'

As soon as they come to a halt, Elliot swings his door wide open and is off, the balloons trailing him towards the merriment.

'You forgot the present,' Susie shouts after him. 'Oh, to be young again.'

Ashley's hand reaches for the car door, frozen mid-motion as Danny's grip catches her arm. She turns around.

'You OK, darling?' he asks.

The sunlight shining through the windscreen catches the

carved dark shadows under his large brown eyes. Come to think of it, he hasn't been himself for the past few weeks. She has put it down to him working late most nights but now wonders if it's more than that.

'Fine. Let's go.' She leans over and kisses him before climbing out of the car to the spirited sound of kids having fun and the alluring scent of charred meat and sweet smoke. Typically, the intoxicating aroma of a barbecue ignites her senses. Danny cooks one most Saturday evenings during the summer months, but today, the smell is overpowering.

Lee's tall, imposing figure approaches them. He's a distinguished-looking man with black-framed glasses that offer an appearance as intelligent as he deserves to look. He steers the conversation towards the ongoing festivities.

There's a shake to his voice. Something is off about him. Ashley senses it immediately. He was OK when she bumped into him in town that morning. Lucy had sent him out for more tonic water and lemonade, and he'd thought it highly amusing that she'd texted him another seven items to add to his list since he'd left home. But now he's trying too hard to be jolly.

'Do you have those tools, Lee? I might as well put them in the car now,' Danny says.

Lee's eyes, ordinarily sharp and focused, seem distant, troubled. 'I'll get them.'

Ashley's eyes narrow, her attention riveted to Lee as he scoots off towards the garage. 'What's up with him?' she says. 'He seems jittery.'

'I thought the same.' Danny nods towards the marquee. 'It's probably the stress of putting on a show like this. I'd be jittery if I was in his shoes.'

Lee reappears clutching a tool bag. 'Here you go.' He opens the bag, his hands unsteady as he showcases the contents to Danny. 'One of these club hammers and bolsters should do the trick.'

'Thanks, mate.' Danny clicks open the boot of his red Audi and dumps the bag inside.

Lee casually drapes an arm around Ashley. His arm is trembling. Or is that her imagination? 'Come and get a drink.' He is talking in a higher pitch than normal and sounds as if he's trying too hard, forcing enthusiasm into his words.

'Are you OK, Lee?' Ashley asks.

'Sure, why?'

'You seem a little on edge.'

He forces a smile, but Ashley can sense the tension in his voice. 'Blame my wife.'

THREE

'What's Lucy done now?' Danny asks with a laugh, trying to lighten the mood.

An awkward pause follows as if Lee is going to say something. Instead, he chews his bottom lip. Ashley stares at him. Lee has always come across as the unflappable type.

'It's nothing. She just has me running around like a lunatic.' Lee ushers them towards the party. 'Go and have fun. I've got some jobs still to do.'

Ashley gives Danny a puzzled look, but he ignores her. They approach the gathering, passing the kids whooping and hollering on the inflatables. Elliot has already kicked off his trainers and stripped down to his swim shorts and is climbing the stairs to the top of the slide with Grace, a blonde girl who looks the image of Lucy.

'Look, Mum,' he calls out, laughing at the excitement of what's to come.

How she admires his love of life. He is so like Danny.

'Where's Susie gone?' Ashley says.

'To the bar, if I know your sister. Go and find a table, and I'll put some cream on Elliot.'

The catchy beat of OMC's 'How Bizarre' spills out from the speakers stationed at the entrance of the marquee. Ashley steps into the bustling tent of around sixty guests engaged in lively banter, the hum of intermingling voices with intermittent raucous laughter playing with her senses. Her gaze instinctively finds Lucy.

With the graceful figure of a model, golden curls that ripple as she walks, and large baby-blue eyes, Lucy Ellis is a woman impossible to miss. She is a well-known figure in the local community and, judging by the packed marquee, seems to have invited everyone who is someone. You'd never think the party was to celebrate her daughter's ninth birthday. A successful businesswoman, mother of three, PTA chair of the village school, and an avid baker for local fundraising events, Lucy is a woman whose accomplishments could make even Superwoman green with envy. And still she manages to appear impeccably put-together at all times. Ashley stares at her in admiration. How does she do it – effortlessly steal every show she attends?

After stopping to say hello to a couple of mums she knows from the village primary school, Ashley finds a bar-style circular table at the back of the marquee. Danny joins her. She gazes around the venue, astounded at how beautiful it looks in pink: the tablecloths, more balloons, napkins and wrapped presents.

Guests step aside as Lucy glides towards them. The skirt of her paisley maxi dress, sporting a tasteful slit up to her knee, floats around her bare legs. She looks as if she has just stepped out of *Vogue*. Ashley couldn't feel more underdressed in her throwback to the sixties denim shorts with frayed hems and a patchwork crop top. She should've worn a dress.

'Great to see you.' Lucy kisses Danny, leaving a trace of her vibrant pink lipstick on his cheek. 'Sorry, Dan,' Lucy says, wiping it away with a gentle caress of her thumb. 'Let's get you two some drinks. Now, where's Renee?' Renee is the partner of

Danny's brother, Tom. They live in the village near the pub but in separate houses.

Lucy stands on tiptoe, not that she needs to, and scans the crowd. 'She was passing around a tray of champagne.'

'Don't worry. I'll go to the bar,' Danny says.

Lucy touches Danny's arm. 'Stay put. I'll find her for you.'

Moments after Lucy has wandered off, a waitress in a black pinafore dress appears with a tray of various drinks on her splayed hand. Ashley takes a glass of orange juice. Danny grabs a bottle of beer.

They sip their drinks, looking out onto the vast *Country Life*-worthy gardens that stretch down to a dense coppice. 'The gardener must have a full-time job on his hands keeping this in check,' Danny says. 'Can you imagine us having a garden this big?'

Ashley's gaze hovers on the sweep of pink roses. She likes tinkering with the containers and annuals in their garden, making the patio look pretty, but when it comes to the rest, she'd rather lounge on said patio in a deckchair with a glass of wine and a good book. Why does everything have to be big with Danny? Big house. Big garden. Big car. She stares at him. When did he change? He has always aimed high but seems to have lost sight of what's important since they moved to Thyme End.

'It's beautiful, isn't it?' he says.

'Stunning.' Ashley studies the guests. A whole manner of people are present, from the local dignitary to the village shopkeeper. 'It's more like a royal garden party than a kid's birthday bash.' Ashley wipes the remains of Lucy's lipstick from Danny's cheek.

'Behave.' Danny digs her in the ribs, smirking. There it is. The expression of amusement he used to wear more frequently.

Lucy reappears, bearing two flutes of bubbly. 'Apologies for that interruption,' she says. 'Ah! Someone has already brought you drinks. Have these afterwards.' She puts the flutes on the table.

There is a tugging on Ashley's hand and she turns to find Elliot in his swimming trunks.

'Mum.' His shoulders are curved inwards hugging his body, and he is shivering.

'What're you doing here? Why aren't you with your friends?'

Elliot stares up at her, a pleading look in his eyes. 'Come on the bouncy castle, Mum.'

Ashley looks at Danny and Lucy, deep in conversation. They are standing so close to each other, their shoulders are touching. 'I'm a bit busy at the moment,' she says to Elliot.

He scowls. 'You're always busy.'

His words are like a slap across the face. She eyes Lucy and Danny. 'OK, let's do it,' she says, shaking off the guilt and discarding her drink.

Elliot's excitement is contagious, his cheerful 'Yay!' filling the air.

Ashley looks over her shoulder. Danny doesn't even notice her slip away. She looks to the bar. Where has Susie gone?

Elliot leads her out of the marquee. 'Make sure you take your shoes off, Mum. Come on, it's great fun.'

Slipping off her sandals, Ashley joins the other mothers up for a laugh, now thankful she chose not to wear a dress. The bouncy castle becomes a mass of screeching children, and their mums. A whirlwind of bodies colliding and collapsing in laughter.

After about fifteen minutes, as Ashley starts to tire, and the heat becomes uncomfortable, the classic jingle of 'Greensleeves' wafts through the air, its promise of ice cream turning the tide of the kids' attention. They scurry off the inflatable like ants to food.

Emerging from the bouncy castle, Ashley is a picture of

disarray, her skin sticky with sweat and strands of faded pink hair clinging to her temples. As she swipes a hand across her forehead, her gaze darts towards the gathering in the marquee. Lucy and Danny are no longer in sight. Hearing someone yell, she scans the crowd.

'You OK?' a school mum asks, catching her breath.

'Fine,' Ashley replies distantly. 'Did you hear that?'

'Hear what?' the mum asks, looking nonplussed.

Ashley shakes her head. 'I thought I heard someone yell.'

Elliot's voice cuts through the air, a debate between strawberry or chocolate unfolding in the background. Vanilla is tasty, too. The words dissolve into the sky as a horrifying guttural cry draws Ashley's attention towards the vicinity of the cart lodges. Her eyes dart nervously around, seeking verification from others, but all the other mums have disappeared, and the kids are huddled around the ice cream van, engrossed in discussions about their choice of flavour. Was it a figment of her imagination? No one else seems to have noticed.

Ashley looks for her sandals. There it is again, a bone-chilling howl, unmistakably male. It sounds like Danny, but she is mistaken. Her eyes scan the driveway to see Lee standing by the parked cars. His head is thrown back, his face skywards, his arms flailing by his side.

Ashley grabs her sandals and dashes over to him. The shingle pierces her feet, but she barely notices. As she gets closer, she stops dead as Lee collapses to his knees, his hands drenched in a chilling coat of crimson.

'Help. You've got to help me.' His plea rips through the air.

Ashley rushes for him. 'What on earth has happened?'

His whole body is visibly shaking, his hands quivering uncontrollably. 'No. No,' he stammers, followed by a series of incoherent ramblings. He points to the nearest garage.

The previously lively scene changes to a growing buzz of alarm as guests swarm towards them. The music has died down, replaced by a cacophony of frantic whispers. Ashley, being the closest to the scene, cautiously ventures into the garage. She steps inside, her heart pounding.

Nothing could have prepared her for the horrifying vision that meets her eyes.

Danny is standing holding a hammer. It's the one Lee lent him.

It's covered in blood.

He is covered in blood. His crisp white polo shirt is unrecognisable beneath the sodden red gore.

On the cold concrete floor by his feet, deluged by a gruesome dark-red pool, lies a lifeless body.

And there is no denying who it is.

FOUR

A chilling gasp tears at Ashley's throat.

Lucy, once full of vibrant life, is lying on the concrete, her head smashed to a pulp. The side of her skull is contorted and dented like a punctured football. Blood mingled with shattered bone clumps in her hair.

Ashley throws her hands to her head, her legs weak, as she catches Lucy's sightless eyes rolled upwards into her skull. She looks like some grotesque waxwork figure.

'Danny?' Ashley whispers, her voice struck with disbelief.

Danny's features are a picture of abject horror. A stark terror she has never seen before is etched on his face. He releases the hammer, and it falls with an ominous thud.

'Danny?' she repeats.

But he is not listening. He sinks to his knees, further drenching himself in Lucy's blood. He cowers beside her, his fingers probing for a pulse. A futile act – it's evident she has gone.

Ashley is transfixed, frozen to the spot at the hideous sight before her. 'Who did this?'

Her question hangs in the air, unanswered. She turns around. An audience has formed in the doorway, an ocean of shocked faces swimming before her eyes. She looks for Elliot but can't see him. She hopes all the children are staying entertained at the ice cream van.

Lee is still howling outside, adding to the commotion.

A tall man barges through the crowd. 'Stand back, everyone.' His voice holds an authoritative tone. It's John Farnborough, a police officer who lives by the fire station in the village. Mid-forties, he carries an air of serene conviction. Ashley first met him earlier in the year when he came to the local primary school to talk to the children in their morning assembly – parents too if they wished to attend – about life in the police force. Elliot had begged Ashley to go along. He wants to be a policeman when he grows up. John marches towards them and turns to the crowd, waving his hands towards the door. 'Everyone, away. No one is to leave the grounds.' He turns to a man Ashley has never seen before. 'Make sure no one leaves, can you?' John steers the man towards the flow of people ebbing away, digging out a phone from the pocket of his cargo shorts. 'And get someone to keep the kids out of the way,' he calls after him.

Ashley stands aside, staring down on Danny, feeling like a pawn lost in a sinister game of chess. 'What happened? What did you do?'

Danny looks at her, his face a picture of puzzlement. 'What? No! I didn't do anything, Ash.'

Hearing John reporting a murder, Ashley zones out, staring at her husband.

Murder.

Danny. Murder. It can't be. Her husband wouldn't hurt a fly. His demeanour is gentle and patient.

Danny offers up his blood-covered hands, similar to Lee's from moments earlier.

It shocks her back to the present. Ashley steps backwards. Elliot. She needs to find their son.

Events unfold in a whirl. A firm hand lands on Ashley's shoulder and remains there as a stranger guides her towards the garage door. She can't help looking over her shoulder before exiting – a last-second vain hope that it's all a nightmare.

But it's not.

It's a horror story just beginning.

Outside the garage, Lee is leaning his bottom against the bonnet of a car, his hands covering his face, weeping uncontrollably. A mum from the school has her arms around his shoulders, pulling his head into her chest. She glares at Ashley, shaking her head. 'What the hell?' she mouths.

Ashley's mind reels, her thoughts scattered like Lucy's blood across the garage floor. Danny being in the garage? It doesn't make sense.

Susie appears, as confused as everyone else. 'What's happened?'

Ashley briefs her sister. 'Go and find Elliot, will you? Make sure he comes nowhere near here.'

'Everyone in the marquee. Now.' John's commanding voice breaks from the garage door through the discordance. 'No one must leave the grounds.' His voice rises, sharp and urgent. 'I repeat, no one. This whole area needs to be sealed off.'

Sealed off? What is happening?

Ashley glances towards the garage, a place now adulterated with fear. Danny's presence there messes with her head.

Two children appear, strawberry ice cream smeared around their lips and melting from the cones, dripping down their wrists and arms.

One of them, a boy from Elliot's class who Ashley doesn't know that well, laughs. 'Has someone died?'

The other one shouts out, 'Is there lots of blood?'

John beckons over the school mum next to Lee with a wave

of his hand. 'Please keep the children away.' He bellows to the crowd: 'Everyone, please proceed to the marquee. No one – I repeat, no one – must leave the premises.'

The crowd surges away. Panic and confusion drain the colour from their faces as people look over their shoulders. Whispers fill the air, punctuated by the scrunch of footsteps across the gravel.

Danny emerges from the gloomy expanse of the garage.

Lee springs into action. A fierce determination has transformed his usually placid face. His feet propel him off the car bonnet, and he strides over to Danny like a man on a mission. He shoves him. The ominous smack of his hand against Danny's chest amplifies his accusation. 'What did you do to my wife?'

Danny staggers backwards, his face a picture of trepidation coloured in shades of grey. Panic wells up in his eyes. He raises his hands in a pacifying gesture, his palms turned towards Lee, as Lee steps forward. 'Easy, mate,' Danny pleads, his voice a strained whisper.

'Easy?' The word echoes Lee's disbelief and rage. Another thud vibrates through Ashley as Lee shoves Danny again, his words playing the blame game.

Ashley tries to intervene, but Susie holds her back.

'Mate, come on,' Danny says.

'Mate? Don't call me your mate. We're not mates.' Another strike as Lee yells further accusations Danny's way.

'Get a grip. I didn't do anything. I found her like it.'

'What were you both doing in there in the first place?'

Before Danny can answer, the wail of police cars sounds in the distance, their sirens slicing through the tense atmosphere. Ashley's gaze flits between Danny and the unfolding chaos, a sense of dread sinking in. She has never been so scared in her life.

Lee's fingers curl into a fist as he hurls himself at Danny. 'You bastard. I'm going to kill you. Do you hear me? You're a dead man!' he roars, each stutter of words an open declaration of war.

The sound of hurried footsteps snaps Ashley's attention as Danny's brother rushes over to form a barrier in front of Danny. It's the first time she has seen Tom today. He looks as shaken as everyone else. His partner, Renee, tries to pull him away from the trouble.

Tom shakes her off and places a hand lightly on Lee's heaving chest, trying to defuse the explosive tension. 'Why don't we all just calm down?'

Danny gazes around the scene with a look of utter confusion. Finally, his eyes lock onto Ashley's, his gaze a silent plea for help. 'You don't think I did this, do you? You can't.'

John joins Tom. They loop their arms under Lee's armpits to restrain him.

'Easy, mate,' John says, repeating Danny's earlier plea.

Lee points to the garage. 'That hammer. I lent him that hammer. He put it in his car earlier. You need to arrest him. Before I get my hands on him.'

Confusion remains on Danny's face. The look of someone who has awoken from a nightmare and is so shaken they don't know what to do with themselves. 'You can't think I did this.' He holds his hand up, an offer of defence. 'I'd never hurt Lucy. Never!'

From up the picturesque drive, an army of vehicles appears, lights blazing, sirens wailing.

'What happened, Danny?' Ashley asks.

Her husband looks at her with a blank expression. 'I don't know. I found her like that.'

The tension in the air is palpable, a storm brewing, and Ashley is standing at the eye of it, petrified.

Before she can speak, the police set to work, securing the scene. Two uniformed officers separate them. She dodges one to try to talk to her husband, unable to process what the hell has gone on. All she knows is that whatever has happened, their lives will never be the same.

FIVE

An aura of eerie urgency develops around her as the small army of police officers swarm the site. A man introduces himself. Ashley doesn't catch his name. All she hears is his title: the scene of crime officer. Two ambulances arrive. Ashley stares on in a daze, feeling like an actor performing a bit-part role in a tragedy. But this is no play. It's real life. And it has threatened her world. With a silent plea, she begs the bile rising in her throat to stay put. Not here. Not now.

Two female police officers seal off the garage area, the blue and white barrier tape rippling in the gentle breeze that has picked up, fluttering across the proceedings as if trying to cool the situation down. The charred smell of the barbecue wafts over from the caterers trying to dampen it down. One of the officers attempts to shepherd those who have been slow to comply with instructions towards the marquee. A few stubborn lingerers hesitate, their eyes wide with shock, but the police officer's stern instructions sweep them away, pushing them beyond the cordoned line. 'Please proceed to the marquee immediately. Now,' he urges. The command in his voice echoes through the crowd, unyielding.

A frail arm reaches to touch her. 'Ashley,' Oriana Lewis says.

Ashley has been giving Oriana private art lessons most Monday evenings for the past six months at her home, Thyme End Hall, that sits in a commanding position at the entrance to the village. It's a sizeable property on the Thyme End Hall estate that Oriana inherited from her parents. Although she is a digital artist, Ashley graduated in Fine Art, and her passion for painting in oil has continually enriched her life. Her ability to absorb sight, sound, feel and touch enables her to use her artistic prowess to create some remarkable pieces in what is essentially a hobby for her now. Lucy introduced Ashley to Oriana when she heard Oriana was looking for an art teacher.

'I was just on my way home.' Oriana coughs, adjusting her bright-orange headscarf. 'I only stopped by to bring Grace her present, and I heard this fracas. What on earth has happened?' The corners of Oriana's lips rise in an attempt to smile. But it's a weak attempt because there's something very sad about Oriana. She's dying. Skin cancer that spread to her lungs before her husband even noticed the odd-looking mole in the small of her back. One of her dying wishes is to finish a collection of paintings of the estate before she passes, hence the weekly lessons. Her husband, Aaron, a stout man with steely features, twenty years younger than his wife, nods hello.

'It... it's Lucy.' Ashley doesn't know how to finish her sentence. Lucy and Oriana were close. Oriana has a son, Simon, by her first husband, and Danny and Lucy were at school with him and used to spend their summers up at Thyme End Hall. When Lucy was a kid, her mum died unexpectedly, and Oriana became like a mother to her.

Ashley has grown fond of Oriana, and she has enjoyed their lessons. They have rewarded her with a sense of giving back. The older woman is a feisty character who knows what she wants and is determined not to let her illness drag her down.

Ashley admires her tenacity. After the fourth lesson, when she discovered the truth about Oriana's imminent journey to the other side, she refused to take any further payment for her time, despite Oriana's constant reminders not to sell herself short.

A police officer separates the two women. 'Mrs Morgan. I'm DC Partridge. Can we talk?' She is tall, slim and blonde, just like Lucy. But that's as far as it goes. DC Partridge's hair is pulled back tightly into a bun at the nape of her neck, and she is wearing smart trousers and a linen shirt, no floaty dress or diamond earrings. She moves with deliberate efficiency that commands Ashley's attention. 'I need you to recount the course of events for me.'

Ashley calls out, 'Oriana,' as she is ushered away, but she doesn't hear her. Her heart sinks. Oriana is going to be devastated when she hears the news, which she can be only moments away from learning. Ashley turns to the police officer. 'I wasn't there. I didn't see it happen. I arrived afterwards.' She is struggling to constrain her spiralling thoughts. She scans the scene. What has happened to Danny? 'Where's my husband?'

'He's talking to another officer,' the DC says, her expression impassive. 'Just tell me what you saw.'

'My son,' Ashley says. 'I want to see my son.'

'All the children are safe and are being looked after,' DC Partridge says, her grip firm on Ashley's elbow. 'Let's find a quiet spot so we can talk.'

She steers Ashley with a determined urgency towards a towering magnolia tree to the side of the long drive. The sickly sweet fragrance from its cuplike flowers delivers a waft of nausea.

Retelling what she witnessed, Ashley stares blankly at the scene unfolding as the police officer fills her notebook. Her focus inadvertently lands on John Farnborough, deeply engrossed in conversation with a man in uniform snapping his hands into a pair of latex gloves. Another detective, perhaps?

But detectives don't wear uniforms. Or do they? She doesn't know. She's never met one in real life.

Lee's loud voice cuts through the air. He is talking to a burly, thick-set man, his voice raised and aggressive. 'I've told you, arrest him. He murdered my wife!' Lee gestures towards Danny, now being escorted towards the house, pointing a finger of culpability in his direction. A look of venom and hatred pulsates through every muscle of Lee's body. A look Ashley could never imagine him capable of.

The attending officers thwart Lee's repeated attempts to attack Danny. The sight anchors Ashley to the chilling reality – her reality. Where friends become enemies, and accusations imbue the air like a death warrant.

Something lands on Ashley's arm. Mistaking it for an annoying fly, she swats it away, only to realise it's DC Partridge's hand. 'I'm sorry,' Ashley says.

'You mentioned you were on the inflatables with your son, Mrs Morgan?'

Ashley catches sight of Danny but can't make out what he is saying. She is too far away. But she can tell from his desperate body language he is protesting his innocence. He laces his fingers and cradles his hands on top of his head. Frantically, he looks across at Lee, anxious, and then his eyes dart towards her. Fear. Panic. Dread. His face screams it all as their worlds crumble in unison.

DC Partridge's voice breaks through her thoughts. 'Mrs Morgan, did you hear me?'

Ashley turns her attention to the police officer and answers all her questions mechanically. She was on the bouncy castle with Elliot. No, she doesn't know why Danny and Lucy were in the garage. Yes, Lee did lend Danny that hammer when they arrived at the party. Yes, she knows the deceased well. Not as well as her husband, no.

The questioning takes what seems like an age. When the

DC has finished, she takes Ashley back to the marquee. But Ashley needs to find Elliot, so she scans the scene for her little boy instead of ducking inside. She doesn't feel that she can leave in case they bring him to her, so she asks the DC what's going to happen to Danny, as they wait outside. The officer offers up little information, though, in fairness, why should she? On the face of it, it's pretty simple. A woman gets her head smashed in by a club hammer. The hammer is found in the hand of a man at the scene of the crime. He is covered in the victim's blood. Said hammer was lent to the man less than an hour beforehand. Case closed.

Ashley inwardly groans.

This is beyond real.

Susie and some mothers are minding the kids, trying to retain normalcy and distracting the children from the grim reality on the other side of the estate. They take surreptitious glances towards the crime scene every few minutes.

Where's Elliot? Ashley looks towards the inflatables. There he is, bouncing around with some other kids. That doesn't bode well for all the ice cream they've scoffed. She can't see any of Lucy and Lee's three children.

Within the confines of the marquee, people are standing around in pairs, silent in shock, or in small groups, creating a dull hum with their muffled conversations. This must be the worst event ever to happen in the history of the village. Even the recent death of Roberta Splinter, the MP who drove into a tree just outside the village a few weeks ago, pales in comparison. Murder doesn't happen in places like Thyme End. Everybody looks out for each other. They help each other. They don't murder each other.

Until now.

Several officers – four or five, maybe – call the guests in turn out the back of the marquee and down into the gardens to obtain their versions of events. The proceedings are orderly and sombre. A silence descends on the gathering as more and more parents grab their children to leave.

'Where are they going?' Ashley asks DC Partridge.

'The police want to clear the area as soon as possible.'

The mothers helping to mind the children take their turn to talk to the officers before slipping off home with their loved ones, while Susie continues her best to entertain the children, placating the ones who appear upset.

A plain-clothes officer Ashley hasn't yet seen appears with John Farnborough.

'How're you bearing up?' John asks, squeezing Ashley's arm.

What a stupid question. How is she supposed to reply to that? 'So-so.'

The plain-clothes officer makes a request – a visit to the station to answer a few questions and provide a statement.

DC Partridge curls a loose strand of blonde hair behind her dainty ear. Ashley has never seen an ear so small. Lucy had small ears, but not as small as the officer's. What an odd observation at a time like this.

'Mrs Morgan, did you hear me? Is that OK with you?'

'It's completely voluntary,' John adds. 'They just want to gather as much information as possible.'

'But I've already told you everything I know,' Ashley says, a hint of a plea in her voice, although she knows she has to do this.

'Still, it would help the investigation.' The officer's tone suggests Ashley doesn't have a choice. 'We need to get as full a picture as possible. I'm sure you understand.'

'I need to take my son home.'

'I think it'd be in your best interest to comply with our requests.'

Ashley looks at John. He nods. She struggles to catch her breath, the weight of the situation repressing her. 'I guess I've no choice, then. But I need to get my son looked after. What's happening to my husband?'

'He's helping our team with their inquiries.'

'I need to speak to him.'

'I'm afraid that's not possible at the moment.'

Ashley reluctantly concedes. What choice does she have?

She turns away, stifling tears she needs to control. She looks across the crowd of people as bewildered as her. Where's Susie? She needs her sister. There she is, talking to a police officer. 'Can I speak to my sister? I need her to take care of my son.'

'Sure.' John follows her over to Susie.

Her sister hugs her. She briefs Susie on the situation. 'I've got to go to the station. Can you take Elliot home and stay with him until I get back?'

'Of course.' Susie squeezes her tighter. 'I can't believe what has happened. Anything I can do, let me know.'

Ashley takes her keys out of her bag and gives them to her sister. 'I need to get someone to give you a lift.'

'I'll organise that,' John says.

Events develop in a fog of bewilderment.

DC Partridge appears. 'Can I drive my husband's car to the station?' As soon as she asks, Ashley knows how stupid this question sounds. Of course she can't. The murder weapon came from Danny's car.

'I'm afraid that won't be possible. A car is ready for you.' DC Partridge raises a guiding arm and chaperones Ashley towards a waiting squad vehicle. Lee is climbing into another marked car. She searches for Danny. He appears in her line of sight, deep in conversation with two officers. He looks so scared, his face deathly pale. Ashley wants to run over to him. But the hostile vibe tells her that wouldn't be a wise move.

As she passes them, she catches snippets of the conversation. 'I was giving her CPR. That's why my hands and clothes are covered with blood.' Danny's voice quivers. 'I thought I could save her.'

The words stick in Ashley's throat as she gets in the car. As the police car drives off, she turns and watches Danny's image recede in the rear-view mirror. A feeling of utter dread grips her stomach. How could this have happened? Her hands ball into fists as she grapples with the fallout of a day that started as one to be endured, and has turned into a nightmare of unimaginable horror.

SIX

Unable to get comfortable, Ashley fidgets in the cramped interview room at the police station in the local town. Her fingers tap an anxious rhythm on the cold metal desk. The room, no bigger than a shoebox, is suffocating, its teal-coloured vinyl floors and walls seeming to shrink with each passing minute. It smells of school dinners and reminds her of a prison cell. Not that she's ever been in one, but she and Danny used to flop onto the sofa every evening to watch crime dramas regularly. Not of late, though. Invariably, one of them has been working. Or Danny has been away on business. It's uncanny how life sometimes unfolds. Never had she thought they'd be starring in their own crime drama.

The image of Lucy lying on that garage floor refuses to leave her. A haunting visage, frozen in a moment of time that she wishes she could delete from her memory. But she knows that's not possible. It's going to stay with her for the rest of her life.

Her eyes dart around the sterile eight-by-ten-foot shoebox. She's not typically claustrophobic, but the room is oppressive. Are they holding Danny in a similar room? Or is he in a prison cell with a bed and a toilet? The thought sends a shiver down her spine.

Don't be silly. Of course he's not. He hasn't been arrested.

Or has he?

She longs to see him, but the police officer who left her there adamantly told her that was a no-go.

Why did she even ask? Her husband is being questioned about a murder. The brutal attack of a woman. And Danny was found with her. Of course she can't see him.

How did she end up here?

The banging and clanging of station life echoes through the walls. Repositioning herself in the plastic seat, she glances at her watch. It has been over half an hour since she was confined to this stifling box. Time drags, and with every passing second, her mind races, conjuring up scenarios and possibilities.

A thought dawns on her. Does she need a solicitor? The officer who led her to this cell said something about one. But she's sure he said she didn't need one. She needs to check. She can't be a suspect, can she? The niggling doubt gnaws at her, adding another layer of unease to the already tense situation. She agreed to attend the station of her own free will. Anything to get her husband out of this massive hole he has dug himself into.

Danny, a murderer? She must remain strong. But why did he go into that garage in the first place? And what was Lucy doing there? And why did he pick up the murder weapon? There are so many questions she wants to ask him. That the police will want to ask him.

The metal door clangs open, and a police officer she hasn't seen before walks in. 'Mrs Morgan. I'm sorry to have kept you waiting.' His tone is friendly, which is a relief. He smiles as if to reassure her.

Ashley relaxes, but only a tiny bit.

'I'm DCI Ben Graham.' He sits down opposite her and

places a black folder on the desk. His hair is flecked with grey, his face lined. 'I'm sorry about the room; we're a little short on space. It's been a busy day. Now, as you can probably imagine, we have lots of unanswered questions.'

A knot of anxiety tightens in Ashley's stomach. She sits up straight. 'Is this going to take long?' Her voice trembles. 'Only I want to get back to my son. It's been a stressful day, and I'm worried about him. I've already told your colleagues everything I witnessed today.'

The DCI nods. 'I completely understand, Mrs Morgan.'

'You can call me Ashley,' she says, her name sounding alien in the foreign setting. The friendliness of the DCI offers a degree of comfort, yet the sterile room seems to swallow her words, leaving her feeling more alone than she's ever felt. Even more so than when her mum died. At least she had Susie with her then.

'I'll make this as quick as I can, Ashley.' He clears his throat and removes his lightweight bomber jacket, hooking it over the back of the chair. His voice is gravelly, like that of a heavy smoker. He doesn't smell of smoke, though, but of the trace of strong black coffee, masked by a hint of minty chewing gum. He runs through the essentials. 'I'll be voice-recording and video-recording this interview. Do you understand that?'

She nods.

'This is a voluntary interview, and you are free to leave at any time. I appreciate all this must've been a terrible shock for you, but I need to ask you some more questions to aid our understanding of what happened today. Some of these questions you may find hard to answer, but please do so as thoroughly as possible. The more information we can gather, the better. No matter how trivial you think it may be. Do you understand?'

Ashley nods. 'Do I need a solicitor?'

'You're not under caution, and, as I said, this is a voluntary interview, so no. But you are entitled to one, so please let me know if you would like me to arrange one for you.'

'Has Danny got a solicitor?'

'I can't comment on your husband, I'm afraid.'

'We have a solicitor we work with for our business. Can you put my husband in contact with them to help?'

'He would've been given the opportunity to get a solicitor. Now, can I get you anything before we start?'

'Could I get some more water, please?' She pushes the empty plastic cup she was given when she arrived across the desk.

'Of course. While I'm out, think about whether you want me to arrange a solicitor for you.'

'How long will that take?'

'I can't say for sure. A few hours perhaps. Think about it. I can easily arrange one for you.'

The door bangs closed, leaving her alone again. She drops her head to her chest. Perhaps a solicitor is a good idea. But solicitors cost thousands of pounds. Money that she and Danny simply don't have. Besides, Danny needs legal help more than she does.

How did they find themselves in this mess?

Visions of Lucy's eyes rolling in her head turn Ashley's stomach. Her breathing quickens.

She's not just scared. She's terrified.

Because she's not stupid. She knows the reality of her situation.

By the end of the day, her husband could be charged with murder.

SEVEN

DCI Graham returns. 'Have you decided?'

'Let's just get on with it.'

He resumes his place opposite her, stifling a yawn. 'OK. Now, first of all, one more time, from your perspective, please run through the events of the day.'

Ashley understands the necessity of recording her version of events in a formal statement, so she runs through exactly what happened in as much detail as she can remember, from arriving at the party to leaving for the station. She stumbles over her words as she describes the appalling scene of Lucy with her head caved in.

'Take your time, Ashley. I appreciate this is stressful. If you need to take a break, we can do that.'

Ashley relays the altercation between Lee and Danny as DCI Graham writes his notes, offering no comment or opinion.

'How did you know Lucy?' he asks.

'Danny and Lucy are childhood friends.' She pauses momentarily before adding, 'Were childhood friends. And I know her... knew her... through Danny. We've also had business dealings with her and Lee since moving to Thyme End.'

'What kind of business dealings?'

'Danny and I run a design and marketing company for small to medium-sized independent property developers, and, as you probably already know, Lucy and Lee are property developers. We've done the marketing for some of their sites.'

'What does that entail?'

She gets asked that question all the time. She reels off the standard answer. 'We provide a range of services – brand design, business cards, brochures, leaflets, flyers, that kind of thing. Any kind of marketing, really. I also design websites for clients.' She explains how she takes architects' drawings and designs CGIs – computer-generated images – of houses, outside and inside, to bring a property to life. 'We also provide detailed floor plans, site plans, 3D animations and street scenes, where you add people and cars, et cetera, to a site plan to bring the whole development to life. And virtual tours of properties, too.'

'So Lucy and Lee are your clients?'

Ashley nods. 'Yes, I suppose you could say that.'

'Suppose?'

'Well, they're friends too.'

'What exactly have you done for their company?'

'I work on the technical side of the business.'

He gives an encouraging nod. 'Would you mind elaborating?'

She feels as if she is repeating herself, but she explains again what she has done for Lucy and Lee.

'And Danny?'

'He doesn't get involved in the technical side of things. He spends most of his time out on the road, drumming up new business.' The set-up suits them. Danny is much better at face-to-face contact. He has the personality for it. Everyone loves Danny. He could sell a raincoat in the Sahara. Ashley is more reserved and is happier behind the scenes. 'And when he's in the office, he deals with most of the admin – running the finances, project management, facing off to the lawyers, that kind of thing.'

'So you were close to Lucy?' DCI Graham then asks.

'We haven't known each other that long, but she has been my closest friend since we moved to the village. We socialised because of her friendship with Danny, and because our kids are best friends.'

DCI Graham flits through his file. 'That's Grace and Elliot?'

'Correct.'

'And Danny and Lucy?'

'She and Danny are close.' Another pause. 'Were close, I guess I should say.'

'How close?'

What kind of question is that? Her mind flits to when Danny introduced her to Lucy shortly after Elliot was born. They'd come from London to visit Danny's parents, who own a thatched cottage on the outskirts of the village. It was a late summer day, a hint of the earthy smell of autumn approaching in the air, and they'd gone for a walk through the village. Ashley will never forget the shriek she heard when they'd stopped to reposition the blanket she'd put over the pram to shade Elliot from the sun. She'd turned to see this beautiful woman dressed in white, floating across the village green towards them like an angel. The way Lucy had embraced Danny made Ashley think she was an ex-girlfriend.

'How close?' the DCI repeats.

And the way Lucy had clung to Danny's arm that first time cemented the thought in Ashley's mind that they'd been previous lovers. However, it was something he later denied.

She shrugs. 'They were childhood friends. They knew each other for most of their lives.'

'Was there an intimate relationship between them during those years?'

'No.' Her answer comes out louder, sharper, than she anticipated. 'They've always just been good friends.'

Haven't they?

That's what Danny has always claimed. But during their business meetings with Lucy and Lee, and the occasional social gatherings she hasn't been able to avoid, Ashley has questioned in her mind whether that is indeed the truth. Thoughts that deep down she has never really been able to banish. Not that he has ever lied to her.

Not that she knows of, anyway.

'Would you say Lucy and Lee had a strong marriage? Were they happy?'

'I think so. Lee has always seemed laid-back. Lucy did her thing; he did his.'

The detective clicks the lid of his pen on and off. On and off. The sound grates on her. 'Thing?'

'I don't know.' Ashley shrugs. 'They ran their business together, but Lee enjoys his golf and hanging out with his mates. Lucy was more driven – by business, by life. And was always involved in something in the village.'

He scratches his head. 'Something? Can you be more specific?'

'She was the chair of the school PTA, so she was always doing stuff for them. You know, arranging fundraising activities, extracurricular stuff for the kids.'

'Stuff?'

'Organising school discos and parties. And she was always involved in village events. Like Danny, she loved Thyme End. Generations of her family have lived there. Everyone knew Lucy. Everyone liked Lucy.' Her voice cracks. 'So I can't understand who would've wanted to do this.'

DCI Graham's eyes meet Ashley's square on. Again. 'You said Lucy and Danny were close. I understand from talking to family and friends that Lucy could be quite tactile with your husband. How did that make you feel?'

Who the hell said that? What family? Susie? No, not Susie. She'd never say that to a police officer. He must mean Tom, Danny's brother. He was the only family member there today. Or perhaps he means Lucy and Lee's family.

'What do you mean?' she asks, although she doesn't need to. She knows exactly what he means. Lucy was one of those women who invaded personal space and crossed personal borders. Especially where Danny was concerned. She was what Ashley would call a touchy talker. After they moved to the village and started to get involved with Lucy and Lee on a business and social level, Ashley couldn't help feeling put out by how much Lucy would touch Danny's shoulder, cling to his arm, pat his thigh when they were seated next to each other. It alarmed her. Until Ashley convinced herself Lucy was like that with everyone, men and women alike. It was just her way.

'I'm not trying to trip you up here, Ashley. I'm just trying to get the full picture.'

'Danny and Lucy were, I suppose you could say, a bit like brother and sister. There was never anything more than friendship between them.'

DCI Graham frowns. 'And Lee, did he have an issue with it?'

'An issue with what?'

'The nature of Danny and Lucy's relationship.'

'No. There was nothing to have an issue with. They were just friends.' She clenches her jaw, trying to keep calm.

He joins his hands behind his neck and leans backwards, extending his upper body into a stretch. 'As far as you are aware, did Danny and Lucy ever have a falling out? Has he ever said anything about wanting to hurt Lucy?'

This guy is trying to trip her up, despite what he says. His line of questioning is making her feel highly uncomfortable. Perhaps she does need a solicitor.

'What kind of a question is that? Not at all. He would never hurt anyone, let alone his best friend.'

But as she says these words, the knot in her stomach tightens. She thinks back to last Monday morning. Lucy had requested changes to a CGI Ashley had designed for one of her developments. Nothing out of the ordinary – terms of business allow for two changes before the final completion of each project. But that had been the fourth change Lucy had requested, and Danny's words echo in Ashley's thoughts.

He'd said he could kill that woman.

EIGHT

Visions of Lucy's blood torment Ashley.

So much blood.

DCI Graham cocks his head. 'Are you sure?'

'Sorry?'

'Are you sure Danny's never said anything about wanting to hurt Lucy?'

Did the DCI sense her pause?

Ashley's spine lengthens. 'Let's get something straight here. My husband would never hurt anyone.' Ashley is trying to hide her indignation, but the words shoot out her mouth a little too defensively. She glances at her watch. She hopes Elliot is OK.

'You haven't lived in the area long, have you?' the DCI asks.

Why the sudden change in the line of questioning?

Ashley shrugs. It depends on what you call a long time. It feels like a lifetime to her. 'Nine or so months.' Lucy once joked with Ashley that you're not classed as a proper local in Thyme End until you have lived there for at least twenty years and seen a generation born in the area. That's the kind of place it is.

'And where did you live before?'

'London.'

'A big change for you then.'

Ashley nods. The move was inevitable. Ever since they met at university, Danny always said he wanted to return to Thyme End to live one day. When he took her to meet his parents, Ashley understood the appeal of the dreamlike country village, but she wasn't sure she wanted to live there. London was her home. She'd lived there all her life. But after Elliot came along, Danny's desire to return to his roots became more urgent. London wasn't a place to bring up a child, he said. With knife crime rife in the city, the countryside would be a much safer bet for them. 'The crime-rate in Thyme End is non-existent,' he'd said. 'It's a close-knit community, one where everyone helps and supports each other. Think how great it'd be to have neighbours and friends living close by who look out for you. And think how convenient having my parents living around the corner would be. Babysitters on tap.'

Ashley wasn't so sure it was a great trade-off. Danny's mother is a tricky character.

But they could have more freedom to go out together as a couple, he said. After a dreadful experience with a babysitter in London, who they'd caught watching porn on their TV, they'd stopped going out. They'd either entertained their friends at home or taken Elliot with them. Danny also said life in the country was more relaxed. But given his all-consuming drive for the success of their business, she had yet to experience the slower pace of life he claimed was a given.

Danny started looking at houses for sale in the village, but she couldn't match his keenness to move. What little family she has – her sister and a cousin she regularly met up with – lived only a Tube ride away. Moving to Thyme End would mean she wouldn't see them as much. But when his mum told Danny about the small development of five properties being built on the edge of Thyme End, Danny suggested viewing one of the houses in Juniper Close.

Ashley never expected to be swayed by a new-build. Old houses are her style. Beams and decorative ceilings, original wooden flooring, nooks and crannies. But despite her preconception of new homes, she could imagine adding her passion for an eclectic range of colours, patterns and textures to transform the magnolia walls into a home of beauty. But she still wasn't sure she wanted to move there.

They held off. He understood, he said. She had to be ready as well. But she couldn't fail to notice his frustration when all five houses sold. 'I guess it wasn't meant to be,' he'd said, clearly disappointed.

But when one of the sales fell through, he persuaded her to have another look and then to agree to the purchase. In fairness, she has taken some pleasure in stamping her mark on the modern four-bedroomed detached. Not that they need four bedrooms. But she is still hoping more children will come along. It is a far cry from their poky two-bedroom flat in Camden Lock that was only as big as half the downstairs space. They could have used one of the large double bedrooms as an office, but sensibly, they had The Hub installed in a vain attempt to establish a healthy work-life balance. Running their business from their Camden home, where the open-plan lounge and kitchen doubled as an office that spilt into the bedroom and even the bathroom, with brochures on the floor next to the loo, had got out of hand years before.

The DCI asks several more questions before coming out with, 'And how would you consider your husband's state of mind? Has anything been bothering him lately?'

'What're you suggesting? You don't honestly think Danny is guilty?'

'If you could answer the question, please.'

'He was fine. He *is* fine. No murderous intentions, no mood swings. Just Danny.'

Although this isn't strictly true, either. There has been a

change in her husband over the past couple of weeks. He has seemed withdrawn and preoccupied. When she questioned him about it, he said he had a lot on his mind with the business. He'd had a couple of disappointments with deals he'd thought were a given. Ones that he'd stayed up late to prepare for and was confident he'd won, but which had gone to a competitor at the last minute. So, lately, he has been working all hours devising a new sales pitch.

The business has a cash-flow problem too, which has caused him a headache. A client, Pickstones, went into liquidation, owing them seven thousand pounds. Money no small business can afford to lose. He has been stressed over that.

And then there was that argument with Tom a couple of weeks ago. It was so out of character for Danny to yell at his brother, which is pretty commendable as Tom can be a difficult character at times, but Danny was very tired. He'd left home early that morning, way before six, to meet a client, and he didn't arrive home until gone seven that night. So, all this is plausible. When you run a business, the responsibility for its success never leaves your side for a single minute.

DCI Graham lays his pen to rest. A lump appears in her throat with the next question that slips from his lips.

'I'm sorry to ask, but how would you describe your relationship with your husband? Would you say you have a strong marriage?'

A shiver runs through her. Has he just read her mind? Sensed her hesitation? She swallows hard, knowing her answer could change everything. Once merely confining, the room now feels like a trap about to snap shut.

'Yes. Very strong.' Danny is her world. And she is confident she is his too.

His next question falls like a guillotine, cutting through the silence. 'And does your husband have a temper, would you say?'

'I thought I was giving a statement. This is feeling more like an interrogation.'

He greets her with a stoic expression.

'No! He does not have a temper. And he's certainly incapable of wielding a hammer and smashing his childhood friend's brains in.'

Unperturbed, DCI Graham allows a pause to linger, ignoring her outburst. He is a cool character. He knows how to press all the right buttons and with what pressure. 'Do you know anyone who could've wished Lucy harm?'

Ashley drums her fingers, her mind a whirlwind of grim thoughts.

'Anyone at all?'

Ashley shrugs. 'I'm surmising, but a bad business deal, perhaps. Jealousy for having made her fortune. How should I know?' You're the detective, she wants to add but stops herself. There's no point in antagonising the guy. She needs all the people she can get on her side. Her heavy sigh fills the room, resonating with a weariness she is finding so damn hard to mask. She needs to control herself, but DCI Graham's line of inquiry has touched some raw nerves. 'But certainly not my husband.'

'OK, thank you. We're nearly done here.' He taps his pen on the desk. She wants to yell at him to stop. 'Last of all,' he says, lifting his head until his eyes meet hers, 'is there anything else you can tell us? Anything that may help us with our line of inquiries?'

Ashley gives a defeated shake of her head. 'I don't think so.'

'We'll leave it there then. Thank you for coming to the station. I'll need to get your signature. Then you can get back to your little boy.'

'I want to speak to my husband.'

'That can't happen.'

She knows there's no use in arguing with him. 'When will he be home?'

'I'm afraid I can't answer any questions related to your husband's, or anyone else's, case.'

Frustrated, she says, 'Our car is still at Lucy and Lee's house. How do I get it?'

'I'll have to check that for you. I can arrange a car to take you home, but you may need to wait a while. Like I said, we're extra busy tonight.'

'It's fine. I'll call a cab.'

Ashley leaves the station drained and numb. The detective's questioning has left her exposed and vulnerable.

She slips into the taxi she had to wait an agonising half an hour for, the world outside a blur. The radio is playing hip-hop music, and the car smells of musky deodorant.

'Whereabouts in Thyme End?' the driver asks, clicking a button on his meter.

'Juniper Close, please.'

'Right you are.' He pulls away from the station.

Ashley clings to her handbag, her knuckles white.

She has just lied to the police.

NINE

When they arrive in Thyme End, the taxi driver navigates his way over the baby humpbacked bridge synonymous with the village and past the unusual number of cars parked outside The Ugly Duckling for a Sunday night.

Ashley shudders. Villagers are out in abundance, spilling onto the neighbouring green and getting precariously close to the large duck pond. No doubt they are discussing her husband and the murder of his childhood friend. Their heavy chatter sounds into the taxi. She slides her body down the seat, staying hidden until the taxi driver pulls up outside her house.

Utterly drained, Ashley pays the driver and gets out the cab. The next-door neighbour, a woman who has lived in the village for over thirty years, has resumed her usual position, looking out her lounge window. Slightly amused, Ashley often wonders if the woman sleeps in the spot in case she misses anything happening in the close.

She enters the house to find Elliot waiting for her in the hallway, his head dropped and shoulders slumped, his arms hanging heavy. If they were any longer, his knuckles would be dragging along the ground. He must've seen the cab pull up. In stark contrast, Rufus, oblivious to his owner's trauma, capers around, tail wagging.

'Steady on, boy,' Ashley says, her voice hollow. She squats down and hugs Elliot. 'Are you OK?'

Rufus nuzzles his nose between them to join the affection. Ashley buries her shaking fingers in his fur, an anchor in the storm that has ripped their lives apart.

Susie appears. 'I'll let him out for a wee,' she says, taking Rufus' collar and leading him to the kitchen. The patio doors squeak open.

'Where's Dad?' Elliot asks, breaking away from Ashley's hug. His face is flushed from too much sun, and his eyes are small from exhaustion.

She needs to get him to bed. 'He's helping the police.'

'Why? What's he done?'

'Why don't we go upstairs and get you in the bath?'

'Dad always runs me a bath on a Sunday.' His bottom lip wobbles. 'I was waiting for him.'

She finds her jovial voice. An attempt to save her son from crying. He is so much more emotional than he used to be when they lived in London. His maturity seems to have regressed. 'Tonight, you've got me.'

'I don't want a bath,' he protests.

'Shower then.'

'I don't want to.'

'I tried to get him in the bath, but he was adamant he wanted to wait for you guys,' Susie says, coming back in. 'Come on, sweet pea. Go with your mum. You need to get clean.'

Ashley thanks her sister and turns to Elliot. 'You're covered in sticky suntan cream, and you've been running around with no shoes on. Shower it is.' She takes his arm and leads him upstairs.

He wriggles in protest. 'I don't want to.'

Ignoring his screams, she lugs off his T-shirt. He usually

undresses himself but tonight she just wants to get him to bed. Reluctantly, he agrees to have a shower.

'Make sure you wash your hair. I'll be back in a minute.'

Ashley runs downstairs and heads straight for the fridge.

Susie is boiling the kettle. 'I'm so sorry, Ash. If I'd have known you'd be so long, I would've insisted he had a bath.'

'No worries,' Ashley lies. It would've been much better if Elliot was already in bed. Taking a fresh bottle of Chardonnay from the fridge, she opens a cupboard and grabs an oversized glass usually reserved for red wine. She holds it up to Susie. 'You want some?'

'I was going to have a cup of tea. I don't know what to do.'

'What do you mean?'

'I'm meant to be on that flight to Frankfurt early tomorrow morning, remember? But I don't want to leave you.'

Ashley sighs. How could she forget? Tomorrow is a big day for her sister. A presentation to the board of her company that could win her the promotion she has been hankering for since her divorce. 'I'm so sorry. I forgot. You go. Now. Go home and get some sleep. It's a big day for you. I told you; you needn't have come today.'

'It was the only chance I had for a visit. I haven't seen you guys for a month. I've missed you. But I kind of wish I hadn't,' she says with a wry smile.

'I'll be fine.'

'We didn't even get the chance to catch up today. I'll come back tomorrow. As soon as the plane lands, I'll come straight back.'

'What about work?'

'I'll move some stuff around.'

'Don't worry about me. Danny will be home by then.'

Susie looks as if she's about to say she's not so sure she agrees about that, but instead she says, 'I'll always worry about you. That's what big sisters do. What happened at the station?'

Ashley contemplates how much to reveal to her sister. Should she tell her that she wasn't entirely transparent with the police? That Danny hasn't been himself lately? That he said he could kill that woman, meaning Lucy?

But she doesn't want to give Susie anything to worry about with such a big day ahead. So she gives her sister the bare facts.

'The police quizzed me when you left the party.' Susie explains that she was asked the same as all the guests with the added question about Danny's state of mind. 'Of course I said he would never hurt a fly.' She then asks the question that must be on everyone's mind. 'Who do you think could've done this?'

Ashley shrugs. 'I haven't got a clue. But it must've been someone who was there today.'

'Unless someone slipped in and then out. Surely they have CCTV in a house like that?'

'Apparently not around the garages. Tom had been working on the lighting there and Lee had been telling him about the security cameras he was planning to have installed.' Ashley finishes the glass of wine. 'Look. You go. I promise I'll keep you updated.'

Susie holds out her fisted hand. Ashley mirrors her sister's actions. They fist-bump. A gesture that signifies a pledge between them that can never be broken. 'Promise?'

'Promise,' Ashley repeats and hugs her sister.

After seeing Susie out, Ashley returns to the kitchen. The faint click of the bottle cap loosening reverberates through the room. It's so quiet. It reminds her of the nights Danny is away on business. Pouring liberally, she fills the glass, sighing heavily as she takes a thirsty gulp. She needs it.

She stands leaning against the worktop, sifting through texts on her phone. Several people have sent messages asking if she is OK. What has happened to Danny? Is there anything they can do for her? Even some mums from school who weren't at the party have got in touch, proving one of her greatest fears about moving to Thyme End. Everyone knows everyone else's business. It doesn't bother Danny, but Ashley is more of a private person. She preferred the anonymity of her big city life. She listens to a string of voice messages, asking the same as the numerous texts, deleting each one. Other than Danny, she doesn't want to speak to a soul.

She thinks about their London flat on the top floor of a converted pub with its timber flooring and retractable skylight in the living area that provided access to an unofficial tiny roof terrace where they used to spend their summer evenings with a bottle of white or red. The yearning to be back there makes her swig another mouthful of wine.

The phone rings again. One of their clients, Mike Booker, is calling. Is he kidding? It's Sunday bloody evening. What does he want? She lets the call go to voicemail, deleting several messages she has no intention of replying to before listening to what Mike has to say. He doesn't hide his disconcerting tone, asking her to call him immediately. If Danny were there, he'd tell her to call him straight back – Booker is a newish client who they want to retain. There's no use upsetting anyone in their line of business; their hefty mortgage won't pay itself.

She finds Mike's number in her list of contacts. 'Hello, Mike. Is everything OK?'

'Sorry to bother you on a Sunday, but I was preparing for a meeting early in the morning and noticed you didn't send the site plans through as discussed on Friday.'

You want me to do this on a Sunday evening? Ashley wants to ask, but knows better. She has often had to work on a Sunday evening lately, clearing her desk and emails ready for the week ahead.

'Can you ping them over as soon as? Like, now?' His tone doesn't disguise this isn't a request. It's a demand. 'I'm meeting a potential buyer on site first thing. I can't go without the plans.'

'I'm so sorry, Mike. I'm sure I sent them.' Sure? She's

certain. That's why she was late picking up Elliot from after-school club on Friday. The plans took forever to load. It's annoying. She'd asked for the technical files so she could start working on those images weeks ago. But she can't allow for the fact that everything came through to her last minute or that she had most certainly sent the plans over late Friday afternoon affect her response. 'I'm just putting my son to bed, and I'll send them straight over again.'

'Thanks.' The phone cuts out.

Ashley ensures the line is disconnected before swearing at the screen. 'Rude bugger.'

'When is Dad going to be home?' Elliot asks as Ashley helps him into his Cat in the Hat pyjamas that Danny bought for him before Elliot was even born. He'd gone on a work trip to some marketing conference in Florida when he was still at the house-building company he worked for before Blue Banana Studios became profitable enough for him to leave.

'I'm not sure, darling. These things take time.' Ashley wonders how many times he is going to repeat that question. 'Get into bed, now. I'll read you a story.'

'But—'

'I know, Dad usually reads to you on a Sunday. But you've got me tonight.'

She tucks him under the sheet and lies beside him. The wine has gone to her head. Hardly surprising since she hasn't eaten since breakfast.

Elliot picks up Champ, his well-worn teddy bear that Tom bought for him when he was born, the perfect uncle present. The bear's fur, once plush and soft, has thinned out in places, especially around the neck where Elliot's growing hands used to hold it. 'Will you and Dad still be able to come to sports day tomorrow?'

She inwardly groans. She'd forgotten about that. She was thinking of keeping him home for the day. She doesn't want to go. She very much doubts Danny will want to go either. He might not even be home by then. She can just imagine the gossip. It spreads faster than chicken pox in a village like Thyme End. But if she knows Elliot, he'll insist, leaving her with little choice. 'One of us will be there.'

'I want you both to be there. I'm going to win the running race.'

Maybe it won't go ahead? Maybe the headteacher will decide it'll be too much. Ashley kisses the top of his head. He is like his dad in so many ways: competitive, determined, and always up for a challenge.

Picking up from where Danny left off, Ashley barely gets through three pages of the latest Secret Seven story he was reading to Elliot before Elliot's eyelashes, long and dark like Danny's, flutter closed. His breath slows to the gentle lull of sleep. She waits for five minutes, staring at the rhythmic rise and fall of his chest, thinking of Lucy, her head lying in a pool of blood. What the hell! They were mingling with a murderer today.

She plants the tenderest of kisses on Elliot's temple. 'I love you, darling. Sweet dreams.'

Downstairs, Rufus anxiously stalks his mistress, waiting for his evening feed. Ashley fills his bowl and stares on absently as he wolfs down the helping of dried food and water. Her phone pings, breaking her out of her trance. It's a message from Tom, asking if he can come over. She ignores it. She doesn't want to see her brother-in-law at the moment. She doesn't want to see anyone.

Her phone is nearly out of battery. She hooks it up to the charger on the side by Danny's well-thumbed cookery books and pours herself another glass of wine. Not so big this time. She needs to keep a clear head. Although work is the last thing she wants to face, she has to stay strong for her family. Mike Booker won't be happy if she doesn't send those plans. It could cost them a new client.

'With me, boy,' she calls to Rufus, who has retired to his bed by the fireplace in the lounge. She grabs her wine and the key to The Hub, and walks along the garden path, pausing before unlocking the door. Someone nearby has cut their grass – a lush scent she has grown to appreciate about living in the country. She stares at the blue and orange sunset fading fast to a subtle purple in the evening sky. It's photogenic. Danny loves a sunset, too. On an ordinary summer's evening, they would be sitting on the patio, their hands cradling glasses of wine as they watched the sun go down. It seems a world away until they will do that again. She shivers... if they ever will.

'What the hell, Danny?' she whispers into the oppressive silence. Her eyes squeeze shut as if to blot out the reality of what has happened to her family. She takes a gulp of wine. It goes down easily. Her heart sinks as the reality hits her.

Her husband is being questioned for murder.

The murder of his childhood friend.

TEN

In the sanctuary of their home office, Ashley sits at her desk, their loyal hound at her feet. The smell of lavender lingers in the air from the burner she keeps on the edge of the desk. It improves the harmony of the place. The downside of running your own business is that it's never-ending. And even when you don't feel like it – as is the case right now – you have no choice but to keep going.

Yes, she and Danny have the flexibility to take a few hours out here and there. They never miss Elliot's school events – instinctively, she checks the monitor to see Elliot still sleeping – but, in reality, eager to expand the business, Danny has piled her workload even higher this past year. Opportunities have been coming thick and fast. And while there's no notion of turning business away, they have got to the point of being over-stretched. And despite the drama she has been dealt, the show must go on.

At a minimum, she needs to resend those files to Mike Booker, and rearrange Danny's schedule for tomorrow. If she recalls correctly, he was due an early start with a new prospect down towards Dover first thing in the morning, with several meetings with other prospective clients scattered throughout the day in the surrounding area. These appointments simply aren't going to happen.

She sits at her glass desk, which mirrors Danny's opposite, and fires up her iMac, trying to process the thoughts buzzing around her head like white noise. Lee's vehement accusations are taunting her. The notion of Danny attacking someone in such a ruthless and violent way is beyond comprehension, let alone that person being Lucy.

What drove Lee to say the things he did? 'I lent him that hammer. He put it in his car earlier. You need to arrest him. Before I get my hands on him.' He couldn't have been thinking straight. But after what he had confronted, who can blame him?

A wave of nausea reminds her she saw Danny dump the bag containing the hammer in the car. So how the hell did it end up in his hand in that garage?

'Damn!' A software refresh. She could do without that right now. Those updates can take a couple of hours. She thumps the desk, desperate for the system to restart. Why now? She's exhausted.

Ashley scoots around to Danny's desk, hoping his machine hasn't played the same unfortunate game. Thank goodness they share passwords. The device lights up as if it's wishing her good evening. Logging into her account, she opens a new email, typing Mike Booker's address into the To field. Clicking on the attachment button, she selects the files she knows she sent on Friday and presses Send, only to see the rainbow wheel of doom spinning on the screen. Her fist hits the desk again. Why is the world against her today?

A photo of Danny and her on their honeymoon in Sicily ten years ago falls forward, banging flat on the desk. She picks it up. The glass has smashed, a crack running between their faces, splitting them in two. She makes a mental note to order a new frame. Standing the photo up, she clasps her hands in front of her chin as if she is praying. 'Come on, come on.' The spinning wheel of doom is still turning. Why the hell does this happen when you least need it?

Her eye aimlessly catches their company brochure sitting in his filing tray. She recently redesigned it to showcase their suite of products. She picks it up and flicks through the glossy pages. The shiny, smooth coating catches the light. She runs her thumb along the edge of the page, emotion sweeping through her as she skims the contents. Even if she says so herself, the designs are eye-catching. They have sweated blood to build their business, and she's proud of their offering.

She checks the computer. The email still hasn't sent.

'Come on. Hurry up.'

She turns her attention back to the brochure. As she reaches the last page, she gasps. Attached to the inside cover is a fluorescent-pink Post-it note, and the words scribed on it clench her gut in another spasm of unease.

Danny, you were great. Can't wait until next week for a repeat performance. h

ELEVEN

With a trembling hand, Ashley tears the note from the page, etching each word into her mind.

A lowercase h... H for Hayley? That's who Danny met on Thursday and he stayed the night away so he could also meet her and her business partner on Friday.

The screen flashes, reminding her why she is there. The email has gone to Mike Booker. With systems up and running again, she composes an email to send to each of Danny's contacts he was due to be meeting tomorrow as she continuously eyes the Post-it note. Her words dance around the grim truth as she offers her profound apologies. Unavoidable circumstances have necessitated the need to reschedule. Danny will be in touch to arrange another time at their convenience.

She touches the Post-it note, her eyes glued to the square of pink, transfixed by the familiarity of the tone of the message. Turning to the screen, she googles Clampitt Homes, where Danny met with Hayley Williams on Thursday... and Friday. Suddenly, she wants to know what Hayley looks like.

The company's website appears at the top of the search

engine. It's a poorly designed site. Ideas for improvement immediately spring to Ashley's mind; she can't help herself. She clicks into the founders section. There are only two partners. Hayley smiles back at her, standing beside an attractive man who reminds her a bit of Danny. Not so much his looks but more the air of alertness about him.

Ashley stares at the redhead with ocean-blue eyes for a minute. Hayley is stunning. She tries to convince herself that, despite her evident beauty, Hayley is not someone Danny would go for. She is clean-cut and pristine. The polar opposite to Ashley, who is more of a free spirit and dresses accordingly. Danny has always said he adores her boho unconventional taste in clothes. But people change.

She massages her neck. It's full of knots, twisting with the tension of the day. There's probably a perfectly plausible explanation for what she has found.

She hovers the mouse over Danny's email account. Is this an act of betrayal? Perhaps. She can't snoop through his things. Not after the last time. She promised herself never again.

A noise from the garden startles her. What was that?

Troubled, she gets up and warily opens the office door. Rufus follows her. She shakes her head. She's being paranoid. If there was anyone there, Rufus would've barked.

Returning to her desk, she checks Elliot on the monitor before retrieving her wine glass. She slowly takes a sip. What she is about to do is wrong. Very wrong. Checking up on your husband doesn't bode well in any marriage. She hates herself for the doubts gnawing away at her. She thought she'd got over these feelings.

It stems back to her childhood. Her father was a serial cheater. Her mother told her and Susie after he died that he'd had more women during their marriage than she'd had cooked breakfasts. But in the name of love, her mother had put up with his shit, and because of that, the shadow of her father's deceit has cast a long, stifling shadow over Ashley's life. She spent her teenage years listening to her mother's howls from behind her parents' bedroom door or to them constantly bickering and sniping at one another. She wished they'd just divorced and freed Susie and her from the constant trauma. She has always vowed to herself that she'll never turn into her mother, but despite her attempts to leave the past behind, her father's betrayal has lingered in her subconsciousness, sometimes convincing her that her insecurities have some credibility.

After Elliot was born and she accused Danny of having an affair, she promised herself she would never doubt him again. She wasn't well at the time. She actually wasn't well for most of the first year of Elliot's life. A breech baby, he was born by emergency caesarean as there were concerns about the position of the umbilical cord. The obstetrician was taking no risks. She suffered excessive bleeding and needed a blood transfusion. Following that, she developed a bladder infection that spread to her kidneys, and she ended up spending a fortnight in hospital. The traumatic ordeal had been a world away from the serene scene she'd envisaged of giving birth naturally in the comfort of her home. But it has never stopped her from wanting another baby.

Danny was working another job at the time she accused him, while squeezing in every spare hour possible to set up Blue Banana Studios. Ashley was on maternity leave but trying to be a new mum while helping Danny with their business and dealing with the postnatal depression that hit her like a truckful of bricks breaking the national speed limit. So when Elliot was about two months old, and Danny hadn't come home until gone four o'clock one morning, she'd fallen apart and accused him of having an affair.

It was so irrational of her. She knew that afterwards. But

after enduring a whole day and night of Elliot's constant colicky wailing, her head had been a mess. Danny had been entertaining a client in London who took him to a nightclub in the West End. He had the receipts to prove it. Not that he showed them to her. She hated herself to the core, but she couldn't help looking through his wallet to find them. And she hated herself even more when they backed up everything he had told her.

Although he tried to hide it, Danny was hurt by her accusations. And after it all blew over and she'd sought help from an understanding GP, she was deeply ashamed. Danny wasn't her father. He would never cheat on her. Marriage is for life, he said, the hurt on his face torturous. Why bother taking vows if it's not?

So why is she distrusting him now?

She returns to Danny's desk. Thoughts continue to whizz around her head, churning up memories she'd rather keep buried. She needs to square her actions away in her mind. Maybe other important emails are waiting in Danny's inbox? Work emails that need a reply. That sounds reasonable enough. He said earlier that he'd need to catch up on his emails sometime that evening.

She turns to another eerie noise from the garden, drawing her attention to the house. Getting up, she opens the doors and pokes her head outside. The branches of the tall ash tree at the side of the garden sway ominously, throwing shadows against the back wall of the house. An owl hoots in a nearby field. But, apart from that, everything seems normal. She keeps the doors open and returns to her computer.

She checks the monitor, ensuring Elliot is still asleep, and types Hayley Williams into the search box. Danny connected with Hayley while carrying out one of his routine cold-calling sessions. Fifty prospective clients, twice a month, on the first and fifteenth, like clockwork. A task many would shy away from, but not Danny. He embraces it every time with inexplicable gusto. Ashley doesn't know how he does it. He either gets the phone slammed down on him or reaches a receptionist who takes his details and promises someone will call him back. Of course, they never do. But sometimes, he's fortunate and gets to speak to the right person.

It's all about breaking through the barrier of the gatekeeper, but Danny is easy to chat with. Once he connects with the right person, he always ends up with at least a face-to-face meeting from his efforts. His secret weapons? His natural charm, lightly sprinkled with a hint of innocent flirtation and his gift of the gab. People are drawn to his charisma like a moth to a flame, and once he makes a connection, it usually ends in the client giving Blue Banana Studios a shot.

It was during one of those initial calls that luck was sitting on his shoulder. He'd phoned at precisely the right moment when Hayley Williams's PA had taken an early lunch, so Hayley had answered the phone. Ashley had been there, and, at the time, she couldn't help smiling at how Danny had worked his magic to nail a meeting with another potential new client.

Ashley pulls up Danny's email account and scrutinises a string of emails between Hayley and Danny, but the correspondence is all professional: details of the new developments Hayley and her business partner have planned. And then the email sent Friday afternoon that Danny had told Ashley about, detailing the work Hayley would like to commission from Blue Banana Studios. It isn't big – a 3D site plan and CGIs for five styles of houses – but it is a start. Ashley well knows this is how businesspeople in their field operate. You do a good job, and future work is offered.

Self-reproach drifts over her. Why is she doubting her husband? She smacks the palms of her hands against her forehead. What is she thinking? She should be helping him, not questioning his actions.

Her head is a mess. Visions of Lucy's bloodied face won't leave her.

She reaches for the brochure and removes the Post-it note.

And rereading it, she gasps as her attention is drawn to the person's initial, written in lowercase. It's not an h.

It's an l.

TWELVE

The security light attached to the pergola snaps on, throwing a blinding fluorescent LED glare across the garden. Rufus stirs, craning his head, his growl low and hostile.

Ashley's heart skips a beat. What was that?

She gets up from the desk and cautiously walks to the door, her senses on high alert. Silhouetted against the backdrop of the house, a tall figure is stomping towards her. She goes to shout for help as the figure comes fully into view.

'Tom! You frightened the life out of me.' She grimaces at her choice of words.

'Hope you don't mind me letting myself in. I called, but I wasn't getting an answer.' Danny's brother's stocky frame fills the doorway. 'I didn't want to knock. I thought Elliot would be in bed.'

Ashley checks the monitor. 'He is. I only popped down here to send a couple of emails.'

Rufus springs towards him.

'Hello, boy. How's my favourite canine friend?' Tom squats down, his large hands roughly caressing the dog's ears and neck. Rufus is beside himself, lapping up the attention. Tom is no stranger to their house. He regularly drops in to see them. He's a great uncle, and Elliot adores him.

Ashley has always felt a little sorry for Tom, though she has never understood why. He's a scruffy chap, with a lonely demeanour, despite his relationship with Renee. It's as if he could do with a good scrub up and a bunch of new friends.

Ashley can't resist glancing at the Post-it note, even with Tom right in front of her. That is most definitely an 'l', not a 'h'. Isn't it? Which client has Danny recently met whose name begins with L?

The taste of wine mixed with bile burns her throat as a thought enters her mind. L for Lucy? Was something going on between Danny and Lucy?

She snaps the brochure closed and tosses it back in the filing tray. Surreptitiously, she puts the computer in sleep mode, her heart beating tenfold.

'I left you a couple of messages.' Tom looks up at Ashley. He has a heart-shaped face where his hair has receded and a beard he could pay more attention to. 'Any news?'

Ashley shakes her head.

'What happened at the station? Did you manage to see him?' Tom asks.

Ashley shakes her head again. 'I made a statement and left.'

Tom doesn't understand. His brother is being questioned about a murder. He wouldn't be allowed to see anyone other than those connected to the law.

'I still can't believe what's happened.'

'Me neither,' Ashley murmurs.

The Post-it note toys with her. No way. Not Danny and Lucy. The thought stirs a cocktail of betrayal she didn't know could taste so bad: anger, sadness, confusion, rage and even grief for the loss of something she can't quite put her finger on. The trust she and Danny have always held in each other, perhaps?

'Renee sends her love. She said she'll see you in the morning.' Tom stands up and folds his arms, his bushy eyebrows knitted in confusion. He moves from one foot to the other. 'What're you doing down here? You're not working, I hope.'

The look on her face answers his question. With a disapproving grunt, Tom places his hands on his hips.

'I'm just sorting out a few bits. Danny has meetings in the morning that I've had to shuffle around. We can't afford to lose business,' she says, defending her presence in The Hub when her husband is being questioned for murder.

Tom is a different animal from his brother – more of a slow-moving tortoise to Danny's busy shrew. Tom has never understood how she and Danny possess such relentless drive. Tom is an electrician, and like many of the tradesmen he works with, he is on the tools early every morning, but you rarely see him working much past four in the afternoon. He is more about having a healthy work-life balance. If you can call dropping into the local pub for three to four *swift* pints at five o'clock every day healthy! He used to have his own company but couldn't cope with the business element, so now he works for a national house builder on new development sites in the region. A conservationist at heart, he hates every minute of it, but the bills need to be paid.

Tom perches on the side of Ashley's desk, picking at his cuticles. She can smell beer on his breath, which is not unusual. 'What's going to happen to him?' he asks.

Ashley feels the pain in Tom's forlorn face. The day must have been traumatic for him. He and Lucy were childhood sweethearts, inseparable throughout their teenage years until Lucy announced she had a place at university, and the relationship had ended. Tom was devastated, and, on the rebound, he married a blue-eyed peroxide blonde. They divorced on the grounds of her adultery less than two years after Tom put a ring on her finger. Ever since, he has headed to The Ugly Duckling in the village every day after work, where he puts the world to rights with whatever other willing local is propping up the bar alongside him before going home for a ready meal. Or, if it's a night he's seeing Renee, something she has cooked.

Tom clears his throat. 'I'm worried about him.'

'Once he's spoken to them, they'll let him go,' Ashley says. 'Which reminds me, I need to go back inside. I left my phone on charge.'

She eyes the Post-it one more time before standing up.

L for Lucy.

THIRTEEN

Ashley sits at the granite breakfast bar, checking her phone while Tom fills the kettle. She'd rather be alone, and she has told Tom as much, but he hasn't taken the hint. He appears edgy. Doesn't he always? Then again, so is she.

'Can I nab a beer?' he asks.

She'd rather he didn't. She can tell he has already had quite a few. She knows what's coming. She's been there before with Tom when he's had one too many. He'll start rattling on, spilling the local gossip, and he'll never leave. As Danny has always said, if you're looking for a sure-fire way to spread news around the village quickly, simply tell Tom. His brother doesn't mean to be spiteful. It's just Tom having no filter. If he were here, Danny would suggest they'd best stick to a soft drink before politely telling him it's time to leave. She wishes he was here instead of his brother.

Tom heads to the fridge. 'You don't want to join me for a beer?'

'I need to keep a clear head for when Danny gets home.'

If he gets home. Why does she have a niggling doubt she won't be seeing him tonight?

Tom opens the fridge and helps himself to a bottle of Bud, sipping it while he chats away.

Ashley sifts through the texts on her phone. More messages from well-wishers, disguising their nosiness for an update in words of sympathy. One from Oriana brings tears to her eyes. The poor woman. As if she doesn't have enough to contend with.

I'm devastated. I can't believe my girl has gone. I hope you're bearing up. How is Danny? Love Oriana X

Ashley quickly replies.

It's a nightmare. I hope you're OK. I'll call you tomorrow. Love Ashley X

'What do you think?' Tom's words pull her away from her phone.

'Sorry?'

'You haven't listened to a word I've just said, have you?' Tom gulps his beer. 'Those fat-cat developers! It looks like they're going to get their way. The government are going to sanction their plans. The village will be flattened without a second thought to the local residents. It's scandalous. They'll be coming for Thyme End before we know it.'

Ashley is stumped. Her husband, Tom's brother, is being questioned by the police about his friend's murder, and all he can talk about is the bloody village? 'Tom, we've been over this. Danny says to look to controlling the controllable. We can't get stressed about something that may never happen.'

'But it *is* going to happen. Our lives will be ruined. We must do something.'

The elephant in the room trumpets. 'Tom! Lucy is dead,

and the police are questioning Danny about her murder, and all you can talk about is developers building more houses.'

Tom appears as surprised by her outburst as she is. 'I'm sorry,' he says. 'It's only words. I don't know what to say.' There's a pause. 'How're you holding up?'

Ashley's eyes glass over again. 'So-so.'

'And Elliot?'

She clears her throat. 'I'm trying to play it down, keeping things as normal as possible. He doesn't fully understand the impact of it all. I've just said his dad is answering some questions and helping the police. Thankfully, he was exhausted from the party and pretty much fell straight to sleep.'

'We'll get through this.' Tom crouches down and rubs Rufus' neck.

Guilt hits her for her outburst. 'This must be difficult for you.'

'I'm finding it hard to process. Which is probably why I was wittering on about work.'

Ashley rests her elbows on the worktop and drops her chin in her hands. 'What do you think happened?'

'You found them.'

She stares at the beam of light shining off the worktop. 'Danny had blood all over him, and he had that... hammer... in his hand.' She holds out her hands, mimicking Danny's position earlier. The blood caked in Lucy's hair torments her. She clenches her jaw. L for Lucy.

Tom walks to Ashley's side and puts his arms around her. His large frame shrouds her petite body.

She's taken aback. Tom seldom displays physical affection. Whenever she used to hug him when they saw each other, he never reciprocated. He simply stood as stiff as a board, resisting the embrace. So she stopped hugging him.

'I wish I'd had the chance to talk to him. Find out what he was doing in the garage,' she says.

Her phone buzzes. Another text from one of the mums at school who means well but should be minding her own business. That's the downside of living in such a tight-knit community. Everyone wants to know what's going on in your life. She hates it.

Tom releases his arm from her shoulders and swiftly drains the remnants of his beer. 'Can I tell you something?' With a troubled expression, he settles himself on the stool beside her at the breakfast bar. 'I didn't mention it to the police when they questioned me at the party.'

Ashley stares at him quizzically. There's an undertone in his voice she doesn't like and his face is etched with unease.

'I was at Lucy and Lee's house Wednesday after work, fixing the wiring for the new security lighting on their cart lodges.'

A sense of foreboding creeps over her. 'And?'

'Lee left to pick up their youngest daughter from some club.'

Tom pauses as if debating whether he should divulge the next piece of his news.

She leans back on the stool, bracing herself for what he is about to reveal. 'And?'

'Danny... Danny was there.'

Ashley's mind races back to Wednesday. Danny was working from home in the morning, and in the afternoon he went out to see a prospective client on the outskirts of London.

Plans that never involved a visit to Lucy and Lee's house.

FOURTEEN

Tom hesitates, his fingers tapping his bottom lip. An internal battle of whether he should divulge further information appears to be written in the deep lines on his forehead.

'He and Lucy were arguing. I saw them through the window and heard their raised voices.' He speaks fast, as though he wants to banish the thought from his mind.

Ashley's stomach turns. She can't remember Danny saying he'd been to Lucy and Lee's house at all, let alone telling her that he and Lucy had argued. 'What were they arguing about?'

He shrugs. 'When I asked him about it, he denied it. He said they were discussing business.'

'You must've heard something.'

'I didn't. Honestly, I'd tell you if I did. It was probably nothing. Forget it.'

Is he lying? He must be. Danny would have told her.

'Have you spoken to my parents?' Tom asks.

'No. I was thinking of calling them but thought it best for Danny to do that when he gets home.'

'That's what I thought, too.'

'I don't want to appear rude, Tom, but would you mind

leaving? I need to get to bed. As you can imagine, I've had the day from hell. And you know Elliot, always up at the crack of dawn.'

'I'll look after him for you tomorrow. I'll call my boss and tell him I'm not coming in. He'll understand, given the circumstances.'

'He wants to go to school.'

Tom raises his eyebrows. 'Do you think that's wise?'

'Not at all. But he said he wants to go. It's his sports day. And instinct is telling me to keep things as normal as possible for him.' Her voice wavers.

Normal? Who is she trying to kid?

The house is silent, save the odd familiar creak and squeak of a relatively new home settling down for another night. Ashley stands at the kitchen sink, staring out the window. The intense darkness makes for a mirror. She stares at her face, haunted by the day. She can't work out whether she is irritated or alarmed at the lack of information about Danny. He should be home by now, surely? She briefly considers calling someone, but who? Maybe her sister? Forever pragmatic and logical, Susie would offer a reasonable explanation about the Post-it note and why Danny and Lucy were arguing. But it would be selfish to disturb her. She's got an early-morning flight to catch. And to what end, anyway? A pity party is not Ashley's style.

With a weary sigh, she tears herself away from her trance-like state. Bed is the only sensible option. It's gone ten o'clock, beyond her normal bedtime for a Sunday night. She fills a glass from the tap and waters the herb planters growing on the windowsill, before wandering around downstairs, methodically checking all the doors are locked. A nightly ritual her husband usually performs.

On autopilot, she pours two glasses of water, shoulders off

the kitchen light, and proceeds upstairs in darkness. It's airless. She places the drinks on the landing table and opens the window, inviting a breeze throughout the upstairs hallway. But the night is as breathless as her.

She checks on Elliot. He has removed his pyjama top, kicked his sheet onto the floor and is sprawled on his back, his skinny limbs extended like the points of a star. Ashley lightly kisses his forehead and slips out of the room.

As she picks up the glasses of water, the unexpected sound of a knock at the door jars her. Water splashes over her fingers and runs down her wrists. Who the hell can that be at this hour?

Rufus barks. She puts down the glasses and approaches the window, trying to catch a glimpse of their unexpected visitor, but she can't see who is at the front door from that angle.

She hurries downstairs, fearful that whoever it is might knock again and wake up Elliot. Ashley tugs Rufus' collar, quietening him. She pauses at the door. She's not sure she wants to open it at this time of night without knowing who it is.

A fist thumps on the door again and she hears her husband's voice. 'Ash, open up.'

She swings open the door. 'At last,' she says, breathing a huge sigh of relief. 'I've been worried sick. What the hell has happened?'

FIFTEEN

Danny bursts into the house. Even in the darkness, she can see his face is as pasty as the unfamiliar grey polyester tracksuit he's wearing.

She hadn't even considered the police would need to take his blood-stained clothes.

Rufus goes mad, jumping up Danny's front, his tail wagging. Danny brushes the dog aside and storms past her, his presence a whirlwind in the otherwise still house. Ashley comforts Rufus and tells him to return to his bed before tailing Danny like a shadow into the kitchen.

'What's happened?' she asks again, her voice tight with tension.

Danny snaps on the light, filling the room with harsh artificial brightness. He snaps it off and flicks the switch to the muted glow of the under-cupboard lighting. Ashley stares at him in confusion as he pours a glass of water and downs it in one, instantly refilling it. Her question remains unanswered.

She steps to his side and grabs his forearm. The scent of alcohol hovering in the air confuses her. Is that him or her? A deep sniff answers her question.

'You've been drinking.' She can't help the annoyance overriding her anxiety. All this time she has been waiting for news of him, he has been out drinking somewhere. Where? Who with? He's got a hell of a lot of questions to answer.

He fills the kettle and switches it on, the sound loud against the tense silence. The coffee tin scratches along the worktop.

She takes it from his grip. 'Let me do that for you.'

He places his hands against the sink, his arms ramrod straight. His gaze locks onto the same window she was staring out of only five minutes earlier. A shroud of darkness seems to have draped over him, a shadow of fear Ashley has never seen before. His furrowed brow is almost menacing. It unsettles her even more.

'Talk to me. What's happened? Where've you been?' she pleads. The sound of her voice is as grating as the tension between them.

'I needed a drink,' he answers, his voice hollow.

The inadequacy of his response tears at her heart. 'You could've called. I've been sick with worry. Who gave you a lift back from the station?'

He doesn't answer.

She watches him. He is in an almost trancelike state, the same as her earlier. Her heart is heavy with a mix of emotions: concern, confusion and a sense of trepidation, all swirling in the heavy silence overpowering the room once again.

'Who brought you back from the station?' she repeats.

'John Farnborough.'

'The policeman who was at the party?'

'That's right.'

'You went for a drink with him? Why? Didn't you think to call me?'

Danny turns his head, glaring at her. 'Give it a rest, Ash.'

His words are like a kick in the teeth. This is not her Danny.

Never before has he spoken to her like that. The shock and disappointment are painful. She needs answers, though.

'What *has* happened? What did the police say?'

His face is tight with tension. 'Don't you think I've had enough questioning at the police station? Back off.'

Tears, threatening to burst, burn her eyes. What *is* going on with him?

Regardless of the day's events, the Post-it note is still plaguing her mind. And the argument Tom mentioned he had with Lucy. Anger rises through her.

'I have a right to know.'

Elliot appears at the kitchen door, rubbing his eyes, halfway between slumber and wakefulness. His hair is sticking up, and his face is flushed from the heat. 'Dad!' He stumbles over to his father.

'You should be in bed,' Danny barks, pointing at the door. 'It's late.' He places his hands on Elliot's shoulders, turns him and pushes him towards the door. 'Bed now!'

Elliot turns to look at Ashley as he leaves the room, his crest-fallen face a second kick in the teeth.

Ashley gasps at her husband's aberrant behaviour. She glares at him. 'That was out of order.' She rushes after their son, who is ascending the stairs three at a time on all fours like Spider-Man. She catches up with him as he flings himself on his bed and buries his head in the pillow. She kneels by his side, stroking his hair. 'Don't worry. Dad has had a bad day. It'll all be OK in the morning.'

What is she thinking? There's no way they will get over what happened that quickly.

If at all.

'Why is he mad at me?' Elliot asks between silent sobs. 'I haven't done anything wrong.'

'He's not mad at you, darling. You're right; you've done nothing wrong. He's just upset. Now, please, get some sleep.'

She stays curled up next to him for a quarter of an hour, hoping it will give Danny time to compose himself. She gently pats Elliot's back. A ritual she knows always sends him to sleep. Dread for the days ahead coils in her stomach, which is turning as fast as her thoughts. What's going to happen to their little family?

When she returns to the kitchen, Danny is in the same spot he was when she left him, his hands ruffling Rufus' red wheaten coat. Two whisky tumblers sit on the worktop, the amber fluid glowing in the dim under-cupboard lighting. She pauses, leaning against the door frame.

Danny stretches out his arm in her direction, a welcoming invite into his loving embrace. She succumbs, relieved the mood he arrived home in has subsided. Laying her head on his shoulder, she can feel a slight tremble from his body. He smells of whisky and uncertainty.

'I'm sorry, darling. You don't deserve this.'

She stays locked in the comfort of his arms, fearing she is grasping onto the final fragments of normality.

His voice is hoarse, as if it's weak from countless attempts to defend himself. 'They asked questions. So many questions. I swear they're trying to pin it on me.'

Ashley lifts her head, unfolding herself from his hold. '*What?* How can they?'

Worry masks his good looks. She has never seen him so scared. 'There's more to come tomorrow.' He shakes his head, the corners of his mouth downturned.

'*More?*'

'They haven't finished with me yet. I've got to be back at the station in the morning.' He sighs heavily. 'They only let me go on the proviso that I don't leave the village and I return tomorrow morning for more questioning. Oh, and I'm not allowed to contact anyone else, especially Lee.'

'What the hell! How could they think you'd hurt Lucy? You've known each other forever.'

He takes a long breath. 'It was like a fucking circus down there. I had to wait ages before they came to speak to me.' Reaching for the tumblers, he hands one to her. They normally clink glasses, but there's nothing normal about tonight. Uncharacteristically, he downs the three inches of fluid in one, as if he won't get another chance, and bangs the glass down on the worktop.

'I can't believe they want you down there again. What time have you got to go back?'

'Eight-thirty.'

'I'll give you a lift.'

'It's fine. You need to join that client call. We've got to stay on top of things, Ash. I've spoken to Tom and asked him for a lift.'

'But he has been here. He never got a call,' she says, confused.

'I spoke to him, literally, five minutes ago.'

'Didn't they keep you long enough today?'

With an unsteady hand, he slides the bottle of whisky towards him. He unscrews the cap and drops it on the floor, shattering the tense silence. He pours himself another double measure. 'It seems not,' he murmurs. He downs the drink in one. 'I'm telling you. They're trying to lay this on me.'

They exchange accounts of what has happened since they each left the party. Ashley shares the probing few hours she spent with DCI Graham, and Danny briefs her on the straightforward questions that grew increasingly demanding as the afternoon progressed to evening.

'What were you doing in the garage?' she asks quietly.

His jaw tightens. 'I went to the car to get my cigarettes. I fancied one, just one.'

Before they moved to Thyme End, Danny had been a packet-a-day smoker. He was constantly climbing out the skylight window in the kitchen area of their London flat to the roof terrace for a smoke. He even had a golfing umbrella up there for rainy days that he kept in a small lock-up that housed a couple of camping chairs and cushions. But he went cold turkey after doing the sums on the hefty mortgage Ashley wasn't keen to take on. She can hear his words. 'Come on, Ash. I'll quit. I promise you. Three hundred pounds a month, I'll save. Then we can easily afford the mortgage.'

It's a promise he never kept. He hasn't fully returned to his bad habit, but he started keeping a packet in the car and having the occasional smoke at social events, which escalated to one or two at the weekend. It riles her. Not that she says anything.

Now she thinks about it, she thought he smelt of smoke when he came home on Wednesday. When he had that meeting with Lucy that she knew nothing about. She jokingly asked if he'd been down the pub, but he said it was in her imagination.

'I thought I heard a scream from the garage, so I went in there.' His voice wavers. He thumps his fist on the worktop, startling her back to the moment. 'That's when I found her.'

'Was she already dead?'

He replies with a solemn nod. 'Whoever did it must've escaped out the side door.'

'And why... why were you covered in so much blood? What were you doing with that hammer?' The questions fall into the room like a lead weight.

His voice breaks. 'I felt the need to hold her. She was my oldest friend, Ash. Then I thought, CPR, try CPR. I wasn't thinking straight. I was a mess. *She* was a mess.'

Ashley repeats, 'And the hammer?'

He groans, slamming his fist into his forehead. 'It was lying on her chest as if it had been dropped there. I moved it to the floor to do CPR. Why I picked it up afterwards, I can't tell you.

I was kind of incredulous that it could cause that much damage. I told the police the same. They didn't seem to understand.'

'So, let me get this straight. Someone went to our car, got the hammer and went to the garage to murder her.'

He shakes his head. 'No, no. You've got that wrong.'

'Got what wrong?'

'It wasn't the same hammer.'

SIXTEEN

Ashley stares at Danny wide-eyed. 'What do you mean?'

'The hammer that killed Lucy wasn't the same one that Lee lent to me. That's what the police told me. So they must've found the hammer Lee gave me still in the car. Apparently, Lee kept a number of similar hammers in the garage.'

Ashley reaches for her husband's hand.

It wasn't the same hammer Lee lent to Danny. That's a relief. She couldn't believe that Danny would have hurt anyone, but all the police interest... Ashley couldn't help feeling a little uncertain until hearing this confirmed.

'I doubt very much I'd be standing here now if it was the same one.'

As they sip their drinks, the conversation trails off into another whirling void of silence.

A thought comes to her. 'What was Lee doing by the garages?'

'I don't know. He came in and saw me holding the hammer and started yelling. I froze.'

They stare at each other, a look passing between them that asks, *Are you thinking what I'm thinking?*

'It couldn't have been Lee,' Ashley says. 'He adored Lucy. But what was he doing out there?'

Danny shrugs. 'I don't know, but I'm sure the police will be grilling him too. Have you heard from him?'

'No. I was thinking about sending him a text but didn't know if it was the right thing to do. Not after what he said to you.'

'I never want to speak to that man again. You should've heard him. He accused me, Ash.' His voice cracks. 'He accused me of murder.'

'I heard. I was there, remember. It was probably just the shock of it all.'

His brown eyes, smaller than they usually appear, stare at her, the hurt in them transferring further pain her way. 'How could he? I thought we were mates.' His shoulders begin to shake. 'I can't believe she's gone.'

Ashley tries to console him, but he rotates his shoulders, escaping her embrace.

'You are allowed to cry, you know,' she says, upset at his coldness. Danny is the warmest person she has ever met.

He closes his eyes, leaning over the sink and scrunching the pain and torment in his face. 'If I break down now, it won't do me any favours.'

Ashley shakes her head. That's Danny all over – always got to keep strong. Always got to keep going no matter what.

'Who could've done this, Danny?'

He shrugs. 'That's what the police kept asking me. I honestly have no idea. Everyone loved Lucy.'

Did they? Ashley's not so sure everyone did. Not that she would ever admit that to anyone. Lucy was too perfect. No one can be that flawless. Ashley had often wondered when they'd met – business and pleasure – about the performance that went on behind the scenes. There was something about Lucy that Ashley had never quite trusted. Maybe because of how touchy-feely she was with Danny. But whatever, she didn't deserve to be murdered.

'To think amongst us at that party was a cold-blooded killer. Poor Lucy. Her poor kids.' Ashley sips her drink, desperate to ask Danny about the Post-it note. She has never been one to skate around an issue, however sensitive, but now is not the time. Danny will be upset when she brings it up, so she needs to choose her moment wisely. But maybe it's better to get it out in the open? A moment's hesitation, a heartbeat's pause, she swallows the questions she's dying to ask him and instead she says, 'Where did you go after the police station?'

'To the pub. I'm sorry I didn't call, darling. I was so wound up, I needed a drink.'

She looks at him, her eyes narrowing. 'The Ugly Duckling?'

'No. The Rose and Crown. That's where I asked John to drop me off.'

Why The Rose and Crown? It's on the other side of the village. 'You never go in there.'

'I didn't want to bump into any of the regulars at The Duckling.' He swigs his drink and slams the glass down. 'And now I need to wash this bloody day off me and get to bed.' He kisses her cheek. 'Coming?'

Ashley nods. 'I'll be up in a minute.'

She watches him leave the room, his head hanging as if the weight of the day has left him too exhausted to hold it upright. Tipping her drink down the sink, she rinses the glasses. A hangover is the last thing she needs in the morning.

While Danny is in the shower, Ashley dumps the duvet in the spare room and finds a sheet in the cupboard. The oppressiveness of the summer heat is too much for a duvet tonight. Besides, she needs to feel less confined. Her mind is in turmoil, a vortex of unsaid words and unasked questions she wants to confront Danny with.

She opens their bedroom window. An ever so slight coolness enters the room. She climbs into bed, her mind in overdrive. She wants to ask him so much, but since he came home, she has been walking on the eggshells of his predicament. But there's one question she can't let pass.

He gets into bed. Droplets of water cling to his wet hair, and a slick sheen of sweat accentuates the furrowed lines on his forehead. He reaches to turn out the light, but Ashley intercepts his bare arm, his skin hot to touch.

'I need to ask you something.' Her voice is a whisper in the quietness of the room.

'I'm done in, Ash. I can't talk anymore tonight.'

And she can't wait until the morning.

Undeterred, she continues. 'Why were you arguing with Lucy the other night?'

The mattress sinks as he turns to face her, frowning. 'What night?' Is that apprehension she can detect in his voice?

'Last Wednesday, you were meant to be in London seeing that new client, but you were seen, and heard, at Lucy and Lee's place arguing with her.'

His jaw clenches. He remains quiet.

'Danny?' She squeezes his arm, coaxing him.

'What?' he snaps.

She can't stand this. 'What were you arguing with her about?'

'Who told you this?'

Her lips twist to the side. 'Tom.'

'Bloody Tom. He can't keep his nose out of other people's business. It'll be around the village, and the police will jump on it, and that's me done for.'

'Danny?' she persists.

He rakes his hands through his hair, audibly grinding his teeth.

'What were you arguing about?'

'Work. A disagreement on a development. I disagreed with her tack. As simple as.'

Her heart is pounding. Is he telling her the truth? 'Which development? I don't understand.'

Danny raises his voice, cutting her off. 'Enough, Ash. Stop. My best friend has been bludgeoned to death, and I found the body. What's more, the police think I did it. I can't take any more tonight.' He switches off the light and turns his back on her.

She looks at him in horror. It's as if she is in bed with a foreign being, a stranger with Danny's voice, not her loving husband. They never go to sleep without kissing each other. Even when they've had a silly argument. And he always spoons his body round hers as they fall asleep.

Ashley doesn't know what to do. She wants to find answers to all the questions spinning around in her head. Several times, she reaches out her hand to prod him on the shoulder, but each time, a voice tells her to leave it. They can talk in the morning.

She turns out her light and stares at the shadowy figure of her husband, the man who has transformed into a stranger right before her eyes.

And for the first time in their marriage, he is scaring her.

SEVENTEEN

Ashley struggles to sleep. The heat is relentless.

Sweat beads on her forehead and the sides of her nose. Wiping it away, she lets out a long sigh, but it doesn't take the weight of her anxiety with it. She reaches for her phone. The digital clock tells her another sixty minutes have passed since she last looked. It's now gone four o'clock.

She glances across at Danny. Thoughts of yesterday swirl around her mind, as restless and intrusive as the summer heat. She repositions herself on her back, staring at the moonlight stretching across the room. The more she thinks about it, the more she is sure he has not been himself of late. A change in him that began when she agreed to move to Thyme End.

How she wishes they were back in their London flat. Life was better there, despite the chaos of trying to run a business from a room that also served as the living quarters for their small family. Danny was less stressed in those days. They were happier. She's sure of it. He had more time for her. He has always been enthusiastic about Blue Banana Studios and poured everything into building a company that would support them all, but since they moved to Thyme End, he has been hell-bent on wanting even more from the business. He's not at home as much, always out on the road chasing a new client or pursuing another line of inquiry. And when he is at home, late nights in The Hub have become more frequent.

And what about that time last week when he was still in The Hub gone midnight? She went down there, dressed in a skimpy nightie, to seduce him to bed. He acted strangely, as if she had caught him doing something he shouldn't be doing. Not even the attire that usually gets him going had the desired effect. He barely looked at her, brushing her away with body language that firmly told her he was busy.

Or has her imagination got the better of her?

With an impulsive surge of energy, Ashley jumps out of bed and slips into her dressing gown. She's exhausted but wide awake, sick yet hungry, a strange combination. As she goes downstairs, she yawns, rubbing her eyes as Rufus greets her, wagging his tail in the hope of an early-morning walk. She tickles the top of his head as he ambles by her side into the kitchen, where she takes a bottle of apple juice out of the fridge. She doesn't bother with a glass.

Finding the key, Ashley creeps along the garden path to open up The Hub. From her desk, she stares at the back of Danny's iMac. She wonders how many potential secrets it holds. What a terrible thought to have. They've never had secrets.

Never.

Or have they? Has he?

Walking to his desk, she sits down and peers around their ultra-modern office with its glass furniture, white walls and a large piece of abstract art she painted at Danny's request. What they've achieved is remarkable. But she can't help wondering the ultimate price they could pay for their success.

Hesitant at first, she finally gives in to the curiosity she no longer has control over and opens the drawer to his desk. She regularly glimpses towards the house nervously, in the unlikely event Danny has woken up. The drawer is as tidy as a neat-freak's house – the total opposite to her desk drawers, which are an organised mess. There's a home for everything in his. That's Danny for you. He is meticulously tidy. Each section of the wooden divider stores office materials, from paperclips to highlighter pens, scissors and Post-it notes. A stapler and a plastic business card holder shaped like an opened envelope slot along the side perfectly.

Ashley grabs the card holder, removes the cards and sifts through them. They are mainly from clients: people Danny has met along the way, a couple of local cab firms, their NHS organ donor cards, a loyalty card for a garden centre they visited as winter gave way to spring, and a photo of her holding Elliot when he was still a baby. Nothing out of the ordinary until she comes to the last one. It's for a firm of solicitors in the local town: Barton, Blake & Co. Ashley reads the details. Shirley Simmons: Head of Family Division. She flips the card over. Written on the reverse is the name 'Patricia Cartwright' and, underneath, today's date, 4 p.m.

She stares at the photo of her and Danny on their honeymoon in the cracked frame. Why is he meeting with a solicitor? He was meant to be in Dover today.

Ashley wanders back to her desk, flipping the business card between her fingers. Who is Patricia Cartwright?

Ashley fires up her iMac and steps behind the large yucca plant that creates a natural screen around the far left-hand corner of the room that houses a kettle, cups and their mini fridge to keep milk and cold drinks to hand. She also stores a stash of Dairy Milk and Galaxy bars in the side section for those days when only chocolate will do. Come to think of it, there've been a lot of those lately.

The faint scent of Danny's sandalwood aftershave lingers in the air, an invisible cloud of what she thought was, only a day ago, a loving and trusting relationship. She takes a deep breath, clinging onto the smell as if the comforting familiarity can ward off her insecurities. Removing a bottle of water from the fridge, she unscrews the cap and drinks it in one uninterrupted gulp, trying to rationalise why Danny is meeting with this woman today without telling her.

When her iMac comes to life, she quickly checks the news. When she looked last night, she could find nothing about the murder, but now it's plastered across the front pages of several sites, each featuring the same sizeable photo of Lucy at her best. She is sitting on a boat surrounded by Lee and her children, her beautiful smile accentuating her perfectly symmetrical face. From the age of the kids, it must have been taken recently. Probably when they nipped down to Cornwall during the Easter break. Danny thought it ludicrous that they'd dragged the kids all that way for four days, two of them spent travelling. But Lucy was too busy to take any more time off work. The image captures her hair gaily blowing in the wind like a flag. Designer sunglasses are perched on her head. Lee's arm is around her shoulders, his adoration evident in the affectionate way he looks at her.

As she reads the story, Ashley can't escape the gravity of the situation. The woman in the photo, so full of life and love, now reduced to a tragic headline and a few lousy paragraphs summing up her fate. She shudders, her mind racing with questions. Detectives are appealing for anyone with any information about the murder or any suspicious events leading up to it to call the police immediately on the number provided.

A mix of emotions swirls within her. Sorrow for the loss of the woman she has known for such a short time and confusion about the man she thought she knew so well.

She googles Barton, Blake & Co. It's a traditional firm with offices along a backstreet in the local town and claims to have an unrivalled reputation for first-rate service. Ashley has never heard of it. They still use an old uni friend who works at a firm up north for their business matters. They found it much cheaper than the same services in London and the south.

She types Patricia Cartwright in the search bar and clicks the go button. It loads instantaneously. A photo pops up on the screen. It's a flattering shot of a thirty-something blonde woman from the waist up. Her hair is scraped back into a tight bun, and the perfectly ironed collars of her shirt sit neatly on the lapels of a navy suit jacket with gold buttons. Beneath the image, it says, Patricia Cartwright: Divorce Lawyer.

A chill runs through Ashley as she skim reads the woman's bio that claims, by way of her commitment and meticulous attention to detail, Patricia Cartwright is one cut above everyone unlucky enough to cross her.

Ashley clicks on Danny's diary. When she was cancelling all his commitments for today, she can't recall seeing a meeting with this woman.

She is right. There is no meeting scheduled for four o'clock today. The timeslot is blank.

She shivers again despite the humidity.

Why is Danny due to meet with a divorce lawyer this afternoon?

EIGHTEEN

Nothing is making sense. Her whole world is collapsing around her.

Ashley peers through the doors of The Hub. Outside, the first hint of dawn glows across the sky. Part of her doesn't want morning to arrive so she can delay the inevitable confrontation with her husband. But Ashley isn't a woman to crumble. She knows she can't let Danny return to the police station before he has explained himself.

She rereads Patricia Cartwright's bio and rechecks Danny's diary to ensure she wasn't mistaken. The 4 p.m. meeting is definitely not there.

She sits in the unsettling quiet, swallowing the bitter taste of betrayal. She has to go and talk to him.

When she returns to the house, Rufus is dozing by the door but springs to life when he sees her. 'Go back to sleep, Rufi,' she whispers and tiptoes back upstairs.

She quietly slips into bed beside Danny. He is snoring gently. She reaches out to wake him up, but the hand of reason pokes her shoulder, asking if this is the best way to tackle the situation. They are both exhausted, and he has to return to the police station in fewer than four hours. Wouldn't it be better to let him sleep a little longer? Her too. They have a hell of a day ahead of them. She lies on her back, staring at the ceiling.

What feels like only moments later, she glances at Danny's side of the bed. It's empty. Where is he?

She reaches out and grabs her phone. It's teeming with messages she hasn't got the time or the stomach to read. It's six o'clock. She must have fallen asleep, although her burning eyes protest she hasn't slept a wink.

Jumping out of bed, she stops and sits down, clutching her head. She shouldn't have drunk that whisky last night. Not on top of all that wine. She barely ate yesterday either. What had she been thinking? She grabs the side of the bed. Keep it together. She must keep herself together.

She snatches summer joggers and a tie-dye T-shirt from her wardrobe and runs downstairs. Danny can't leave for the police station before she has spoken to him. He has some explaining to do. If he has been seeking the advice of a divorce lawyer, then he can bloody well be a grown-up about it and tell her straight. But why would he even be considering it? They are happy together, aren't they? The Post-it note enters her thoughts.

The smell of coffee hits her halfway down the stairs. Searching in the lounge and then the kitchen, there's no sign of her husband or the dog. Danny has either taken Rufus out for a walk or he is in The Hub. At least that's what she hopes. He wouldn't have left without talking to her first.

She walks into the kitchen and heads to the patio doors. He is in The Hub, sitting at his desk. His elbows are resting on the desktop, his hands supporting his bowed head as if he is reading something.

The kettle is still hot to her touch. Danny loves his morning coffee as much as she does. She reboils the water and pours them both an extra-strong cup.

As she approaches The Hub, Danny is no longer sitting at his desk. He is on all fours in the corner by the small kitchen area, with his back to her. What is he up to?

She bends down, places the cups on the decking, and quietly opens the door. Kings of Leon's 'Use Somebody' fills the room.

She stares at him, confused. 'Whatever are you doing?'

Danny startles. He peers around. 'Bloody hell, Ash. You scared the life out of me.' He looks like crap, washed out, as if he hasn't slept all night either. But she knows he has.

'What *are* you up to?'

'Nothing.'

'You must be doing something. Why else would you be on your hands and knees down there?'

'My ring. I was playing with it, and it fell off. I can't find it.' His clipped reply offers her no comfort. He turns to face the wall. 'There it is.' He reaches out a hand. Standing up, he twists his wedding ring around his finger.

Ashley steps back outside and picks up the two cups of coffee. 'We need to talk.'

'Ash. Please.' He glances at his watch. 'I've got to be at the police station soon. And there's stuff here I need to take care of first.'

'That's what I want to talk to you about.' Ashley hands him a cup of coffee. Taking a deep breath, she walks over to his desk and retrieves the business card. 'Have you got something to tell me?'

Danny looks at the card, then at her. A mixture of irritation and bewilderment clouds his face. 'Where did you get that?'

NINETEEN

'I found it in your drawer,' Ashley says.

'Checking up on me now, are you?' he says bitterly.

'Can you blame me?'

Danny runs his hand through his hair. 'Don't go there, Ash.' He is referring to the time after Elliot was born, and she doubted him. She knows he is.

She reaches across his desk and grabs the brochure with the Post-it note attached to the inside of the back cover. 'And what about this?' She unsticks the note and slams it in his hands. 'Who is this from?'

He reads the note, frowns, then, seemingly understanding the connotation of its meaning, smiles. 'Ash, come on.'

Her pulse is racing. 'No, you come on. Tell me the truth. Are you looking for a divorce?'

He laughs. A genuine, wholehearted laugh. She realises it's been a while since she saw him do that so freely. She steps backwards, affronted.

He pauses, then says, stammering between laughter, 'Ash, you've got it all wrong. That note is from Larry. Larry from the golf club. We got through to the quarter-finals of the four-balls last month. Remember me telling you? I had a blinder that day. I told him about the great work you do, and I showed him our brochure after the game when we had a drink in the bar. I got a phone call from a client.' He scratches his head. Is he talking a little too quickly? 'I can't even remember who. It might even have been Lucy. I went outside to take it. It went on a while, and Larry had to go. He left the note. His wife owns that coffee shop next to the barber in town. The one I take Elliot to. She wants some signage for her shop. Not the type of work we usually take on, I know, but I said I'd speak to you about it. It's only a bit of graphic design, but you never know where it might lead. I forgot all about it. I'm sorry.'

'And what about the divorce lawyer?' she asks as she digests his explanation for the Post-it note.

'Lucy introduced me to Patricia a few weeks ago.'

'When?'

'I went to Lucy's for a meeting. Patricia was there.'

'What meeting? You didn't tell me.'

He shrugs. 'I forgot, I guess.'

'The same as when you met with her on Wednesday?' She can't help the accusatory tone in her voice. 'What was Patricia doing there?'

'She's a friend of Lucy's.' He pauses, thumping the palms of his hands together. '*Was* a friend of Lucy's.'

'So why have you got a meeting with her?'

'It's not with her. It's with her cousin, Peter. Peter Clarke. He's a property developer and lives in Faversham. I was going to stop there today on my way back from Dover.'

'Why didn't you put it in the diary?' She's sounding desperate, clutching at straws of accusation, and she hates herself for it.

He shrugs. 'I forgot. I'm sorry.' He thumps the side of the desk. 'For fuck's sake, Ash. I feel like I'm back at the station being grilled by the coppers.'

She recoils into her chair.

Danny's jaw tenses. He sits on the corner of her desk. 'We can't let this get to us, Ash. Come here.' He opens his arms.

She shuffles the chair along to him and falls into his embrace. Laying her head on his knees, she looks up at him. 'I'm sorry. I don't know what's got into me.'

'It's been an unbelievable time.' Danny drops his head backwards. Looking up to the ceiling, he slowly releases a large puff of air. 'And it's not over yet.' He kisses the top of her head. 'I'm really concerned about what the police are going to throw at me today. We need to keep strong, darling.' He releases her from his hold. 'I got up early to go for a run to clear my head, but now I don't have the energy. I'm going to have a shower and get Elliot up.'

'You upset him last night.'

'I know. I feel terrible. I don't know what came over me,' he says. 'I'll talk to him. You coming?'

'I need to do a couple of things. I'll be in soon.'

He guides her face towards his and kisses her, saying, 'I love you,' before taking his cup and walking back to the house.

She lied to him. She has nothing to do. Nothing urgent, anyhow. But she needs a minute to breathe before she faces the day.

Because she's not entirely convinced her husband has just told her the truth.

TWENTY

Ashley sits on the bed, a towel wrapped around her hair like a bird's nest, cradling her thoughts. She stares at the floor, waiting for the wave of nausea riding through her since yesterday to subside.

Fewer than seven hours of sleep a night never agrees with her. She'll spend the day feeling as if she's wading through mud. Her concentration levels will be non-existent as well, which only heightens the feeling of sickness. She's got deadlines to meet today.

The shower clicks off. Through the gap in the door of their en suite, she sees Danny step out of the shower. He grabs a towel and wraps it around his waist. His body, toned from running and the regular fifty press-ups and one hundred sit-ups regime he practises every morning without fail, glistens with droplets of water. On any other morning, she'd suggest they go back to bed. But it's not any other morning when your husband is due at the police station for questioning on the murder of his childhood friend.

Her phone beeps. A message from Susie asking if she is OK.

Ashley notices another couple of texts that Susie sent late last night.

She replies.

Can't talk. Danny's home, but he's got to go back to the station. Speak later. Good luck for today. You know you can do it. Ash x

Danny still hasn't answered her question about what exactly he was doing at Lucy and Lee's house on Wednesday. He said it was a business meeting, but why so secret?

L for Lucy. She can't stop that thought flashing in her mind. L for Lucy. L for Lucy.

He dries himself, his muscles as tense as her nerves, before spraying deodorant under his arms and down the line of hair that leads to his groin. The sweet smell of vanilla wafts through the room.

Or Lee? But why would Lee have sent him a note like that?

Her thoughts turn morbid. She can't help herself. What if he was having an affair with Lucy and something went wrong? It could be the last time she smells that scent.

Her mother always said you never truly know anyone. Not really.

Surely the police would have arrested him if they thought he was guilty. Unless they simply didn't have enough to go on. His explanations all seemed rational. Is she a fool to doubt him? Is she overthinking this?

She pushes the thoughts away. There's nothing healthy or helpful in them. Besides, she has always vowed she'll never turn into her mother. Danny is nothing like her father. Nothing.

He exits the en suite and grabs a pair of khaki Bermuda shorts and a plain black T-shirt while she slips into her underwear.

Clenching her jaw, she blurts out, 'You never told me exactly what you were doing at Lucy's place on Wednesday.'

Pulling the T-shirt over his head, he pushes his arms into the sleeves, swiftly pulling the hem over his taut abs. He clears his throat. 'The new Squires project in Newton. She wanted twelve CGIs by next week, and I told her that wasn't possible. You know how demanding she can be. Besides, she and Lee owe us money. That was the main reason I went there.'

She squints at him. That sounded well-rehearsed. As if he knew she would challenge him again on his covert meeting with Lucy. What better way to deflect than to hit on the grating nerve of cash-flow problems.

'What do they owe us for?' she asks, taken aback to be learning this for the first time.

'They still haven't paid April's bill.'

'How much was that?'

'Just over five grand.'

'What's the delay?'

He pauses. A little too long for her liking. 'She said she was waiting for a client who had run into difficulties to pay her. Not our problem, I know, but she asked for a few more weeks.'

'What about May's bill? I did that set of CGIs for her and that walk-through. And don't forget the website for the new development. And she asked for all those extra changes at the last minute.' Guilt hits her for talking about money when a dead person is involved. It's disrespectful. But she needs to know. She is surprised Danny allowed this to happen. They are still repaying the hefty loan they took out to cover the property taxes and moving costs. 'Please tell me you charged for those?'

'Of course I did.'

'So how much was their May bill?'

'Roughly the same.'

Ashley's face screws up into a ball of disbelief. 'So they owe us over ten grand.'

He nods, rolling his eyes. 'Nearer eleven in total.'

'Why didn't you tell me?'

He lifts his arms and quickly drops them by his side. 'I didn't want to worry you, Ash. Not after Pickstones went bust. I sort out the finances, you do the technical stuff. We're a team, remember.'

'But...'

He disappears back into the en suite and shuts the door. Conversation closed.

She's peeved Danny hadn't told her about all of this. If they're a team, she should know everything. And why is Lucy and Lee's company strapped for cash? They're loaded.

She finds the weather app on her phone. It's going to be even hotter today. She chooses a navy checked summer dress, hastily slipping it over her shoulders. She bends down to search for her leather sandals in the bottom of her wardrobe. Has she even unpacked them yet? Several of her boxes from the move still clutter one of the spare bedrooms she uses as an art room. Her room. The one she decorated herself that has the retro vibe of their London flat. Maybe her sandals are still in there. She can't be bothered to look, so she settles for her white Converse. Danny has unpacked all of his stuff, but it's as if she can't quite accept that this is their permanent home. They won't be returning to London.

Picking up her phone, she slips it in her pocket as Danny comes out of the en suite. He walks over to her side of the bed. He's shaking.

He grabs hold of her, squeezing her shoulders. 'Listen, Ash. I need you to do something for me.' There's an edge to his tone. One she hasn't heard before.

She looks at him quizzically.

'If – and it's only an if – the police call you in for questioning again, please don't mention the argument with Lucy. It was nothing. But it won't sound like nothing to them. I'm going to talk to Tom on the way to the station and tell him the same.'

He lifts her head with both hands and gently kisses her forehead. A gesture he has performed many times. One that usually brings comfort and a sense of unity. They're meant to be a team. But it sure doesn't feel like it today.

'You understand, don't you?' he says.

'Of course.' The lack of conviction in her voice is noticeable.

'I'm going to say goodbye to Elliot and get going.'

'Do you mind not going in to him? He wants to go to school today, but I don't think it's a good idea. I'd rather he slept for longer while I get myself together.'

Danny nods knowingly. Once Elliot is up, the house becomes a different place. The hushed hallways echo with exuberant chaos. 'Sure. You've got that, then?'

She frowns at him. 'Got what?'

He speaks to her as he would speak to Elliot. 'Don't mention that argument to the police if they ask to speak to you again. In fact, never mention it to anyone.'

'You do know what you're asking me to do, don't you?' She leaves the unsaid words hanging in the air.

'But it was nothing.' He smiles, a feeble attempt to make light of a very dark situation. 'It'll only lead to more problems for me. Besides, they're probably done with you now.'

He comes across as if he's talking to a prospective client, trying to wheedle them into a sale. But what is she so worried about? She has already withheld information from the police when she failed to mention that Danny had said he could murder Lucy. But that was on her terms. She chose not to.

But now, essentially, if it comes to it, her husband is asking her to lie for him… or withhold what could be relevant information… in a murder case where the police believe he is a suspect.

TWENTY-ONE

Ashley is in the kitchen preparing breakfast when Danny comes downstairs. She is listening to the news on the radio.

'Have something to eat. I'll make you some eggs if you want,' she says, as the newsreader announces the funeral being held today of the local MP Roberta Splinter, who tragically lost her life when her car hit a tree just outside Thyme End.

Danny walks over to the radio and abruptly switches it off. The news of the MP's death had shocked him. He had known the woman since he was a child. 'No thanks, I'm going to get going.' He still looks dreadfully pale. The dark rings that have formed around his eyes a stark contrast to the pallor of his skin.

Ashley can't bear to look at him. 'Isn't Tom picking you up?'

'I thought I'd walk to his place. Get some exercise. Have a quick coffee with him. Who knows how long they're going to keep me cooped up in that hellhole all day.'

Ashley flinches. Danny rarely swears. Unlike her. She can be a right potty mouth at times, especially in the throes of her artistic frustrations. But only in private. She mainly swears at her computer screen when a design refuses to cooperate, or at one of her paintings when it's not going her way. Yet, hearing that raw edge in Danny's voice now, so out of character, is threatening.

And he hardly ever goes to Tom's place. It's a tiny house, and Tom is a hoarder. Danny finds it claustrophobic.

She nods. There's an awkwardness between them. One she's never felt before. An unspoken tension that has been building for the past few weeks as he has become increasingly obsessed with the business, piling on the work.

He kisses her again. She returns the gesture, but her kiss lacks conviction.

'You won't forget that nine o'clock call, will you?' he says.

Is that all he can think about? Work?

'I think it'd be better if I put it off until tomorrow when you're here, and I'm more with it.'

It's an online meeting with one of their new clients who Danny is super excited about. A client who could take Blue Banana Studios to the next level, he reckons. They have eight new developments and want to discuss the technical aspects of the marketing material. Usually, they do these calls together. Danny owns the client relationship and is much better at running the meetings.

'No. We can't postpone it,' comes the flat response. His countenance softens. 'Stay strong, darling. We can't let business slip. You can do this one without me. And don't be late.' He kisses her a final time. 'I'll be home as soon as I can.'

She glares at him as he walks to the door, astounded at his ability to still put business first when he is off to the police station to be quizzed about a murder.

He turns around and walks back over to her, pulling her towards him. 'When all this is over, we should take a break. It's been ages since we went away. We still haven't rebooked that trip to Venice we had to cancel during Covid. Elliot's older now, so we can take him, too. I'd love that. Or he could stay with Mum and Dad and just the two of us go. In fact, let's do that.

We need some chilled-out time together. Just you and me. I'll look into it when all this mess is over. What do you say?'

She nods, despite the uncertainty bubbling away inside of her.

He squeezes her tightly. 'I love you so much, darling. I hate to see you so worried, but we need to keep strong. Together, we'll get through this.' He kisses her one more time, before turning away.

The front door clicks closed. So slick compared to the rickety old door of their London flat. Ashley walks to the lounge window and watches Danny stride up the street, his head dropped. A storm of doubt thunders about in her head. What was he really arguing about with Lucy last week? Clashing over a business matter with a client is not Danny's style. Putting aside his relationship with Lucy, something doesn't quite stack up. Blue Banana Studios is basically a supplier. Why would they be having an argument over business? Lucy would preside over all business matters for her company. It wouldn't be Danny's place to question her, argue with her, surely? Were they arguing about the money Lucy and Lee's company owe them? But why didn't he say that if that was the case?

She lies on the sofa; half an hour's sleep will make her feel better before she gets Elliot up. But she's too wired. There's no way she'll be able to drop off. She's better off preparing herself for that nine o'clock call. Keep busy. That's the best thing to do at a time like this. She considers going up to her art room. Getting lost in one of her paintings always helps when she's unsettled. But she's not in the mood, and she doesn't want to ruin her latest project. It's a painting of their London flat. Squares of each room showing the retro vibe she loved so much. Not the clean lines and cream-and-coffee curtains Danny wanted for their Thyme End house.

After making a large cup of coffee, she checks the child monitor is working. 'Stay here, boy,' she says to Rufus. 'Look after Elliot.'

She heads to The Hub and sits at her desk, where she drops her head in her hands, weary – so drained from the stress and lack of sleep. She switches on her computer. Typically, she writes her to-do list for the day as she waits for it to wake up, but all she can do is stare at the screen.

Her phone rings. It's Susie.

Ashley accepts the call. 'I thought you were meant to be on a flight.'

'It's been delayed. I'm in the airport lounge, so I thought I'd check up on you.'

The familiarity of her sister's voice provides comfort Ashley didn't realise she needed. She updates Susie on the events since they saw each other yesterday, stifling tears as she relays the nightmare she is living. 'So Danny is currently on his way to the station to answer more questions.'

'You're kidding me.'

'I wish I was.'

'Danny murder someone? That's bonkers.'

'I know, but I'm scared. Really scared. He was found at the scene of the crime covered in her blood. What does it look like?'

'What was he doing in the garage?' Susie asks.

'He said he went back to the car to get his cigarettes, and he thought he heard a scream, so he went to look.' She explains about the hammer being a different hammer to the one Lee gave him earlier.

'I thought he gave up smoking,' is all Susie can say.

'So did I,' Ashley says with contempt. 'He's been having the odd one at weekends and when he has a beer.'

'Naughty.'

'He's been so stressed lately.'

'Why?'

'You know that client I told you about? The one that owes us seven grand? They went bust. Filed for bankruptcy, so we might as well say goodbye to that money.' She hopes Lee will still pay them.

Susie tuts. 'That's so unfair.'

'Tell me about it.' Ashley sighs heavily. 'All those hours of work, but what's money when you've got a crisis like this on your hands?'

'Poor woman. Poor family... poor you.'

'There's something else.'

'What?'

She tells her about the Post-it note and her initial suspicion that it was from Lucy.

'But it wasn't, so stop beating yourself up,' says Susie.

Ashley's tone lowers. 'What if he's lying?' Panic creeps into her voice. 'I don't know what to do with myself.'

'This is Danny we are talking about. He will be cleared. And any way, you keep strong. That's what you do. You know how to. You always were a tough cookie.'

'I know. We'll get through this.'

'It's all over the news, you know.'

'I saw.'

'Apparently, someone was seen leaving the grounds by a gap in the fence to the side of the property. Did you read that?'

'No. I never saw that.' Does that mean the police might have another suspect? 'Someone from the party?'

'It didn't say.' An airport announcement drones in the background. 'Listen, I've got to go. My flight's been called. There's a perfect explanation for everything, so keep strong.'

'I know.' Guilt strikes. She should be trusting her husband, not doubting him.

'I drove to the airport, and I've packed a bag. I can come straight over as soon as I land. If you want me to. The flight back is at two o'clock UK time – so, depending on traffic, I could be with you around five-thirty.'

Ashley pauses. She'd like nothing more. Susie has always been the constant in her life. Her family, best friend and confidant, all rolled into one blanket of security. 'You've got work in the morning.'

'I can work from yours. I've got my laptop. See how the day pans out. Catch ya later. Love ya.'

After ending the call, Ashley clicks on the news to find a new picture of Lucy giving a talk at the school. Ashley remembers that talk. It was after the Christmas play, and Lucy had addressed the audience, thanking members of the PTA for their efforts that year and adding that new members were always welcome. Ashley can't bear to look at it. She reads the latest report about a person seen leaving the party through a gap in the fence that Susie must've been talking about. The police are urging that person to come forward. Who could that have been?

She gets up from the desk and walks to the fridge for a bottle of water, inexplicably glancing to where Danny was on all fours earlier looking for his wedding ring. She can't help thinking how strangely he has been acting recently, distant, as if he has had more on his mind than he has been letting on.

Fragments of doubt enter her thoughts. She tries to sweep them up with positive thoughts, but she can't. She frowns, noticing a faint chink between the carpet tiles in the corner. It looks out of place. Curiosity wins out. Stepping over to the spot, she drops onto her hands and knees. One of the tiles is slightly smaller than the others. Not a noticeable amount unless you look closely. She touches the tile. The corner is loose. Using the nails of her thumb and forefinger, she prises it back.

What the hell? Her heart slams into her chest as she questions if her eyes are deceiving her. Set in a section of the concrete floor is a safe the size of two shoeboxes stuck side by side. She reaches to touch it, the matte-black surface rough against her fingers. When Danny was designing The Hub, he said he was considering installing a safe but never told her he had actually gone ahead with it. The sight of it screams a betrayal of their mutual trust.

Her breath catches in her chest, as the office closes in on her, like the walls of a lift creeping towards her, threatening to swallow her whole. Summoning her strength, she shakes off the dread, replacing it with resolution.

What has her husband been hiding from her?

TWENTY-TWO

Tiny, high-pitched beeps of the digital keypad cut through the silence of the room as Ashley tries to open the safe. Six digits stand between her and whatever secrets her husband is keeping from her.

She bites her lower lip, her thoughts pinging around as she punches the numbers of Danny's birthday in rapid succession. The safe remains locked. She tries another combination – her birthday. Again, the safe stares back at her, a black void of silence. She attempts Elliot's birthday, their wedding anniversary. Still nothing. Her heart hammers in her chest, her hands shaking. Usually, he uses one of those combinations for his passwords. But not this time.

Think. Think. What else would he have used?

Sitting on her heels, Ashley puffs out a large breath. She has to figure this out.

A possibility comes to mind. The date they set up their business. That's a passcode he has used before. His face, packed with enthusiasm and bursting with pride as he filled out the online paperwork and bought a domain name for her to get cracking on building a website, flashes in her thoughts. She taps in the six digits. Every beep echoes through the room until, finally, bingo. A thick click sounds as the first piece of the puzzle slots into place.

Ashley frowns. Maybe this isn't as bad as she thought. Surely he wouldn't have made it so simple if he had anything sinister to hide from her? Or perhaps he never thought it would come to this? A saddening thought reminds her of the dark place their relationship is at.

She opens the heavy door of the safe. Observing the contents, she gasps. Her heart beats even faster. Inexplicably, she lifts her head and quickly peers around her as if she is doing something she shouldn't be and expects to be caught. Reaching down into the bowels of the safe, she pulls out the contents one by one and lays them on the carpet, her confusion deepening. An iPad and a very old phone she has never seen before, two notepads, and probably the most mysterious of all, given their current financial predicament, a bundle of cash.

She studies the items, incredulous. Picking up the wad of the cash, she flicks through the crisp twenty- and fifty-pound notes packaged together in what looks like five-hundred-pound packages. She spreads them out on the floor and makes a quick calculation. Her face registers utter shock. There is over twenty thousand pounds there. What the hell is Danny doing with all that cash? More to the point, where did he get it from, and why is he concealing it from her?

It doesn't add up. Nothing is making sense.

Picking up the phone, she contemplates its significance. It looks cheap, a throw-away. A pay-as-you-go, perhaps, like a burner phone? Is Danny some sort of secret agent? A spy, possibly? She openly laughs. What a senseless idea.

Pressing the button on the side of the phone, she switches it on. So many thoughts are rushing through her mind, the prominent one being what the hell is Danny doing with all of this? The screen of the phone lights up, asking for a passcode. She grunts in annoyance. Of course it would. It wants five digits this time, though, not six. She attempts the combinations she tried with the safe, minus the last number, but to no avail. Then she thinks. Their business banking app requires a five-digit code. Danny uses the month and year they set up the business, 0107, but repeats the first number. She punches in 01070. But it's not that either.

Tossing the phone on top of the money, she picks up one of the notebooks. Her heart falters. She bought it for Danny when Blue Banana Studios was just a pip in his thoughts. He came home from work one day with two bottles of Merlot, thoroughly fed up because he'd been passed over for promotion at the company he worked for back then. Unfairly, in his mind. He'd been the company's top salesperson three months in a row. He deserved the Sales Director role. As he unscrewed the cap of one of the bottles of red, he told her he'd had enough. They were better than the people they worked for. Together, they could go it alone. By the time they'd polished off the second bottle, they were both slurring and laughing and he'd crammed both sides of four sheets of A4 printer paper with their ideas. The next day, Ashley found the notebook during her lunch hour. Gold stars are sprinkled over the navy-blue cover, and in a white box are the words DREAM BIG: Make it Happen. Come to think of it, she hasn't seen it since. Now she knows why.

She opens it, but hesitates, biting her lip harder and harder. Apart from the time shortly after Elliot was born, and then earlier this morning when she found that divorce lawyer's card, she has never snooped on Danny. She winces. She also accessed his emails the previous evening.

What if the pages are filled with his innermost secrets? Secrets that could undo their marriage, all because she is prying. If she'd found this at any other time or in any other place – in his bedside cabinet or desk drawer – she wouldn't have thought she was snooping. But this is not his bedside cabinet or desk drawer. This is a secret hiding place.

She opens it, taken aback at what she finds. On the inside cover is a pencil portrait of her on their wedding day, the background smudged to a blur. A crimson heart in the bottom left-hand corner adds the only colour to the page. Not that it needs any. It's perfect as it is. She can't believe how much the drawing looks like her, and how he has captured the spirit of her mood to perfection. How he has sketched the glints sparkling from the tiara she was wearing is striking. She was so happy that day. Beneath the red heart, he has written, 'Ash forever'.

Sketches of her and Elliot fill three-quarters of the book, beautiful drawings of them through the years. Why has Danny never shown these to her? She knows he can draw, but she never knew he had such talent. He wanted to study art at uni, like she did, but never felt he was good enough, so he settled for a business degree with marketing. He always said her artwork made his attempts feel like primary-school stuff. But this is far from amateur.

She picks up the second notebook. The cover is a thin brown board, smooth to the touch, and has TOP SECRET in a box printed across the front in red. Unlike the other one, she has never seen it before. Sheets of loose paper stick out from the back cover. She pulls them out. They are the four sheets of paper scribbled on both sides with their ideas for Blue Banana Studios from all those years ago.

With an unsteady hand, she turns the cover and peruses the pages. The mood of the pictures couldn't be any more different to the first notebook. Caricatures of people with quips and anecdotes pack the pages of half of the book. Some of them Ashley knows, and many she doesn't. She turns the pages, laughing at the one of Danny's mother. The way he has exaggerated her nose, her meddlesome temperament bouncing off the page. On the opposite side is one of his father, an oversized smile on his face as he swings a golf club with one hand and holds one of his many golfing trophies in the other. Tom is there, too, propping up the bar in The Ugly Duckling with a pint in his hand. His mouth is significantly out of proportion. She grins at the following drawing of their favourite client, a property developer from the Midlands. Flicking through the pages, she recognises other clients and people they know, but not all, though it's evident which people Danny likes and which he doesn't. Why has he never shown these to her before? Is this the life of a salesman? A coping mechanism to deal with the challenges, rejection and success.

Ashley places the money and notebooks back into the safe but keeps the iPad and phone out. She closes the door. It locks with a heavy clunk. Placing the carpet tile in its original position, she stands and walks to her desk with determination. She sits down and props the iPad in front of her. It's an old model. The screen is scratched. She turns it on. She needs to find out what it holds. Then, perhaps, she can work out what the hell her husband is up to.

TWENTY-THREE

Ashley tries Danny's passcodes to fire up the device. The ones she had used to try to open the safe and the phone, his usual choices, but, frustratingly, none of them work. Think. Think. What could Danny have used? She needs to be careful. She only has two attempts left.

Elliot was playing around with the passcodes on Danny's usual iPad a couple of weeks ago and must've typed in the wrong one because what he thought it was didn't work, and Danny ended up having to erase the iPad via the computer and reset it. It was such a pain. He wasn't happy. Not happy at all. With hindsight, apart from last night, it was the only time she has ever seen him be angry with Elliot. She realises that was about the time when Danny's behaviour started to change. He'd come home from a day in the Midlands jittery and distressed. He'd passed a dying deer on the road coming into the village. It was whimpering. He called the police to put it out of its misery but waited with it. That's the kind of guy Danny is, isn't he? Not a man who hides stuff from his wife or would hammer a woman to death.

And, come to think about it, that's also when the calls started...

On a few occasions lately, when they've been in the kitchen, he has stepped into the garden to a take a call. He always said they were business-related. Even though he'd never taken business calls elsewhere before, she never thought too much about it until now. She's never had any need to. Danny is her husband. She trusts him.

Ashley checks Elliot on the monitor before switching on her iMac. He is still sleeping soundly. She types *How to unlock an iPad if you've forgotten the code* into the search bar. It's a half-hearted attempt. Deep down, she knows it's impossible without a lot of drama. She's right. The only way is to put it in recovery mode, which deletes all the data settings and passcodes.

There has to be a backup, she thinks. But what if there isn't? Or Danny has changed his Apple ID password? Or it's not connected to his Apple ID. She can't chance it. She needs to find the passcode.

And then it dawns on her. What if this iPad is not Danny's? What if he's storing it for someone? And what if that someone was Lucy?

Opposing voices fill her head. One demands she go to the police. Another tells her not to be so stupid. Danny will have a plausible explanation for keeping a phone and iPad hidden from her. It could make things worse for him.

But what if it all has something to do with Lucy's murder? The thought raises the hairs on her arms. Is she protecting a criminal? A killer?

She grits her teeth. Why is she having these nonsensical thoughts about her husband? The man she promised to have and to hold during the good times and the bad.

Her fingers brush aside the cold metal of the iPad. She breathes deeply. Never has she felt so out of control. How could he have kept all this from her? The chilling shock creeps in. If her husband has concealed from her all she has discovered in the last twenty-four hours, what else lurks in the shadows?

She's teetering on the edge between trust and betrayal. She opens Danny's email, curious to see if anything else appears out of the ordinary. Scrolling through her husband's tidy inbox, Ashley can't find anything that seems unusual. Danny is so organised. He files all emails in appropriate 'Admin', 'Client', or 'To Action' folders, so only twenty or so emails sit in his inbox, most of which arrived yesterday or this morning. Some she is copied into; others are potential deals he is working on sealing that he has told her about, mailing lists he is signed up to or correspondence on administrative matters.

She scans the 'Client' folder. There's one subfolder for each of their clients, and one for prospects. Tomorrow's Housing Today – Lucy and Lee's company – piques her attention. She opens it and reads the recent email exchanges between Lucy and Danny. She is copied in on some where appropriate, but not all. She scrutinises each one. But despite Danny and Lucy's personal relationship, their business correspondence appears very formal. Danny's tone is as professional as if he were conversing with any other business colleague or client. From reading the exchanges, one would never guess Lucy and Danny had been childhood friends.

Ashley opens the 'To Action' folder. A particular email stands out because of the address. It has an Eastern European feel to it. She clicks it open and comes across a chain of messages with an external agency based in Poland. Poland? She isn't aware of any business dealings in Poland.

She reads the conversation between Danny and Krzysztof Adamski from Warsaw, her heart thumping so hard, she can hear it in her ears. Danny has been negotiating the price with this Krzysztof guy for creating CGIs for a housing development in Surrey of fifteen hundred executive houses. Ashley frowns. She would normally create the CGIs for their clients. And she's never heard of this housing development being built in Surrey. Why has Danny never mentioned it to her? She examines the latest correspondence. Why the hell has Danny outsourced this work without discussing it with her first?

She googles Krzysztof's website. From what she can gather, he is a one-man band doing what she does for Blue Banana Studios, but she guesses at a considerably lower cost than they charge clients. She looks at the contact page. There's no phone number, just an email address. A feeling stirs in her stomach. The same one as when she found the divorce lawyer's business card in his desk drawer. But this time, it's more profound. She links the two discoveries and can't work out if her imagination is running away with her, or if her husband has plans that don't involve her.

Her hand shoots over her mouth, silencing the sobs trying to escape. Has he been looking to outsource her work so he can set up a separate business? One that he is developing without her? Is that what the twenty grand is for? Money he has been siphoning from their company for his getaway? And the iPad and old phone – do they play a part in his intended escape from his life with her?

But it doesn't make sense. Money has been tight for them since they moved to Thyme End. With interest rates rocketing, the mortgage costs more than they'd budgeted for each month. She knew they should've got a fixed-term deal, but he'd disagreed. And there hasn't been spare cash to take from the business. Or has there? Perhaps she needs to check the accounts. Besides, the notes are crisp and new, as if they are fresh off the print.

She rereads the correspondence, focusing on Danny's intent, but the conversations are as she would expect. Every sentence is professional and true to Danny's style.

Her breath quickens as she intensifies her search. But she can't find anything else to raise her suspicion. Apart from the emails with Krzysztof, everything strikes her as everyday business matters.

She needs Danny here now to give him the opportunity to explain himself. And, hell, does he have some explaining to do. She calls his mobile, only to get his answerphone. Of course she does. He's not going to have his phone on while he is being interrogated by the police.

She hovers the mouse over his personal email folder, conscious the click of her finger will take her snooping to another level. Hunting through his business emails is one thing. Prying through his personal ones is another. This is breaking the boundaries of her moral code. A downward spiral she has no desire to get stuck in. It's wrong on every level. Zero justification. But, then again, so is concealing a stash of cash, an iPad and a phone she knew nothing about. And that's without mentioning the safe she never knew existed.

How have they come to this? Theirs was the perfect marriage. Friends have often commented on how close they are. Susie, twice-divorced and now on her third engagement, admitted one drunken night – back when the two of them had met for one of their weekly rendezvous in London, a ritual Ashley deeply misses – that subconsciously she thought she was searching for a Danny. And as her sister popped open a second bottle of Prosecco, she stated, in a loving way, how lucky Ashley was to have met a man who only appeared in her dreams. Ashley struck gold the day she met him, said Susie. 'Everyone needs a Danny in their lives, darling,' she'd slurred, staring at the brand-new sparkling diamond on her finger. 'I fear I still haven't found mine.' A year later, Susie is wearing a different guy's ring.

Ashley takes a deep breath and dives into Danny's personal emails, apprehensive that she might hit rock bottom. She soon realises she's scanning for emails from Lucy. She knows Lucy's private address because they regularly exchanged emails about the kids and school matters. An email titled: *I need your help* flashes like a beacon. A warning to take a closer look. Lucy sent it two weeks ago.

Two weeks before she was savagely murdered.

Why the hell was Lucy asking for Danny's help shortly before her death?

TWENTY-FOUR

The first line irritates Ashley, which in turn bothers her. The woman is dead, for heaven's sake. Lucy shouldn't irritate her. That's not just mean, it's cruel. But she's irritated anyway.

> Hi Dan

She hated how Lucy usually called him Dan. No one else does. And the lilt with which Lucy pronounced it was as if she believed it was her privilege to call him that. A childhood tie that no one could ever undo. It was almost as if she had some sort of a hold over him.

Ashley continues reading.

> Hi Dan
>
> Just a quickie. I was speaking to the Head yesterday. The school playground equipment desperately needs replacing. The sandpit dates back to our days there. Remember those? Lol. I've been looking at options to replace it all. As a general ballpark figure, we're looking at around five grand. This

includes a couple of benches and a climbing frame. Also – and this is between you and me – another autistic kid is joining the school in the autumn term. I'm looking to include some kind of sensory equipment for them, but I'm not sure of the requirements/cost of this yet.

I'm asking local businesses for donations. Lee and I will be putting up £2500. Speak to Ash. See what you can do. Would appreciate your support.

Also, I have an update on the Bridle project. I'll email you separately about that.

Speak soon.

L x

Ashley jumps at a noise from the garden. What was that? It sounded like the gate behind The Hub clicking closed. The one that opens onto the footpath leading to the fields. She leaves the desk and peers out of the door, gasping loudly to see a shadow disappear around the side of The Hub. Someone is there.

Fear rushes through her, freezing her to the spot. She looks towards the house. Rufus is lying at the patio door. Surely he'd be barking if someone was in the garden? Perhaps he can't hear anything.

With shaking hands, she quietly opens the door and listens. The back gate clicks open and quickly closes. Finding a shred of bravery, she tiptoes to the side of The Hub and peeks around the corner. There's no one there. Gingerly, she creeps around to the back of the building. The gate is closed. She strides over and opens it, looking up and down the footpath, but it's empty. Did she imagine it?

She runs to the house to check on Elliot, her stomach in her throat. Rufus wags his tail and follows her to the stairs. The need to see her son physically, not on the monitor, overwhelms her. Dashing up to his room, she finds him still sleeping. She stands at his bedroom door watching him for a minute. He is dead to the world.

Returning to The Hub with Rufus, she tries to calm her nerves. Her life is spiralling out of control. What the hell is happening? She rereads Lucy's email, puffing out a large breath. It doesn't add up. Danny said Lucy and Lee's company have a cash-flow problem, which is why they owe Blue Banana Studios money. But they can afford to fork out two and a half thousand pounds? She shakes her head, trying to find a plausible excuse, but she can't.

It's the first she has heard about the school playground equipment, but then again, she could easily have missed it. She's not one who rides in the circles of school gossip. As the chair of the PTA, Lucy would probably have got wind of it first to spearhead the efforts to replace it. A stab of guilt strikes her. Whatever she felt about Lucy, there was a good side to her. A very good side when it came to supporting the local community. How many other businesses would agree to fronting a fundraising effort with such a generous donation?

Danny hasn't replied to the email, but it looks like he has seen it. Maybe that's what has been stressing him out. He would have wanted to support Lucy's appeal, Ashley is sure. But they don't have any spare cash to donate.

She scours the other emails in his inbox, feeling dirty at her betrayal. Grubby behaviour, soiled with wrongdoing. But he has brought this on himself. At least that is how she packages it in her fraught mind. Even if she stops now, she knows she'll find herself back here at some point. Danny has left her with no choice.

She sifts through several emails he has signed up to from property alerts to home gadgets, recipe ideas to gardening centres, and companies advertising their wares, until she comes across one from an old uni friend inviting Danny and Ashley to their house-warming party next month. The invitation shows a picture of the friend and his wife standing arm in arm in front of their colonial-style house in the West Country. The guy is dressed in chinos and a custard-coloured shirt, and the woman in a beige dress and matching heels.

The perfect couple standing in front of the perfect house.

Ashley cringes. She and Danny had a similar photo taken not so long ago when they moved to Thyme End, minus the beige dress and high heels. Ashley never wears high heels. They give her backache and serve as a painful reminder of her mum, who wore them to impress her dad. And beige? No, Ashley opts for vibrancy in her wardrobe. Danny's smile wasn't too dissimilar to the one his friend is wearing in the photo. But Ashley's smile nowhere near resembles the wife's.

Danny has replied to his friend's email saying they would love to come to the house-warming party, adding that it has been far too long since they saw each other. He is looking forward to seeing them. He signs off the email, 'Cheers, Dan'.

Dan? When did he start calling himself Dan? Is it a name reserved for only the oldest of his friends?

Ashley also doesn't recall Danny mentioning the party to her. She glances at the date: the thirtieth of July. Dread seeps deeper into her bones. What is going on? It's her sister's birthday that day. Ashley has bought theatre tickets for her and Susie. So there's no way she would have agreed to go to this house-warming party. So who was he planning on taking?

She toggles to his diary. The thirtieth of July is a Saturday, but she recalls blocking the day out so he knows he has to look after Elliot. Sure enough, there it is. The whole day is blocked out. Was he intending to take Elliot on his own?

Or is this another part of his bigger plan? A plan for a new life with someone else.

TWENTY-FIVE

Ashley's mind races as her finger clicks through more emails. Her stomach is twisted, her thoughts confused.

She has started to seriously doubt Danny. In isolation, what she has found may seem trivial, deserving of a grumble once she has been presented with explanations. But collectively it stinks, and she can't quite understand why. She finds nothing incriminating, only lots of emails on property prices in the local area and deals on the latest air fryers, outdoor pizza ovens and garden furniture.

Until she comes across an email from the bank.

She squints at the screen. It's regarding a new overdraft arrangement for their joint bank account. Why has Danny not told her about this? She didn't even know they were overdrawn.

A noise disturbs her prying. She gasps loudly, jumping. She's so jittery, her nerves a mess, but it's only Elliot standing at the door, clutching Champ to his chest as if he needs protection.

'I didn't know where you were,' he says.

'Sorry! I didn't hear you on the monitor.' Ashley thrusts her chair away from the desk and slaps her hands on her thigh, beckoning him to her. He climbs on her lap and buries his head on her chest. He's heavy. She hugs him tightly. 'You always know I'm down here if I'm not at the house.'

'Where's Dad?' His question lingers, edged with innocence.

'He had to go back to the police station.'

'Why?'

She tries to mask her angst. 'He's helping the police.'

The inquisition persists. 'Why?'

Questions. Always so many questions. She unfailingly does her best to answer them. It's important to nurture his curiosity. But this one she simply doesn't know how to answer. 'Because Grace's mum died, and they're asking everyone questions.'

'When will he be home?' he asks, changing the subject as if he can't talk about Lucy. She wonders just how much he has taken in about this whole situation.

'Soon.'

'Can I go and see him?'

'No, darling. Come on, let's go and get you dressed, and I'll make you some breakfast.'

'Can Dad still come to my sports day?'

Damn. That had slipped her mind again. Even if it's still on, she can't send him in. Everyone will know about Danny. All eyes will be on their little family. She can just imagine cliques of gossiping mums muckraking amongst themselves, while looking her way. The wife and son of the man being questioned about the murder of the woman he went to school with there.

'I'm not sure it's a good idea for you to go to school today.'

He hits her arm with Champ. 'I want to go. I can win the running race. I want you and Dad there.'

She relents, not having the fight for a battle.

'I'm not sure Dad will be able to make it, though.'

'But you'll be there?'

She nods, torn into two halves of despair.

'Promise?' Elliot's pleading eyes tear at her heartstrings. They always do.

'I promise, darling.'

She glances at the clock on the computer: 8 a.m. Is it really only two hours since she got out of bed? It feels like a lifetime. They'll have to get a move on if she is going to get him to school on time.

Elliot's voice booms as he leaps down the stairs and skids along the hallway into the kitchen, 'Mum!' He grabs the door frame as if to stop himself from taking off. 'Where's my homework?'

'On the table where you left it,' Ashley replies.

Rufus sits patiently at his bowl, staring Ashley out. She glances from him to the clock as she fumbles with the handle of the toaster.

'What've you been doing? I called you over ten minutes ago. You really need to get a move on.' She winces at the harsh tone of her voice. She mustn't take out everything on him.

'That stinks. You're gonna start a fire,' Elliot says, his eyes like saucers. 'Then we'll burn to death.'

'Elliot. Don't say such things. Eat your cereal and drink your orange juice. Be quick.'

Ashley swears as the toaster pops up two charred slices of toast. Her stomach coils, rejecting the thought of food. Her appetite has been replaced with repeated waves of nausea as thoughts of Lucy and of the safe in their office consume her mind.

'Can I still go to Grace's after school today? Please.'

'That's not going to happen, Elliot. Please don't ask again.'

'But she invited me,' he says, scooping up a mound of cereal onto his spoon.

'No.'

'Is her mum really dead?'

Ashley walks over to the table and sits beside him. She needs help here. They all do. How do you handle the trauma they have been dealt? She's sure any expert would say talking about it would be the best medication, but what to say?

'Yes, she is. Do you want to talk about it?'

He shakes his head. 'Will Grace be in school today?'

'No. I very much doubt she will. You don't have to go in either.'

He thinks for a moment. 'What about sports day?'

'You can miss it.'

'I don't want to miss it.' The exact look of resolve that is part of Danny's make-up plasters their son's face.

What happened yesterday has shaken her to the core, but he seems unaffected in this at least. He obviously knows something is going on but he doesn't quite understand the magnitude of it all.

'If you change your mind, I'll be there to pick you up. And, Elliot...'

'What?'

'Any time you want to talk about what has happened, you come to me, OK?'

He nods. 'And Dad.'

'And Dad. Of course.'

The charred offerings burn Ashley's fingers as she tries to prise the slices out of the toaster. She drops them on the floor, vigorously shaking her hand and cursing under her breath. Rufus whines, a doggy complaint reminding her not to forget his breakfast. Why is everything so much calmer when Danny is at home? Is it because he has a better handle on time? He is pedantic when it comes to timekeeping and so ordered in his approach to life.

Her mobile rings. Ashley takes it out of her pocket. It's Miriam, Danny's mother. She and Danny's father, Derek, are currently on a Norwegian fjords cruise. Ashley can't speak to her in front of Elliot. She can just imagine the conversation. 'Hi! How's your holiday going? And, oh, by the way, your son's childhood friend was murdered yesterday, and the police are currently questioning Danny about it.' But, saying that, Miriam will arrange help of some sort. Danny's mother is good at that – organising other people's lives.

She sends the call to voicemail and casts the phone on the side.

Snatching a tea towel, Ashley swipes the burnt toast onto a plate and drops it into the compost bin. She'll have to grab something to eat later. Coffee is another matter, though. She can't start the day without another cup. Opening the door to the integral fridge, she takes out a bottle of milk, giving it a habitual shake. A fountain of milk spurts a foot in the air before covering the tiled floor and her feet. She must not have screwed the lid on properly when she filled Elliot's bowl of cereal. 'Damn.' The creamy smell turns her stomach.

Lucy's head, caked with blood. That's all she keeps seeing.

'Mum, don't swear.' Elliot stuffs another spoonful of cereal into his mouth.

Ashley grits her teeth. There's no time for this. She needs to be on that call at nine o'clock. Throwing her head to the ceiling, she closes her eyes, dreading the meeting. At least it's over Zoom.

Rufus comes to the rescue, licking up the milk. She grabs an apple from the fruit bowl on the windowsill and tosses it into Elliot's Harry Potter lunch bag.

Elliot drops the spoon from a height. It crashes against the porcelain bowl. The sound goes right through her.

'I don't want any more.'

Usually, Ashley would coax him to finish his breakfast, but she has lost the will this morning. 'Go and brush your teeth and put your shoes on. Be ready in five minutes.'

There's not enough time to walk to school now. She'll have to drive.

He sticks out a foot. 'I've only got one sock.'

'Get another pair out of the airing cupboard. Hurry. Hurry. We're going to be late and there'll be no sports day.'

When he leaves the room, Ashley wipes the kitchen table. It's an old, battered table they bought second-hand off eBay shortly after Elliot was born. The three of them travelled to Croydon to pick it up in a van Danny had borrowed from a mate. Ashley will never forget the experience. It was the weekend after she had accused Danny of cheating on her, and they were hardly talking. The journey there had been fraught, with Elliot crying and a crazy traffic jam that made them over an hour late. And when they finally arrived, the lady with the bleached hair and over-made-up face selling the table had looked so much like her mother, it was as if she had been lifted from her grave to remind Ashley of the person she swore she would never become, which only fuelled her suspicion of Danny.

The table suited their London flat, doubling as a spot to eat and the workspace of Blue Banana Studios, but it's now out of place in their modern kitchen. It's on their list of things to replace when they get some money, along with several other items they can't afford. But Rome wasn't built in a day, she keeps telling Danny.

The bank overdraft Danny was arranging behind her back enters her thoughts. Why has he kept so much from her?

She rinses the cloth and leans against the sink, lowering her head. She wants to go back to bed and sleep all day but knows she's got to keep going for all their sakes. Lucy's dead body continues to swarm her thoughts, intermingled with her discovery of the safe and Danny defending himself against her questioning. Was he lying about Patricia Cartwright, the divorce lawyer? He sounded damn convincing when he said the meeting wasn't with her but with her cousin, Peter Clarke, a property developer he'd planned to meet that afternoon. But he'd never told her he'd met this Patricia woman at a meeting with Lucy. Another meeting that wasn't in his diary.

A nagging doubt drives her to google Patricia Cartwright's telephone number. She knows it's wrong. She should trust what Danny told her. But she can't. Not after everything she has found. The number pops up on the screen of her phone. She should wait until later when she's got more time, but she wants to catch Patricia before the start of the working day.

She hesitates. She doesn't want to appear desperate. With a trembling finger, she presses the number, her heart beating as loudly as the ringtone.

By luck, she gets straight through. 'Patricia Cartwright speaking.'

Ashley introduces herself. 'I'm afraid Danny Morgan won't be able to make the meeting with you this afternoon.'

'Sorry? What meeting?' she says. The clicking of her mouse suggests she is looking through her calendar.

'I believe you have a meeting with him at four o'clock.'

There's a pause. 'I think you've got it wrong. I don't have a meeting with a Danny Morgan today.' There's a brief pause until Patricia says, 'Ah, I think you're confused. He has a meeting with my cousin Peter.'

The knot in Ashley's stomach loosens. 'Oh, that's right. Now I look at the diary entry, I can see Peter Clarke,' she lies. 'Is that right?'

'That's him.'

'I'm sorry to have bothered you,' Ashley says, relieved. 'Could I have his number so I can tell him Danny won't be able to make it.'

There's a scratching sound from the phone speakers. Patricia reels off a number. 'How is Danny? I heard about the events yesterday and him being questioned.'

Ashley clenches her teeth. More evidence confirming her fears about living in a community like Thyme End. Gossip stretches its vicious claws far and wide. 'He's helping all he can. Thank you.' Ashley curtly ends the call.

Danny was telling her the truth.

About that, at least.

She quickly checks her emails. There's one from the school titled: *Sports Day Arrangements*. She clicks on it. It's succinct and signed by the headteacher. Sports day will still go ahead today but will start five minutes early so everyone can gather for a one-minute silence to mark the passing of Lucy Ellis. Due to the weather forecast, please ensure all children are sent to school with suntan cream and a hat.

Walking into the hallway, she calls up the stairs. 'Elliot! We're going now!' She checks his school bag for his hat and the bottle of factor fifty she bought for him.

'I haven't brushed my teeth yet.'

'You're going to have to leave it.' She barely conceals her frustration as Elliot shuffles down the stairs. 'Shoes, now,' she orders. 'And go and get in the car.'

A frown appears on his forehead, his usual enthusiasm wiped from his face at the tone of her words. He's a sensitive boy and, for an almost nine-year-old, remarkably switched on to his emotions. His shoulders drop. 'I miss Daddy.'

The words hit her like a punch, guilt intensifying her gut-wrenching ache. Besides being a typical youngster with zero time-management skills, he is innocent in all of this.

'He'll be back soon, darling,' she reassures him, pulling his shoes from the cupboard and kissing his forehead. 'I didn't mean to upset you.' She opens the front door, her mind consumed with thoughts about how to get into that iPad.

And what else might Danny be hiding?

TWENTY-SIX

An ageing blue Ford Focus turns into the close as Ashley waits to pull out. The driver is waving at her frantically, the car window open.

Ashley groans. It's Renee. With everything going on, she forgot she was coming to clean this morning. She comes every other Monday morning for two hours to give the house a once-over. Danny arranged it when their workloads started to pile too high for them to keep on top of the housework. An unnecessary expense in her eyes, but the messiness had started to get to him.

Ashley braces herself for the onslaught of questions. Like Tom, Renee is partial to village gossip. In Danny's words, they are 'Cut from the same cloth, those two.' She and Tom have been seeing each other for the past two years. And while there's no mention of them moving in together or making the relationship more permanent, there's no denying they make a good couple.

Ashley opens her window. Renee looks as white as Ashley feels, which is hardly surprising. In addition to cleaning jobs around the village, she works as a housekeeper for the Ellises, collecting their three children from school when Lucy was otherwise engaged – which was most days – so she knew Lucy well.

'I'm running late,' Ashley says. 'Just dropping Elliot at school.'

'I'll let myself in.' Her voice is sombre. 'How's Danny?'

Ashley shakes her head and presses a finger to her lips, signalling to the back seat.

Oblivious to Ashley's gesture, Renee continues, 'Such a shocking day.' She shakes her head in disbelief. 'I can't get over it. I spoke to Lee this morning. Poor man. He was taken in for questioning yesterday. Can you believe that? I'm going over to help with the kids when I'm done with you.'

'Do you want to skip ours today and go straight there? I don't mind.'

'I'd rather keep things as normal as possible.'

Elliot opens his window. 'Renee!' he shouts. 'Are you coming to my sports day today? I don't think my dad will be able to come. He's helping the police.'

'Sorry, champ. Aunty Renee is working.'

Ashley doesn't like it when she calls herself his aunty. Tom and Renee aren't married. And after Renee told Ashley one morning, shouting above the vacuum cleaner humming, 'After four husbands, I've concluded I'm better off on my own,' there's no guarantee she and Tom will stay together. She is surprised Elliot even asked her to come along to sports day. He once told Ashley he didn't like her. But that was when they first moved to the village.

As Ashley has got to know her more, she realises Renee unnerves her at times. She has never been able to determine why. When she mentioned it to Danny, he laughed it off. He gets on well with her. But that's Danny for you. He gets on well with everyone.

'Let me see what I can do,' Renee says. 'Maybe I can get your uncle Tom to go.'

Ashley bids her goodbye and closes the window, wondering if either of them will turn up.

Halfway to school, Elliot pipes up from the back, 'Mum, where's my lunch bag?'

'What?' She catches his eye in the rear-view mirror. 'Please don't tell me you've left it behind?'

'You didn't give it to me,' he says in an accusatory tone.

Damn. She debates driving him to school and delivering the lunch bag later, but it's another thing to remember. She doesn't know what the day will hold, other than hours of uncertainty. Unless Danny gets home very soon. But she has a nagging doubt that's not going to happen. He's going to be at that station all day.

Ashley swings around by the old Guild Hall, a white building with oak beams and lath and plaster walls that dates back to the fourteen hundreds. Thinking about the hidden safe, she revs the engine and floors the accelerator, negotiating a precarious U-turn and gunning the car back up the hill.

'Mum, you're going too fast.'

A shiver runs through her. That could've been Danny speaking. Elliot sounds so like him, it's uncanny. Danny is always telling her off for driving too fast. Six points already blemish her licence since they moved here. All those years of driving in London, and she never got caught speeding. Ever since they moved to Thyme End, life has seemed against her.

She brakes. 'It's OK, darling. Look, I've slowed down.'

Minutes later, the car tyres screech to a halt as Ashley pulls up outside the house. She dashes inside to find Renee descending the stairs. What was she doing up there? She always starts in the kitchen.

Renee coughs, clearing her throat. 'That was quick.'

Ashley rolls her eyes. 'He forgot his lunch box.'

Renee holds a rubbish bag in the air. 'I was just emptying the bins.'

Ashley retrieves the lunch box from the kitchen and runs back to the car, panting. The shoelace of her Converse has come undone and catches under her foot. Her arms shoot out to break her fall, but they are too late. A burning sensation strikes her cheek as if someone has slapped her around the face. She lies on the ground, already hot from the sun, processing the throb on her face and the metallic taste of blood in her mouth. Damn, that hurt. She gingerly touches her cheek. Red stains her fingers. She pauses momentarily before picking herself up. A spot of blood drips onto the white canvas of her shoe as she reties her shoelace.

She scrambles back into the car and looks in the mirror. What a mess! She glances at Elliot in the rear-view mirror, lost in his iPad, oblivious to her fall. Finding a tissue in the glove compartment, she cleans up the blood as best she can, her thoughts racing. She needs to get a move on. Elliot is going to be late for school, and she's going to be late for that call.

Elliot shouts at his iPad, an angry response to the game he is playing.

A sense of déjà vu reminds her of an outburst Danny had last week when he was angry with a client for mucking him around.

'Elliot, it's only a game. Chill.'

Arriving at the school ten minutes late, Ashley parks the car and looks at her cheek again. It has stopped bleeding but is red and inflamed, and her eyes are puffy from the lack of sleep. She rushes a dishevelled Elliot towards the reception, nodding hello to a few mums she vaguely knows idly chatting by the school gates. Are they giving her dirty looks? Judging her for sending her son to school after his friend's mother's fate yesterday, or the state of her battered face? Or is paranoia playing tricks with her rationality?

Entering the reception, Ashley apologises profusely for their lateness to the formidable admin assistant gatekeeping the main door into the school from behind a glass window. 'Could I have a word with Elliot's teacher, please?' Ashley asks.

The permed-haired woman pulls the window aside. Her hoity-toity disposition is annoying at the best of times, but today, it's extra aggravating. 'I'm sorry, but class would've already started. If you give me a message, I'll see if I can get it to her.'

For once, given the circumstances, couldn't she have been more accommodating?

Ashley straightens the collar of Elliot's shirt and wishes him a good day. He can come home at any time, she tells him. He just needs to speak to his teacher.

'I'll see you this afternoon for your race.' She goes to kiss his cheek. He steps backwards. 'Sorry,' she whispers.

Damn the village. Ever since he started at the school, he doesn't like to be kissed in public anymore.

With his lunch box swinging in one hand, and his school bag clutched in the other, he marches to the main door. He even walks like his father. A mini-me if ever she saw one.

Ashley returns to the window and coughs to gain the admin assistant's attention. The woman is deliberately ignoring her. Danny has always said about this woman that it's amazing how a snippet of authority can create a monster. The woman continues ticking boxes in a register. Irritated, and in no mood for games, Ashley coughs again. 'Excuse me,' she says, unable to hide her annoyance.

The woman looks over her glasses in Ashley's direction.

'I wasn't sure whether to send Elliot in given what happened yesterday, but he was insistent,' Ashley says. 'If there are any problems, please call me. I'll email the head.' She grinds her teeth and turns to leave.

A group of mums, dressed in designer athletic wear, have gathered at the school gates, ready for their Monday morning power walk across the fields. The hum of their chatter diminishes as their heads follow Ashley's rapid return to her car like a succession of motorists rubbernecking at an accident. She hears their whispering accusations. 'What was she thinking?' 'I wouldn't have dreamed of sending Tilly in under the circumstances.' 'Did you see her face? Has she been hit?' And 'Who do you think hit her?'

How much does she detest Thyme End?

She wishes they'd never moved there.

TWENTY-SEVEN

Ashley drives past the village green. A cluster of school mums has congregated around the two benches close to the low white fence surrounding the pond, chatting in groups of twos and threes. The Monday Morning Gossip Club, they are usually there. But the sisterhood of scandal seems to have several extra members today. And her burning ears tell Ashley exactly why.

Renee is in the kitchen wiping the worktops when Ashley arrives home. She looks troubled. The events of yesterday are affecting them all.

Renee stops cleaning and stands with her hands on her hips. 'Goodness! What happened to your face?'

Ashley presses her fingers along her cheek. It's hot to the touch. She looks at the clock. It's now gone nine. 'I tripped getting into the car.' She walks to the sink and grabs the empty bottle from last night. The faint smell of whisky turns her stomach as she chucks the bottle into the recycling bin.

'It looks like you've taken a right hook. You need to get some ice on that.' Grabbing a glass from the drainer, Renee steps over to the fridge freezer and presses it against the lever of the ice dispenser. Cubes of ice clink into the glass.

Ashley's phone pings with a text. The nine o'clock client is trying to join the Zoom call. Where is she?

Renee wraps the ice cubes into a tea towel and approaches Ashley, holding the package against the gash on her face. 'This'll bring down the swelling. How's Danny?'

Ashley winces, but remains quiet. She would love to unload her thoughts and feelings to someone. But, being a busybody, Renee is a pro when it comes to worming information out of you, and Ashley is fully aware that whatever she says will revert to Tom before the day is over. Danny won't want his brother to know too much. One pint too many at the pub for Tom, and whatever Ashley tells Renee will be spread all over the village like a rash.

Ashley takes the tea towel full of ice and dabs it on her cheek. 'He's bearing up. You know Danny. As tough as old boots.'

Renee bends down to pick up Rufus' squeaky toy from the floor. 'Hopefully, he'll be home soon.'

'I must get going,' Ashley says before Renee can ask any more questions. She swallows the tears she could let loose right now. But it's not the time. She needs to get to work.

During the client call, Ashley finds it hard to concentrate. Her head is pounding, and her cheek is throbbing. Her thoughts are mixed into a cocktail of images of Danny at the police station, Lucy's bloody body lying on that cold concrete floor and the iPad she wants to get into, and it tastes disgusting.

The client hasn't been forthcoming with their wishes and now they are unhappy with the drafts Ashley sent. Danny did warn her about this one being particularly demanding. And it's not for her lack of trying. They want to create a bunch of lifestyle CGI images around a housing development they are building on the outskirts of London. A collection of four- and five-bedroom houses and an apartment block with two-bedroomed flats. Their brief was sketchy at best, so, frustratingly, everything she has presented has only clarified what they don't want rather than what they do. She tries her best, but the guy isn't impressed. She can't stop glancing at the phone and iPad sitting on the edge of her desk.

Another person joins the call. Nicer. More polite. He takes over, explaining what they're after in more detail. Ashley works with him, giving her ideas. There's a rapport. He loves her suggestions. Why can't all their clients be more like this? He brings the call to a close, thanking her for her time and asking her to send some images as soon as possible. They have deadlines they need to meet.

She opens the mood board she has been constructing for another client. She promised it to them by the close of business today, but her creative juices have run dry. What code could Danny have used to get into the iPad? After thirty minutes, she has achieved nothing. It's useless. She's wasting her time. She'll need to come back to that project later today.

Her mind wanders to Danny again. How long will the police keep him? She continuously checks her phone, desperate for news, but the only communication is from people snooping for an update.

She clicks on Danny's diary, debating cancelling his appointments for tomorrow. Four meetings span the day, three on the west outskirts of London and one closer to home. Even if he gets home tonight, they can't carry on as if nothing ever happened. They're going to need some time to get over the trauma.

Maybe they can go away to Venice like he suggested. They haven't had a holiday for a couple of years. Not even a full day off. There's always an email that needs answering or a client project that needs finishing.

What is she thinking? They can't afford to go on holiday. Not with their current money situation.

She'll give it until the afternoon to decide on tomorrow's meetings, and he can make the call. He should be back by then.

Shouldn't he?

TWENTY-EIGHT

The sun shines relentlessly on the playing fields of the primary school. It's like the air on a holiday abroad, nearly as hot as when Ashley and Danny went to Greece that year, but the atmosphere is charged with a cool intensity.

Everywhere she turns, parents are huddled in groups, their conversations hushed, eyes darting towards her where she has purposely positioned herself at the back of the crowd. The knot in her stomach tightens each time she catches a pair of eyes averting her gaze. As soon as Elliot has run his race, she'll be out of there.

Elliot's full-body wave catches her attention. There he is. She smiles, her heart hurting as he scans the space around her to see whether his dad has made it. When the realisation sinks in that Danny isn't there, the corners of his mouth drop, and his shoulders slump until, mercifully, a teacher says something and draws him back to the main event.

At one-fifty-five precisely, the headteacher calls everyone to attention over a loudspeaker. Ashley drops her head as she listens to the brief speech focused on Lucy. What sterling work she did as the head of the PTA, and how greatly she will be missed. 'Let's take a minute's silence as we think about the Ellis family.'

The younger children are surprisingly well-behaved, staff reminding them to put on their sunhats and encouraging them to be quiet. The older ones stare at the ground, their maturity allowing them a greater understanding of the gravity of the situation. As the respectful silence ends, two mothers standing next to Ashley invite her into their conversation. Idle chit-chat about the weather and the excitement of the children. She politely talks with them until a hand lands on her shoulder. She jumps.

'Has he run his race yet?' Tom says.

'I didn't know you were coming,' Ashley remarks.

'Danny asked me to this morning if he couldn't make it. I haven't heard from him, so I guess he's still at the station.'

Ashley nods. 'I can't understand what's taking so long.'

'What happened to your face?'

Ashley touches her cheek. It feels bruised. 'I tripped getting into the car. Elliot's up next.'

'I'll take him back to mine for dinner after this, if you want. It'll distract him until Danny gets home.'

They glance at the starting line, where boys from Elliot's class brace themselves. Ashley's grip tightens around her folded programme, the paper crumpling under the strain.

Elliot's face lights up to see Tom. A shrill whistle pierces the air, and they are off, a blur of limbs and determination. Shouts of encouragement fill the air. Elliot stays in front for the whole race, but as they cross the finish line, another child marginally beats him to the finish. He doesn't take it well, stropping off like a spoilt child towards the school buildings.

'Doesn't he look just like his dad?' Tom laughs.

He's right. If there is one unsavoury trait in her husband that Ashley doesn't like, it's just that. Danny doesn't like losing at anything. He never has.

Before she slips off home, Ashley heads to the bathroom.

While she's in one of the cubicles, the main door opens. She remains quiet, listening to the barrage of gossip volleying between the two mothers as one appears to wash their hands, oblivious to her presence. 'I'm surprised she sent him in today. What kind of a parent would do that?'

'Poor woman. She must be going through hell. You don't think he did it, do you?'

'What do you mean?'

'You don't think her husband murdered Lucy Ellis, do you?'

'Who knows? They were friends for years, apparently. They were at this school together. Trisha told me they used to be an item. Strange he's still being questioned, though, don't you think? But stranger things have happened. Can you imagine the headline: "Village man butchers childhood friend".'

Ashley wants to run out of the cubicle, but she's frozen in shock. She clasps both hands across her mouth, stifling a scream. No. Whoever this bloody Trisha is has got it wrong. It's Tom who used to go out with Lucy. Not Danny.

'That's wicked,' one of the women says. 'I wonder what the motive was. If it was him, that is.'

'I'm not sure it was him. My money is more on the husband. That's what I always say in these cases. Always look at the husband.'

'Lee Ellis?'

'Yep. Renee – the woman who cleans for us – told me a while back how possessive he was about Lucy.'

'She works for them, doesn't she?'

'That's right. She's the housekeeper and an "any job that needs doing" kind of employee, from what I can gather. A right old gossip if ever I met one. She's a very good cleaner, though. Very efficient.'

Another person walks in, and the two women leave. Ashley flushes the toilet and washes her hands. As she heads for the exit, she catches her reflection in the mirror. Her face looks drawn, the weight of the gossip dragging her down even further. She tightens the grip on her bag, reminding herself to remain composed. It's astonishing how people can twist history to suit their repulsive thirst for gossip.

When she gets home, Ashley returns to The Hub, her mind reeling. The iPad is plaguing her, but she tries to immerse herself in the mood board that is due to the client by the end of the day. They've chased her; she must finish it. And there's that suite of six CGIs with a deadline this Friday she needs to work on. They are for one of Danny's favourite clients. He is always keen to do business with them as they pay as soon as he submits an invoice. If she can get the six images to them today, there'll be time to make any changes they want before Friday.

The two gossiping women remain in her thoughts, as do Danny and Lucy, making it difficult to concentrate.

Her phone rings. It's her sister.

'I've just landed. I tried to call you after the meeting and again from the airport. What's happened?'

'Danny's still not home. I need to talk to you.'

'Do you want me to come over?'

Ashley debates whether this is a good idea. Danny could be home any time soon. But, then again, he might not. How long can they keep him? She called the solicitor's officer earlier, but there was no update. 'Would you?'

'I'll be there as soon as I can.'

Ashley can't concentrate. It's too hot, and there's too much on her mind, but she has to complete those CGIs. Otherwise, they'll have to delay sending the invoice to the client, and Danny has insisted they run a tight ship until they can recoup the funds they lost from Pickstones. Not to mention the money Lucy and Lee's company owes them. But it's too difficult to focus.

Her phone rings again, disorientating her. It's the early-morning sound of chirping birds. She frowns. That's not her ringtone. Confused, she grabs her phone. No one is calling. She's going mad. All of this is too much. It's playing with her head.

But then the chirping sounds again. And her eyes stretch open in astonishment as she realises it must be the phone she found in the safe.

Ashley grabs it, but her hand is shaking so much that she drops it on the floor. She scrambles to pick it up. She can't allow it to ring off.

The incoming call shows as No Caller ID.

Gingerly, she accepts the call, lowering the tone of her voice. 'Hello.'

TWENTY-NINE

'Danny.' The caller has a melodic Eastern European accent. 'Krzysztof from Warsaw here. I need help.'

It's the guy Danny has been conversing with by email regarding outsourcing some of their CGI business. The part of the process Ashley is responsible for.

Putting aside her anxiety, Ashley composes herself. Clutching the arm of the chair, she draws in a deep breath. 'Hello, Krzysztof. It's Danny's wife here. Danny is in a meeting at the moment. How can I help?'

'When can I speak to Danny?' Krzysztof says. He has a strong accent, but his English is good.

'He won't be available for the rest of the day, I'm afraid, but we work together, so I can help you with whatever you need.'

'The code for the brick colour in the file Danny sent doesn't exist.'

She pauses. Think. Think. 'Listen, Krzysztof. I haven't been involved in this particular project and Danny's computer is in the middle of an update, and it's taking ages. But if you send the file back to me, I can take a look.' She swallows the ball of guilt in her throat for yet another lie passing her lips. When did she get so good at lying? 'Send the file over as soon as possible, and I'll get back to you straight away.' She relays her email address.

'I send now. Thank you.' He ends the call, wishing her a nice day.

Nice day! If only he knew.

Surprisingly, the phone hasn't locked after the call. It must be because it's so old. Ashley looks at the messages app. It's empty. Contacts? Again, nothing. The recent call from Krzysztof is the only activity. Danny appears to have been studious in keeping the phone clean. Why?

She waits for Krzysztof's email with bated breath. But an hour later when Susie arrives, she's still waiting.

Ashley hadn't realised how much she needed someone to talk to until she hugs her sister as if they haven't seen each other for years.

'Careful, you'll knock me over,' Susie says.

Ashley releases her grip.

'What happened to your face?' Susie asks.

Ashley touches her cheek. It's still sore, but she forgot about the fall in all the mayhem. 'I tripped over my shoelace.'

'Drunk again?' Susie giggles, a sound that would usually make Ashley laugh, but not today. Dropping her designer holdall on the floor, Susie chucks her laptop case and handbag beside it and removes her suit jacket. 'Any news from Danny?'

Ashley shakes her head. 'I've got so much to tell you, though.'

Susie bends down, unzips her bag and pulls out a bottle of Sauvignon. 'Let's open this, and you can tell me all about it. Where's Elliot?'

'He went to Tom's for dinner.'

Susie sticks her nose up. 'Oh.'

'He is his uncle, Suz.'

'I know. I know.' Susie fishes around in her handbag and takes out a packet of Silk Cut and a silver lighter. 'It's just you know how I feel about that guy. He gives me the creeps.' It's so unlike Susie to say a bad word about anyone. She is the kindest person Ashley has ever met. But Susie and Tom don't see eye to eye. He made an advance on her one night after she split with her first husband, and Susie claims she had to fight him off with more persuasion than was appropriate.

'He's good with Elliot. And Elliot loves him. I'm sorry, I didn't even ask you how your presentation went today.'

Susie smiles, nodding her head. 'Good. Very good.' She smiles coyly. 'They seemed pleased.'

Ashley finds some enthusiasm for her sister's good news. 'So you got your promotion?'

'I hope so.'

'When do you find out?'

'I should hear by the end of the week.'

'That's brilliant news.'

'How's he taking all this? Elliot, that is.'

'You know how resilient kids are. I'm worried about him, though. How it's going to affect him.'

Fully conversant with the dynamics of the kitchen, Susie grabs two glasses from the cupboard. Ashley stands at the sink staring at Susie pouring the wine from the reflection in the window. Was it only last night that Danny stood here and invited her into his embrace to confess his fears? It feels as if she has lived a hundred days since then.

'So what's happened?' Susie nods to the garden. 'Shall we sit outside? The pollution in London is shocking in this heat. Frankfurt wasn't much better.' She takes a deep breath through her nostrils. 'I'm gagging for some of your fresh country air. When's Danny coming home?'

'I have no idea.' Ashley opens the patio doors. 'I'll get us some shade, and then I'll update you. You're not going to believe it.' She steps into the garden and unties the strap of the canopy, opening it over the rattan patio table and chairs that

Danny's parents bought for them when they moved in. At the time, Ashley argued that there were more pressing items they needed, but Danny was adamant they also needed garden furniture.

She fetches the iPad and phone, and they sit at the table, the canopy providing shade from the early-evening sun still warm in the blue sky. Rufus stretches himself out by Ashley's feet, his head on his front paws. Susie hands her a glass of wine.

'I can only have one now. I need to jump on a call to the US later.'

Taking a deep breath, Ashley ploughs into the intricate details of the last twenty-four hours while Susie smokes a cigarette, her eyes locked on her sister.

'Twenty grand? What the hell?'

Ashley nods and sighs heavily. 'I know, right? It's all the deception I can't get my head around. When I challenged him last night, he had a perfectly plausible explanation for everything. Of course, I didn't know about the safe then. Ah, and that's something else. He was at Lucy's house on Wednesday. Tom told me. They were arguing.'

'What about?'

'When I asked Danny, he said it was over a work matter.'

'Business colleagues do argue, Ash.'

'I know. It's just...' Ashley shrugs. 'It's just, he never told me he was going there.'

'He doesn't have to tell you everything.'

Ashley knows this is true, but it's not how she and Danny operate. They do tell each other everything... Or so she thought.

'And he asked me not to tell the police about them arguing,' she continues.

Susie twizzles her packet of cigarettes in her hand, a ray of sunshine accentuating her sharply defined cheekbones. 'You can't blame him. I mean, it doesn't look good, does it? He was seen arguing with a woman who, a few days later, was murdered. And he was found with her body. However innocent he is, that won't go down well.'

'Then there was the supposed meeting with the cousin of the divorce lawyer he never told me about.'

Susie raises her eyebrows as she lights another cigarette.

Ashley rolls her eyes. She mimics her sister's voice. 'He doesn't have to tell you everything.'

Susie laughs. Ashley doesn't.

'There was a perfectly reasonable explanation for the divorce lawyer,' Susie says.

'But the Post-it note.'

'There was a perfectly reasonable explanation for that as well.'

'Whose side are you on?'

'Is there a side?' The lines in Susie's forehead deepen. 'Look, Ash, I'm playing devil's advocate here.' She takes another puff of her cigarette and slowly exhales the smoke. 'You two have always been so good together.'

'But he *has* lied. Explain this Krzysztof guy. That reminds me.' Ashley grabs her phone from the table and refreshes her emails, tutting. 'He still hasn't got back to me.'

'Are you sure you gave him the right email address?'

Ashley nods. Unusually, she's annoyed at her sister. Why is she sticking up for Danny?

'The language barrier. He could've taken it down wrong. Or maybe he got caught up on another project. Don't jump to conclusions. It's not healthy. I should know.'

'It doesn't explain why Danny called upon his services without telling me. The safe. The money. The iPad.' Ashley thumps the palm of her hand against her forehead. 'He's got twenty grand sitting in a safe in the office where we work together every single day, and I knew nothing about it. Where the hell did it come from? Explain that. At the very least, it's deceitful.'

'Oh, Ash. I agree with you. There could be a reasonable explanation for everything. But the cash, that does sound very dodgy. But what can you do but wait to ask him.'

'You think it's all dodgy, but you're trying to keep me calm. I can tell.'

'I just don't want you to get worked up any more than you already are.'

Ashley reaches over to grab Susie's hand and gasps. 'Where's your ring?'

Susie scrunches up her face. 'I was waiting to see you to tell you. I broke off the engagement. I was going to tell you yesterday but events got in the way.'

'Were you wearing it yesterday?'

Susie shakes her head.

'I never noticed. I'm sorry.' That's a shame. She liked Paulo. She thought he was good for her sister.

'I know,' Susie says.

Ashley stares at her sister. She has always felt like the ugly duckling beside Susie's beauty. When she once told Danny that, he told her beauty was in the eye of the beholder and kissed her long and hard on the lips. She once wondered if they were actually sisters. But then she reminded herself that their father was the cheating rat in their parents' tempestuous forty-year marriage, not their mother.

Susie sighs. 'But I decided he wasn't for me.'

'Why? He was one of the good guys. He treated you so well. Better than any of the other rotters you've had.'

'I know, I know.' Susie shakes her pretty head, her big brown eyes as wide as her wonderment. 'I'm a girl destined for the bad boys. I blame our mother.' She claps her hands in the prayer position and looks to the sky. 'God bless her soul. And you can stop that face. I don't need pity. I don't deserve it. I'm my own worst enemy.' She laughs. 'I think I may need to invest in a counsellor. What do you think they'd say? "You're a lost cause. You silly woman."'

'You jest, but it might not be a bad idea.' Ashley thinks her sister would benefit from some therapy. She'll never hold a relationship down otherwise. But that's a conversation for another time. When Ashley's sorted out her own relationship.

'Do you ever wonder how you managed to escape our dysfunctional childhood, but I've ended up the way I have? I mean, look at you. Married to a great guy, beautiful kid, successful career.' Susie sweeps her arm around the garden, stopping at the patio door. 'Not to mention this fabulous house.'

'I don't think I've wholly escaped it.'

'What do you mean?'

Ashley has never told anyone, not even her sister, how she accused Danny of cheating after Elliot was born. She has always been too ashamed. She relays the story about that wretched night when she thought she was having a breakdown. Susie listens intently.

'So, I haven't escaped our dysfunctional childhood. I have trust issues.'

THIRTY

Ashley's phone pings with a text. 'It's Tom. He's bringing Elliot home.'

Susie pulls a face. 'I don't want to see him.'

'You don't have to. I'll tell him I'm heading out. I need to take Rufus for a walk. I think it's cool enough now. Do you want to come with us?'

Susie stands up. 'I'll go and get changed. Call me when Tom's gone. Your pots need a water, by the way. You'll lose those petunias if you're not careful.'

Ashley looks around the patio at more wilted victims of the past twenty-four hours. 'I'll do it later.'

She picks up the iPad and phone and returns them to the safe. Elliot will ask whose they are if he comes across them. And it's probably a good idea for Danny not to see them when he comes home. Elliot needs to be in bed before she tackles him over them.

Susie is upstairs when Elliot arrives home. Ashley squats down to greet her son.

'Is Dad here?' is the first question he asks.

Ashley's heart aches for him. 'Not yet. He should be back

soon. Aunty Susie is upstairs, though.' She's hoping Tom takes the hint and makes a swift departure. He knows how her sister feels about him.

'Yay.' Elliot turns to Tom. 'Thanks for dinner.' He swiftly kisses Ashley on the cheek as he passes her, calling, 'Aunty Susie,' as he runs upstairs.

'Any news?' Tom asks, his face sharing her concerns. He seems on edge, his voice throaty as if he is trying to control his emotions. Is it because Susie is there? 'I've not heard a thing from him all day.' He sways from foot to foot.

'Me neither. Not even from the bloody solicitor! If I've not heard anything by the time Elliot's in bed, I'll ask Susie to babysit while I go to the station. I'm going out of my mind here.'

'Just keep me posted, won't you? Mum and Dad are on their way home.'

So it won't be long before she has them to contend with as well!

'That's good,' Ashley says, faking a smile.

It's another lie. She hates lying. 'Liars never prosper,' her mum used to always say to her dad. 'You'll ultimately pay the price for all your deception, darling.' And he did. It cost him his wife and his two daughters.

Elliot goads Rufus mercilessly, leaving the poor dog tugging furiously at Ashley's extended arm.

'Stop, Elliot,' Ashley says, her voice strained. 'He'll knock me over.'

Rufus pulls her along the narrow dirt path to the fields lined with towering bottle-green bushes blocking out the sun, save for some slivers of light breaking through the branches. The path shortly opens onto fields as far as the eye can see in a gently rolling landscape of arable farmland where golden wheat, wispy barley and rich sugar-beet crops thrive in the fertile soil. The odd copse, wooded areas or farm buildings are the only disruption to the scenery. It's a route Ashley walks most days. Usually early in the morning, before Elliot is up. Sometimes with Danny during the day when he is working from home. If the weather is good, they might take an hour's lunch break and head to The Ugly Duckling with Rufus. They order cheese and pickle sandwiches and a bowl of fries to eat in the pub garden. Come to think of it, they haven't done that for a few weeks. Even though the beautiful weather has warranted it.

They pass the stile leading to the expanse of farmland stretching out to the horizon, where Ashley lets Rufus off his lead. Elliot races after the bounding dog.

'What about the date you got married?' Susie pipes up.

'What?'

'For the iPad passcode.'

'I tried that.' Ashley stops walking and stamps her foot on the ground. 'I can't bear it. All this secrecy. All this deception.'

The low buzz of her phone interrupts them. Fishing it out of her pocket, she warily eyes the No Caller ID commanding the screen.

'This could be the solicitor.' Her steps falter as she accepts the call, until she hears the words that shock her world, and she freezes, rooted to the spot. Any remaining traces of blood drain from her face.

Susie looks at her, frowning.

Ashley ends the call, her eyes as wide as the horizon. Her gaze meets Susie's, her face a picture of shock.

'They've... they've arrested Danny on suspicion of Lucy's murder.'

THIRTY-ONE

Susie's shocked expression echoes Ashley's thoughts. 'There must be some kind of a mistake.'

'I need to get back.' Ashley's voice reverberates across the fields. 'Elliot! Rufus! Here. Now.'

'On what grounds have they arrested him?' Susie asks.

Ashley's eyes flit to her sister's. 'The solicitor said the police believe they have reasonable grounds to suspect he did it. Danny asked her to call me and tell me.'

Danny's words echo in her thoughts. He said he could kill that woman.

'Don't you get to make a call when you're arrested? Why didn't he call you?'

Ashley staggers towards a tree, leaning against the trunk. She can't be sick. Not now. Not in front of Elliot.

Susie walks over and rests a hand on her shoulder.

Ashley turns to her sister. 'I'm scared.'

'Don't be,' Susie says with confidence that appears fake. 'They do this so they can keep him in custody to question him some more.'

'The solicitor just said they can hold him for twenty-four

hours before they charge him in the first instance, but it won't be hard to get an extension in a suspected murder case.' Her breathing quickens. 'Which can be up to ninety-six hours.' She pauses, her thoughts making a quick calculation. 'That's four days.' The idea of Danny sitting in a cell for that long haunts her. 'They're assigning him a new solicitor. Same firm, but he's a more experienced member of the team.'

Before she can say any more, Elliot appears. Susie entertains him with a story about the ghastly potato omelette they served on her flight to Frankfurt that morning. Ashley walks behind them, stunned. Is she married to a murderer?

Her phone rings again. It's Tom. She diverts the call to voicemail.

'What's happened, Mum?' Elliot asks. 'Why're you crying?'

'I'm not, darling,' Ashley quickly responds, wiping her eyes. 'The pollen count must still be high. I feel like I've got a touch of hay fever.'

Here we go again. Another lie, but her mind is in turmoil. How can she possibly explain to her child that his dad has been arrested for murder?

And not just any murder. The murder of his best friend's mum.

It's surreal, something out of a nightmare. Anger sets in. She kicks at a stone along the dirt path with her Converse, unable to comprehend how this could be happening. Yesterday morning they were your average family attending a birthday party.

She longs to hear Danny's voice, assuring her this is all a dream, a misunderstanding he'll clear up. But the fear swirling in the pit of her stomach tells her it's way more sinister than a simple misjudgement by the police.

When they reach the clearing to Juniper Close, Elliot abruptly stops walking, his small voice laced with confusion. 'Mum, why are the police here?'

Following his gaze, Ashley spots the marked car parked on

the road outside their house. Three police officers exit the vehicle. One is in uniform and the other two plain-clothed, their faces stern and determined. They advance towards her house. When they reach the front door, one of them rings the bell. She and Susie exchange looks of horror, asking the question: what the hell are they doing here?

Pulling Elliot's hand, Ashley hurries towards them. 'Can I help you?'

The oldest of the trio, a grey-haired man, lanky and all limbs, steps forward. 'Ashley Morgan?' He is dressed in suit trousers and a white shirt, sleeves rolled midway up his sinewy arms.

'Yes,' she replies, her voice shaky.

'Can we step inside, please?' the officer requests, his tone leaving little room for objection.

Paranoia sets in. Have they come to arrest her as well? What has she done? What will happen to Elliot? She doesn't want him staying with Tom. Or Danny's parents.

Curtains flutter and window blinds twitch around the close. The woman Ashley sometimes walks home from school with is hurriedly shepherding her kids inside the house opposite, towels wrapped around their necks, their hair wet. The woman avoids her gaze. She is usually so friendly. The weight of her judgement sickens Ashley. Her neighbour should be supporting her. What happened to the tight-knit community Danny made out Thyme End to be?

Numbly, Ashley retrieves a door key from her pocket, the metal cold against her burning skin. Her movements are robotic, driven by the need to survive this as calmly as possible for Elliot's sake. She opens the door, allowing the police officers into her home. Susie comes after her, as dumbfounded as Ashley, followed by Elliot and Rufus.

The man introduces himself as DI Graves and his two female colleagues, PC Roads and DC Sortie. Their names and ranks blur in Ashley's mind, which has been inundated with fear and confusion.

DI Graves looks towards Susie.

'I'm Ashley's sister,' she says.

Elliot wraps his hand around Ashley's, gripping it like a vice. 'They're not taking you as well, are they, Mum?'

Susie gasps, taking Elliot's hand. 'Of course not, buddy.'

PC Roads, a young woman dressed in uniform, squats so she is at eye level with the innocent child. 'Elliot, isn't it?'

He nods, looking from the officer to Ashley and Susie.

'Can someone tell me what's going on here?' Ashley demands, her voice stronger. She doesn't like what they're putting her son through, let alone her and her husband.

PC Roads ignores her and addresses Elliot. 'Would you mind taking me to your living room while your mum has a chat with my colleagues?' She glances at Susie. 'It would be good if you could come too.'

Elliot's grip tightens. Ashley squeezes his clammy hand. 'It's OK. Why don't you go with Aunty Susie and show the lady your DVDs.'

Susie nods at Ashley. A nod of encouragement that falls flat. Not even her sister can fake her enthusiasm now.

Ashley leads the way to the kitchen. The ball of fear that has been growing in her throat the past twenty-four hours is now so big, she can't swallow it down. 'What on earth is going on?' Her words echo around the room as Rufus laps up the remaining water in his bowl.

'Are you aware of your husband's circumstances, Mrs Morgan?' asks DI Graves, rolling his shirt sleeves up to his bony elbows.

She nods, choking on facts she wishes were fiction.

'He has been arrested on the suspicion of murder,' the officer continues, his tone as steady as her gaze. 'We have a warrant to search the premises.' He brandishes a piece of paper.

'Why?'

'I'm afraid we're unable to discuss the ongoing investigation. We aim to be as quick and undisruptive as possible. But we'll need to take a few things away with us. You can wait in the living room with your son.'

Ashley watches them remove blue nitrile gloves from their pockets and snap them on their hands. She wants to argue with them and scream at them, grab them by their shirt collars and chuck them out of the front door. But she is on the back foot here. 'How long is this going to take?'

'Two to three hours, we hope,' the plain-clothed woman says, her tone indifferent and impersonal.

'Does your husband own a computer or any other device?' DI Graves asks. The question is concise, as if he has asked the same question hundreds of times before.

She nods, her mind swirling with doubt for her husband. What is Danny mixed up in?

'Where does he keep them?'

She nods to the garden. 'His computer is in the office. I don't know where his laptop is. It could be down there, or in his car, which is still at the Ellises' house, I think. Sometimes, he keeps it in the boot of the car between meetings.'

'Thank you. Is the office open?'

A cold chill runs through her despite the stuffy temperature. They are here to confiscate her husband's possessions. Her heart beats in her chest. What if that phone rings in the safe while they are in The Hub? Should she come clean and give them up? Something is telling her that's not a clever idea. It's evident Danny didn't want anyone to know about them. But isn't that perverting the course of justice? Withholding evidence that might help the police? She could get into big trouble. What if they discover the iPad and phone and find her fingerprints on them? Could she get arrested as well?

She doesn't like this. She's an honest, straight-up person.

What the hell has Danny involved her in?

She doesn't want to talk to them. Instead, she robotically walks over to the ceramic pot on the corner table and opens the patio doors. She hands the key to the officer. 'His desk is the one on the right. The other one is mine. I need to keep working, so please don't touch any of my stuff.'

'Thank you. Please wait in the lounge with your son.'

Ashley grits her teeth, knowing it's best to keep her mouth shut, despite her longing to shout at them to get the hell out of her house.

She joins Elliot and Susie in the lounge. Elliot is talking through his precious collection of DVDs with the police constable.

The sisters exchange looks of horror. Ashley can't bear the thought of Susie being wrapped up in all the lies and deceit, but she has been left with little choice.

Ashley tries to remain as composed as possible given the circumstances. 'How's it all going in here?'

'Come and sit with us, Mum.' Elliot turns and addresses the police officer, 'You can watch as well if you like?'

'Thank you, Elliot. I'd like that very much,' the officer says.

Really? Why don't you go and help your mates, Ashley wants to scream at the woman. Then you can get the hell out of my house much quicker. But she knows why. The woman is staying to spy on her. To make sure she doesn't tamper with evidence. Not that there's anything to tamper with. Is there?

Elliot holds out his hand to her. Her heart hurts for him. How is she going to tell him what has happened? She and Danny have always had a policy of truthfulness. Her dad was a serial liar, and Danny has vivid childhood memories of his mother, for good or bad, constantly lying to him. The truth always wins the day in Danny's books.

But what is the truth, Danny?

THIRTY-TWO

'Come on. Let's start this film.' Ashley cuddles up beside Elliot on the sofa, their bodies sticky in the room, airless despite all the windows being open. 'I need to buy that fan,' Ashley says, referring to the purchase she and Danny have talked about over the past few weeks as the heatwave took hold.

Through the lounge door, Ashley sees the female detective in the hallway holding a wad of plastic and brown bags.

'What're they doing?' Elliot looks washed out, his bottom lip curled outwards. 'I'm scared.'

Ashley exchanges a look of frustration with Susie, sitting on the other side of Elliot. She masks her concern with a smile. 'Don't be scared, darling. They're police officers. Their job is to protect us.'

Another corker of a lie!

What has her husband done to her? As well as lying to her, he's made her lie to their son and question their marriage. It's as if she doesn't know him anymore.

'Ride this storm, Ash. Ride this storm.' That's what Danny would say. 'Keep calm. It'll all blow over soon.' But she has an overwhelming feeling that won't be the case. Heavier, rain-laden clouds are waiting, ready to unleash their torrent.

'What're they doing?' Elliot asks again.

'They're having a look around.' That, at least, is the truth.

'Why?'

'Dad was good friends with Grace's mum. Like you and Grace are at school together, Dad was at school with Lucy. She had an accident, and they hope they can find a clue as to how it happened by looking around.'

'But why here? Shouldn't they be looking in Grace's house?'

Questions. Always so many questions.

Ashley stares at him, so astute for his age. 'They'll be looking there as well. Come on, watch the film.' She doesn't want to say much more with the police officer listening. The woman's presence makes her uncomfortable.

Susie's eyes dart regularly to Ashley. They are asking the same question that Ashley keeps asking herself. Should she disclose the iPad and the phone to the unwanted visitors?

A few minutes pass. Ashley peers upwards, to the shuddering sound coming from above. They must be searching through Danny's wardrobe; the drawer below the hanging space always makes that noise. What could they possibly be looking for?

Her phone rings. It's Tom. She should answer it, tell him what has happened. But now's not the time. She stabs the red button.

Her jaw clenches. Her husband has been arrested for murder. It doesn't seem real. Perhaps the police will realise they've got it all wrong before she needs to inform the world.

A text pings. It's one of the mums from school asking how she is. She's in no mood to converse with anyone. Especially people who are only after gossip.

Clicking the Google app on her phone, she searches how to tell children their dad has been arrested for murder or that he is in prison. As she thought, there is no right time or way to relay such news, but honesty is the best policy. Her mind is a whirl. The lack of sleep is playing havoc with her thought process. She can't remember what she has and hasn't told Elliot. She reads on and concludes she doesn't need to say anything yet, other than what she has already told him. If Danny gets charged... well, then that will be a different story.

Danny get charged? It's an impossible prospect to process.

She checks her emails. There's still nothing from Krzysztof. Why hasn't he sent the file? Has he given their conversation some thought and decided it would be too unprofessional to send details to her when he has been conversing with Danny? She checks her spam folder, sifting through the junk emails telling her she has won an electric toothbrush or she needs to claim a one-hundred-pound gift voucher. There's nothing there either.

'Put your phone down,' Elliot insists.

Ashley flinches. It's as if Danny is in the room with them, scolding her like he always does for being on her phone when they're watching TV as a family. It's because of what Danny and Elliot choose to watch. Football, mutant superheroes, Transformers, she has zero interest in their choices.

The police officer coughs, reminding Ashley the reason why she is here.

Her thoughts return to the situation, and now she can't help them playing over and over in her mind like an addictive tune she can't stop humming.

Murder.

Her husband has been arrested for murder.

Where does she go from here?

THIRTY-THREE

The police leave her home pretty much as they found it.

Apart from the absence of Danny's iMac, and the bed not made to Ashley's standards, it's as if they'd never been there. They left an inventory of what they took: mainly a few personal items, and his computer and files from The Hub.

'It'll all be returned when we've finished with it,' DI Graves said, his stoic expression irritating the hell out of her.

Ashley leaves Elliot soaking in the bath. When she gets downstairs, her phone pings with a message from Oriana, asking how she is. Ashley winces. She should have been at Thyme End Hall this evening for Oriana's weekly art class. She completely forgot. Ashley calls her, apologising for having not been in contact.

'I think you've got enough on your plate, dear.' Oriana's voice, shaky and quiet, has lost its usual positivity.

They discuss Lucy's death. Oriana is heartbroken about the murder of the woman who was like the daughter she never had.

'Who could've done such an abhorrent thing? And to hear Danny has been arrested is the most preposterous thing I've ever heard.'

Ashley's eyebrows draw together in confusion. 'How did you find out?'

'Apparently, it's common knowledge.'

'But the police aren't allowed to name people at this stage.'

'I don't think they needed to, dear.'

Ashley grits her teeth. The village grapevine has been producing more of its sour crop.

She joins Susie in the garden, who is drinking a glass of wine. She was only going to have one until her call. Circumstances seem to have changed that.

'What the fuck!' Susie says, shaking her head. She pours a glass of wine for Ashley and slides it across the table.

'Do you think I should've mentioned the iPad and phone?'

'I don't know.' Deep concern is etched on Susie's face. 'Where are they?'

Ashley nods towards The Hub. 'I put them back in the safe.' She panics. Her breathing quickens. 'I didn't know what to do for the best.'

Elliot calls her from the bath.

Ashley sighs. 'I'll be back soon.'

She trudges upstairs, her shoulders stooped.

'Is Dad going to prison?' Elliot asks as he lathers shampoo into his hair.

Ashley shudders. She has been stupidly underestimating what he has been gleaning from the events of the past couple of days.

'Did Dad kill Grace's mum?'

'Elliot! Don't be silly. You can't say things like that.'

'But the police think Dad did it, don't they? That's why they've taken all his stuff.'

'They've made a mistake. A silly mistake, that's all.' She needs to explain the situation to him properly, but that's a conversation for the morning, when she's had some sleep. Not that she can see that happening. All she envisages is a hot and sweaty night ahead while she stares at the ceiling.

On her way downstairs, she checks the news app on her phone. It's there in black and white: a statement from the police. They have arrested a thirty-seven-year-old man on suspicion of the murder of local woman Lucy Ellis. He remains in police custody for questioning. The DCI said, 'We understand this will be an unsettling incident for the local community, but please be assured that we believe this to be a targeted incident where the victim was known to the suspect. Our thoughts are with the victim's family, and we will do all we can to support them as we progress our investigation.'

'I think I've got it,' Susie says when Ashley returns to the garden.

'What?'

'The iPad passcode.' Susie points at Rufus. 'What about this fella's date of birth? Or the day you got him?'

Ashley raises an eyebrow. Just one. An expression that has always amused Danny. 'That could work.'

Susie taps her forefinger on her temple. 'Stick with me, kid.' She stubs out her cigarette. 'Sorry to leave you, but I need to join that call to the US. I'll come straight back down when it's done. Shall we get pizza in?'

'I don't fancy anything.'

'You need to eat, Ash. Your usual? Pepperoni?'

Ashley's stomach turns at the thought.

There's a knock at the door. They look at each other.

'I don't want to see anyone,' Ashley says.

Susie stands up. 'Leave it to me.'

Ashley runs to the lounge, peeping out of the window to the feeding frenzy of iPhones snapping shots as Susie opens the front door. What the hell is happening to her life?

Susie is polite but firm. 'We've nothing to say. Nothing at all. Please leave us alone.' She slams the door shut.

Ashley is aghast to see a group of reporters backstepping along her garden path.

Susie joins her at the window. She pats Ashley's shoulder. A pat of encouragement that attempts to tell her to hang tight, everything is going to be all right.

'I'll come straight back down after the call. Hold your head high, girl, and carry on as normal. You've got nothing to be ashamed of. Danny hasn't been formally charged.'

The *yet* remains unspoken in Ashley's mind.

Ashley paces up and down the kitchen, barefoot. Danny hates her walking around without anything on her feet. He says it's unhygienic, so she doesn't do it when he's around. She adores it, especially in the garden. It grounds her to feel the earth beneath her toes, makes her feel free.

She returns to the patio and sits down, Rufus at her side. He places his paw on her knee. What's that saying: enjoy today because you never know what tomorrow is going to bring? Hell, you don't.

She pats Rufus' paw, her anticipation heightened. She's got to chance it. What has she got to lose now anyway? Rushing to The Hub, she removes the iPad and phone from the safe, peering around the office. Danny's missing iMac and files make the place look bare. She checks the phone to see if there have been any calls. There haven't.

She takes the iPad to the kitchen table, wiping the sweat glistening on her forehead. Rufus dawdles to sit by her side. She taps the screen. It lights up, demanding a passcode. She types in Rufus' date of birth, watching each of the six circles on the screen darkening with the entry of each digit. All the circles clear and wobble. Failure. She winces at the 'Touch ID or Enter Passcode' demand.

She has one more opportunity to get it right. Can she chance it with the date Danny brought Rufus home? She thinks back to that day when they lived in London. She remembers it because it was the night before her thirtieth birthday. It was one of the happiest days of her life. She had always yearned for a dog. Ever since she was a young girl. But her dad had always refused – 'Not another bleeding mouth to feed.' Danny had always said their London flat was too small. Besides, the landlord would never allow it. That wasn't true; the couple in the downstairs flat had a dog. She'd spoken to them; the landlord agreed to pet ownership on a case-by-case basis. So Danny did his homework and sourced Rufus from a dogs' home when he was still a puppy, barely nine weeks old. He knew she would love any dog but was conscious a Rhodesian Ridgeback was her first choice. They were both shocked to see how big he grew. Too big for their small flat, but they found room for the new addition to their little family.

Ashley paces around the kitchen, her stomach in her throat like it has been since the party. Going into the garden, she turns on the hose, giving the plants a good water and deadheading the flowers while she's at it. The iPad continues to consume her thoughts. This is her last chance to get the passcode right. If she doesn't, the iPad will be disabled. But she's got to chance it.

Back inside, she switches on the radio, grabs a glass of water and sits at the table. Susie's voice garbles from the Zoom call she is on from the bedroom above. Ashley types the date Danny brought Rufus home into the iPad as a dreadful thought occurs. Has this action linked to Danny's iMac? Will the police know about the iPad? If so, she'll have to deny it. Say she's just found it.

She shakes her head. Who is she trying to kid? She'd be in deep, deep trouble.

Too late.

The screen lights up.

She's in.

THIRTY-FOUR

Ashley clicks on the email app. Her jaw drops to the floor in astonishment to find Danny has an email account connected to what looks like another company, TE PRO Limited. She opens an email titled: *Confidential*. It's from Lucy.

What the hell?

> Hi Dan,
>
> Please find below the email I was talking about re: location plan. When you get the sample CGIs of the houses, please send them to this group.
>
> Lx

Opening the attachment, Ashley studies the plan. Her jaw drops. It looks like the group is involved in a development comprising three hundred new homes cutting through the Thyme End Hall estate.

Her phone beeps with a text from Tom. She ignores it but

checks her emails to see if there's any news from Krzysztof. She clenches her teeth. Still nothing.

Returning to the iPad, she looks at the group the email originally was sent to and gasps: Guy Rogers, Roberta Splinter, John Farnborough and Patricia Cartwright.

There's another email with some sample CGIs of houses attached that Danny has received from Krzysztof. It appears Danny is providing sample marketing material for this new development. The CGIs are of poor quality. Her head slowly moves from side to side, her eyes wide in bewilderment. Why has Danny used someone else to do this and not her?

Her phone pings again. She's so on edge, she jumps, knocking the glass of water over her phone. Damn. She can't afford for it to get wet. Dashing to get a cloth, she wipes it dry, letting out a sharp cry to see a text from Lee.

Ashley, I need to talk to you. Can we meet?

She frowns at the message. Lee is not a person she expected to hear from. Why would the man who accused her husband of murdering his wife want to see her? What has he possibly got to say?

Her finger hovers over the reply button. Is it a good idea to meet with him? Maybe he's got news that will help Danny. From where she's sitting, her husband needs a hell of a lot of help.

Another text pings.

I need to explain my actions at the party. Please.

Without thinking, she types a reply. If it will help Danny clear his name, then it's worth meeting with Lee, surely? She can always change her mind.

Sure. When? And where are you thinking? Neutral ground is probably the best for both of us.

He instantly replies as if he'd already been composing the message.

Understood. I'd rather go outside the village, though. Tomorrow? At that café at Brewer's Farm where we took the kids for Sunday lunch that time. We can get a table outside. Is ten good for you?

She can't believe she is conversing with this man. Is it safe to meet him? If he believes Danny killed his wife, maybe he wants to do the same to her.

She's being paranoid. Brewer's Farm is popular. It'll be busy. He's not going to do anything to her there. And he wouldn't do anything to her anyway.

She types a reply, arranging to meet him.

What about Elliot? She can't take him with her. If he doesn't go to school, perhaps Susie can look after him while she pops out. She's not even sure he should go to school. She taps her fingers on the table, whispering to herself. 'Lee! What have you possibly got to tell me?'

She parks Lee's message. There are more pressing items on her agenda. She returns to the iPad. It appears the device's sole purpose is for correspondence on the new development, but Danny has only recently joined the conversations. And his job is to provide marketing materials. Who owns TE PRO, then?

A little more digging gives her the answer she needs. The company was set up earlier in the year and the registered office address is in Bristol.

Bristol? She bites her lip. The taste of metal nips her taste buds. Clampitt Homes is based in Bristol. Where Danny met with that Hayley woman, the beautiful redhead, and where he supposedly stayed last week. Did he fake a meeting with Clampitt on Friday morning and stay overnight so he had a reason to visit TE PRO?

Her mind is a whirl of questions she can't answer. She digs further.

The nature of business for TE PRO is listed as 'Development of building projects'. Her heart sinks. How come Danny got involved in all this and hasn't told her? He's her husband, not to mention her business partner. He's always told her everything. They're that kind of couple. She closes her eyes. Aren't they?

She drops her head in her hands, trying to control the emotions running through her. She refuses to cry. She's not the type, but a torrent of tears is damn close.

She slowly opens her eyes and clicks on the people button for the company, holding her breath. Call it a sixth sense, but she somehow knows what's coming.

The screen flashes. She lets out a cry. There is one current officer listed at the same Bristol address.

Lucy Ellis.

THIRTY-FIVE

Ashley pushes her chair away from the table and stands up. She paces up and down the room. 'What have you got yourself mixed up in, Danny?' she says through gritted teeth. And why would he do this and not involve her? Answers to these questions bounce around her head.

The only rational one is money.

She bangs her fist on the kitchen worktop as she storms past. Is that what the twenty grand in the safe is for? Did Lucy pay him to do all the marketing for this development? But even that doesn't make sense. Twenty grand is too much, especially if he uses a guy like Krzysztof to do the CGIs. Besides, Lucy and Lee's company owes Blue Banana Studios money.

And why isn't Lee involved?

Perhaps he is.

The news comes on the radio. An update on the murder of Lucy Ellis. The person who was seen leaving the grounds of the Ellis house has come forward, and the police have eliminated them from their inquiries.

Ashley grabs a bottle of Danny's whisky from the shelf at

the end of the kitchen cupboards. Not bothering with a glass, she swigs straight from the bottle, the burn in her throat as intense as that in her stomach.

The dressing-table chair scrapes along the wooden floorboards above, and the bedroom door opens. Susie must have finished her call. Ashley returns the whisky to the shelf as Susie runs down the stairs to a knock at the door. Who the hell is that, now? Not more reporters trying to get her to sell her nightmare of a story?

'I'll get it,' Susie calls out. 'It's only the pizza delivery.' A minute later, she strides into the kitchen. 'I was quicker than I thought, but I need to join another call later.' She chucks two pizza boxes on the table and stares from Ashley to the iPad. 'I take it you got in.'

Ashley nods.

'And?'

'Sit down.'

Susie obeys. Ashley tells her about the police eliminating the person seen leaving the party through a gap in the fence from their inquiries.

Susie frowns. 'Why not just leave by the front?'

'Strange, isn't it? Obviously they didn't want to be seen leaving. Perhaps they were never invited.' Who could that have been? Ashley can't recall seeing anyone suspicious, but then she hadn't been looking.

Susie opens one of the pizza boxes. 'So, come on. What did you find?'

Ashley grabs her sister's hand. 'I need you to promise me something. This conversation doesn't go any further.'

Susie leans back in the chair. 'I'm your sister, Ash. What kind of question is that?'

'Promise me.'

'I promise. Jeez, what's happened?'

'I've found some pretty devastating things.'

'Porn?' Susie giggles.

But her effort to lighten the mood fails miserably.

Ashley stares at her in horror. 'This is serious.'

'Sorry. I'm all ears.' Susie pushes the other pizza box across the table. 'I got you pepperoni.' She bites into a slice of margherita.

Ashley can't think about food right now. 'Do you remember that night you came over just after we moved in? Lucy turned up. She brought us a case of champagne for a house-warming present.'

'I do. It was a heavy night. How many bottles did we drink?'

'Four.' Ashley doesn't add that she only had one glass before turning to fizzy water. She didn't feel comfortable getting drunk in front of Lucy. Even back then, she realises, she was wary of her.

Susie shakes her head, feigning disgust. 'Shocking behaviour.'

'Do you remember Lucy telling us about some developers that wanted to build a bunch of new houses on the other side of the village, near the windmill?'

'I can't say I do.'

'Danny said no developers would ever be allowed to ruin Thyme End because the locals would fight them off. Juniper Close here was a bit of an anomaly. It sneaked through because it was only five houses and on the outskirts of the village. And there's also Lucy and Lee's development of those two eco-houses on the other side of the village.'

'I don't remember that conversation.' Susie takes another bite of pizza.

'Danny didn't say anything at the time, but afterwards he told me those two houses only went ahead because some generous bribes were passed between Lucy and the local planning officer. I asked him how he knew this, and he said it was one of the benefits of having a brother who spends so much time in the pub.'

'So what's this got to do with the iPad?'

Ashley touches the screen and clicks the relevant file. 'Look what I found.'

THIRTY-SIX

Susie stops chewing, her big brown eyes wide. She looks at the screen.

'It's a plan for a development on the Thyme End Hall estate,' Ashley says.

Susie looks confused. 'Sorry?'

'It's on the right as you come into the village. The one with the blue gates, where I give private lessons for the owner, Oriana Lewis.'

Susie nods. 'Ah, I know where you mean. It's massive.'

'She was at the party on Sunday with her husband. You might have seen them. She was wearing a bright-orange head-scarf. She's got cancer, hence the headscarf. Terminal.'

'Poor woman. I spoke to her husband at the bar.' Susie clicks her fingers several times. 'Aaron.'

'That's the one.'

'Bit of a smooth character.'

'That's him.'

'How come they were at a kid's birthday party?'

'Lucy's mum died when she was a kid, so Oriana has been like a mum to her. She has a son, Simon, by her first husband.

Danny and Lucy were at school with him. Just after we moved here, Simon got married. They held the wedding in the grounds of the estate; it's a pretty impressive place. Danny hadn't seen Simon for years. He said they lost contact as he turned into a knob, which I could kind of see. Loud, City know-it-all. Shamelessly rude and ruthlessly obnoxious.'

'Why go to his wedding, then?'

'Because a load of Danny's friends had been invited, and he didn't want to miss out.'

'Fair enough.' Susie leans over the iPad. 'So, they're looking to sell their land. Is that what you think you've found?'

Ashley slides the iPad nearer to Susie. 'I think so. I'm confused, though.'

Susie narrows her eyes and peers at the screen.

'Here. Look. It's not totally clear, but from what I can work out, Danny is involved in an application for the development of three hundred executive homes.' She points to a map. 'It cuts up the Thyme End Hall estate. This is massive. It'll completely ruin the community. What's more, people who live in the three worker's cottages on the edge of the estate will lose their homes. The schools will be overcrowded, traffic a nightmare, and services will be scuppered.'

Susie frowns. 'Can they do that?'

'If they get the permission. But it doesn't add up. Oriana loves Thyme End Hall. I'm guiding her to finish paintings of the estate she's been working on since she was diagnosed. She's always telling me about her life there and the experiences she's had.'

'So who is the developer?'

'This is the interesting bit. TE PRO Limited.'

'Do you know them?'

'I'd never heard of them, so I looked them up on Companies House. And guess who owns it?'

Susie looks at her blankly. 'Who?'

'Lucy.'

'Dead Lucy?'

'That's right. Lucy Ellis owned TE PRO Limited.'

'Why would she want to develop a piece of land there? I thought you said she was Miss Thyme End herself.'

Ashley holds up her hand and rubs her thumb along her adjoined fingers. 'Money.'

'But I thought she was loaded. Her house is a mansion. That massive party must've cost a good few pounds.'

'I can't be sure, but I've been thinking. Perhaps the company has money issues. They're behind on payments to us, Danny has just told me. But Oriana selling Thyme End Hall for development makes no sense.'

'So how come Danny is privy to all this?'

'I'll come to that.' Ashley opens an email from Lucy. 'I found this.'

Susie looks on quizzically.

'It summarises the various steps in the planning application process and where they are at with it.' Ashley reads it to Susie.

'Isn't this illegal?' Susie asks. 'How on earth do these people think they'll get away with it?'

'Unscrupulous, yes. Illegal, I'm not quite so sure. You could argue there's nothing actually illegal here. I wouldn't mind betting they know this'll cause a major issue with the local community, so they're trying to cover every aspect before it goes public.'

'It doesn't make sense for Danny and Lucy to be involved in all this.'

'I agree. I remember Danny saying that after our houses were built, no significant developments would be allowed to happen in the village. Any submissions or modernisations have been vigorously defended during recent times, prior to the more rigorous listed planning acts passed in the late nineties. But now the government are all up for providing new housing. Do you know there's currently a national shortage of around two million homes across the UK due to planning restrictions and legal barriers that people like those born here in Thyme End – Danny, Tom, Renee... and Lucy – have put up?'

Susie sighs. 'It's one of the downsides of living in the south-east. It's where the country has the biggest shortage of housing.' Susie tells her that she sees it in London too. Houses and flats are sprouting up like weeds everywhere you look.

'I know. We're prime commuter-belt territory here, especially post-Covid, with more people working from home. Five days a week was a problem, but now people don't mind the one-and-a-half-hour trek into London once or twice a week. They see it as ideal.'

'So how come Danny is involved in all of this?'

'There are six of them involved, and it looks as if Danny has only just joined the group. There's no mention of Lee, which is strange. Perhaps Lucy was keeping it from him just like Danny was keeping it from me.'

'Who are the others?'

'Guy Rogers, the local planning officer. Then there's the local MP – Roberta Splinter. Well, she *was* the local MP.'

Susie frowns. 'She lost her seat?'

'No. Her life. Do you remember me telling you about the woman killed in a car accident the other week on that road with all the bends?'

'That's right. She drove her car into a tree. Poor woman.'

'She was on her way to pick up friends to take them to the airport.' Ashley gives a tight-lipped smile as she slowly shakes her head. 'You do a good deed, and bam, that happens. Then we have John Farnborough, who is the local policeman. Remember the man who took control at the party after Lucy's body was found?'

Susie looks at her wide-eyed.

'Then there's Patricia Cartwright.'

'All of them will make a tidy sum out of it, no doubt. So how does Danny fit into all of this?'

'My guess is he was brought in to do the marketing for the development. And that's what he is farming out to this bloke in Poland. That reminds me.' Ashley picks up her phone and checks her emails for news from Krzysztof. 'He still hasn't sent me that file.'

'And Danny never told you any of this? But why?'

Ashley shakes her weary head. 'Hell knows.'

'What's his motivation? He loves Thyme End. He wouldn't want to destroy the village.'

Ashley sighs heavily. 'Between you and me, we've had money problems since we moved here. We were barely treading water, and then interest rates rocketed. And that developer went bust, owing us a truckload of money. My guess is, he got involved for the money.'

'Ash!' Susie says, horrified. 'Why didn't you tell me? I can lend you some money.'

'I thought we were managing, but I came across an email from the bank today about an overdraft arrangement for our joint bank account Danny never told me about. I didn't even know we were overdrawn.'

'How much do you need? I'll transfer some over to you now. Is this what the twenty grand in the safe has to do with?'

'I don't know.' Ashley drops her face in her hands and screams. 'Bloody hell, Danny! What the hell have you done?'

Susie places her hand across Ashley's shoulders.

Ashley shakes her sister away. She's claustrophobic, as if every new revelation is suffocating her more and more. She points to the iPad. 'Look again at those involved. There are some pretty influential figures. But something's not right.'

'In what way?' Susie asks.

'I'm not quite sure. I'm missing something.'

'Do you think you should go to the police with all this, Ash?'

'I can't now. I'd be in trouble.'

'What do you mean?'

'If I was going to tell the police, I should've done it when they were here taking Danny's stuff. They asked me if he had any other devices.'

'Well, I think you should.'

'What? Go behind Danny's back?'

Susie hesitates before saying, 'I hate to say it about my brother-in-law. I've always loved Danny. You know that. But he has gone behind yours.'

Ashley drops her head to her chest. Her shoulders shake. The dam that has been impounding her tears is threatening to finally give way. She slowly raises her head. 'How could Danny have involved us in all this?'

'You know what has just occurred to me?' Susie says, grabbing a napkin and wiping her hands. 'Greed has brought a group of pretty influential figures together to get their own way. And now, Lucy is dead. The local MP is dead. Danny is out of the way and accused of murder. Doesn't it look as though these people are being picked off one by one?'

THIRTY-SEVEN

Ashley snorts. 'That's a bit far-fetched.'

'I'm serious,' Susie says.

'You've been watching too many TV crime dramas.'

'Think about it,' Susie says soberly. 'What if that MP's car accident wasn't an accident? What if someone tampered with the brakes or something?'

'It would've come out, surely.' Ashley picks up a piece of pizza but puts it down again. She's hardly eaten for two days, but she can't face food, especially pizza. The red pieces of pepperoni merged in with the cheese remind her of the blood clumped in Lucy's hair.

'Or what if someone drove her off the road?' Susie points at the screen. 'What if a villager got wind of all of this and is trying to destroy them?'

'Who?'

'Tom.'

Ashley manages a laugh at the absurdity of her sister's accusation. 'You're being melodramatic.'

'He's a proper village boy.'

'You've got it in for him. Tom's a gentle giant. He couldn't.'

'You didn't see the side of him that I did that night. I told you, he was all over me. Wouldn't take no for an answer. Anyway, are you coming outside? I need a cigarette after all that.'

Ashley looks at her watch. 'I need to get to bed.'

'Sorry, I shouldn't have said that about Tom. I was only joking.'

'Were you?' Ashley shakes her head. 'No. There's no way Tom was capable of what happened to Lucy.'

'They say you don't know anyone. Not really.'

Ashley holds up the palm of her hand, a stop sign for her sister's accusations. She checks her phone. Numbered red circles flood her messaging apps, alerting her to several missed calls and messages. She grimaces. She doesn't want to see or speak to anyone. All she wants is to find one of Danny's sleeping pills and disappear into the comfort of the perfect world they lived in before they moved to Thyme End.

Shortly after they moved, Danny started suffering from bouts of insomnia. At the time, she blamed the stress of the move. But now she thinks back, it was when he started to get more involved with Lucy and Lee's business. Or was that a coincidence? She's not sure. She persuaded him to go to the GP who prescribed the pills. She went with him. 'Only for use on a short-term basis,' the doctor said. 'Come back if they aren't working.' Danny only took them for a few weeks. He told her that was all he needed.

'I'm exhausted. I'm going to bed. If I don't get some sleep, I'll never get up for Elliot.'

'You haven't eaten anything,' Susie says.

'I can't face it.'

'You're fading away.'

'I'll save it for lunch tomorrow.'

Susie looks at her watch and grabs her packet of cigarettes.

'One more, and I need to join that call. Think about what I said about going to the police.'

'Withholding evidence is a big bloody deal, Suz. And what if the police speak to you again. You knew about the iPad and the phone as well. You could end up getting dragged into this mess.'

Susie removes a cigarette from the packet. 'On second thoughts, don't think about what I said about going to the police. We can talk more in the morning.'

Upstairs, Ashley heads for Danny's bedside cabinet to find a sleeping pill. It's the only way she'll get some sleep. There they are, at the back of the drawer, behind a tray neatly holding his bedside reading light, the bookmark Elliot made for him last Christmas, a tube of Arnica cream and a packet of tissues. The police don't appear to have taken anything from there, but she could be wrong. She doesn't make a habit of going through his drawers.

She grabs the packet of pills only to find it empty. Damn. He did take them all, then. She's sure he told her they were helpful for a couple of weeks, but he didn't want to get addicted, so he stopped taking them and would leave the rest for emergencies. Had those emergencies transpired, and he'd taken the rest without telling her?

Frustrated, she throws the empty packet back into the drawer, only to spot another packet of the same pills. Confused, she grabs it. He never told her he got another supply. She reads the label. Twelve days ago by the look of it. He must have gone to the doctor and never mentioned it to her. She cries out in exasperation. There's so much he has not told her recently. Too much. Susie's words reverberate around her head. 'They say you don't know anyone. Not really.'

Popping a pill, she swallows it with a glug of water and

plonks herself on the floor, her back pressed against the bed, willing herself to relax. If one doesn't work, she'll take another in an hour's time. Drawing her knees to her chest, she drops her head onto them, deflated. Every hour, she is learning something new about her husband. And nothing is particularly pleasing. How she wishes she could turn back the clock of the past year. She never would have agreed to moving to Thyme End. But Danny was so insistent it would better their lives. She shakes her head. How wrong he was.

One pill suffices. It takes hold, drifting her into a nightmare of police officers and prison cells. But it's not Danny sitting on the cold bench that doubles as a bed. It's her. She has swapped places with her husband after he told the police she was the one who had murdered his childhood friend. My guilty wife. That's what he called her. A prison warden drags her by the arm to take her to the electric chair for her sins. She vehemently resists, begging her innocence.

Startled, she awakes to someone tugging her hand, whispering, 'Mum. Mum. Wake up.'

Ashley opens her eyes. She's woozy. She was so tired, she didn't make it under the covers. Her hand is curled around a packet of pills. Another reminder of yet another discovery about her husband.

The nightmare peters out into the present as Elliot says, 'Someone's trying to break in.'

She sits bolt upright. Is someone in their house? Or has he had a nightmare himself?

'They're in the garden. I can see them from my window,' he whispers.

Ashley follows Elliot into his bedroom. The dream has disorientated her. His room is hot and stuffy, and dark except for the moonlight filtering through the half-open blinds.

He runs over to the window. 'I thought it was Dad.'

'Get down,' she says. 'Don't let anyone see you.'

They kneel by the window ledge. She tells him to stay put while she raises her head to look out into the garden. Her heart beats like hell as she sees the movement of what looks like a torchlight flashing around inside The Hub. She locked it, didn't she? Danny is always berating her for forgetting to lock up. She thought someone came into the garden when she was working in The Hub. Is it the same person? This has something to do with Danny. She's sure of it.

'There's someone there, isn't there, Mum?' Elliot mutters.

She glances at him sitting on the floor, hugging his knees drawn up to his chest. The position her body had taken before she fell asleep. She turns her attention back to the window. Why isn't Rufus barking? He's meant to protect them at such times. Maybe he can't hear what's happening outside.

'Listen carefully.' She takes Elliot's head in her hands.

His innocent eyes stare up at her.

'You know I sometimes say that you must do what Mummy says?'

Elliot nods frantically.

'Now is one of those times. I want you to crawl along the floor and get back into bed. And stay there.'

'What are you going to do?'

'I'm going to let Rufus out into the garden.'

'What if there's someone in the house too, Mum? You could get hurt,' he says, his bottom lip trembling.

'Rufus would be going mad if someone was in the house. Now do as I say.' She leads him crawling back to bed, where she reiterates her request for him to stay put. 'I'll be right back.'

'I want to come with you, Mum.' His voice doesn't hide his agitation. 'Please take me with you.'

'Absolutely not.'

Whatever his dad has been up to, it's her job to protect him.

THIRTY-EIGHT

Ashley opens the door to the spare room. The velvety smell of Susie's perfume hits her. Ashley gently nudges her arm. 'Suz, wake up. I need your help.'

Susie stirs, mumbling in confusion.

'I think someone has broken into The Hub.'

With a suddenness that startles Ashley, Susie springs up like a jack in the box. 'Are you sure?'

Ashley nods. 'Come downstairs with me.'

Susie grabs her hand. 'Call the police.'

'I think it has something to do with Danny.'

'So what? Someone was telling me at the party that there's been a spate of burglaries in the surrounding villages. Call the police.'

'No. Not yet.'

Ashley creeps down the stairs before Susie can challenge her any further. But her sister is close on her tail. The house is in darkness, apart from the slim sliver of moonlight stretching along the hallway.

At the bottom, Susie grabs Ashley's shoulder. 'I really think we should call the police.'

Ashley ignores her sister. 'Rufus, Rufus. Come.' Her voice is a timid whisper gulped up by the quiet.

The dozy dog appears from his bed in the lounge. What did Danny harp on about when he wanted to move to Thyme End? His words echo in her mind, a cruel irony now. 'It's safer in the countryside than living in London. Elliot will have a better life. We'll have a better life.' And yet, all those years they lived in London, no one ever tried to break into their flat.

She pats her thigh. 'With me. Come, darling.' At the kitchen door, she turns to Susie. 'You stay here.'

Ashley hurries to the side of the doors and edges her head around the wall to see into the garden, her knees wobbling like a newborn fawn's. All is dark, save for the eerie twinkle of the torchlight bobbing about in The Hub. With trembling fingers, she finds the key to the patio doors and quietly coaxes them open until there's enough space to free Rufus. Finally, he barks as he bolts into the garden and charges along the path.

She retreats to the side of the doors, out of sight from the intruder, and waits. She's shaking and her breathing shallow and rapid. The barking fades, the silent night replacing her dog's protective tune.

Susie joins her. 'What's happening?' she whispers.

Ashley taps her forefinger against her lips. Slowly, she peers around the wall and peeps outside again. Why is Rufus quiet? In a panic, she opens the door and calls his name. Nothing. She never should have sent him out there. If anything has happened to him, she'll never forgive herself.

'Rufus,' she calls again. 'Here, boy.'

Rufus appears suddenly, a strange object in his jaw, wagging his tail like the dog who got the bone. Breathing a sigh of relief, she lets him in and quietly closes the door, where he drops his prize on her foot. It catches her toe. She swears at the pain. Rufus has quite literally got the bone.

'What the hell?' she says, kicking the meaty knuckle away.

It stinks and leaves a trail of slime that she wipes along the floor with her foot.

'Whoever is out there came prepared to silence him,' she whispers to Susie.

Ashley looks out to the garden again.

A figure creeps out of The Hub like a ninja and slips into the darkness around the back towards the gate. Did they get what they came for, or did she frighten them away?

Opening the patio door again, she listens, hearing what sounds like the back gate shutting and footsteps dashing along the path that runs to the fields. She shuts the door and locks it. 'I think they've gone. Come with me.'

They rush upstairs to the spare room that overlooks the garden. Ashley peers out of the window, hoping to see something, someone, anything, but it's a futile attempt.

Elliot appears, startling her. 'Mum. What's happening? I'm scared.'

'I thought I told you to stay in bed.' Her tone is too harsh. 'I'm sorry, darling. You made me jump.' She strides over to him and scoops him up into her arms.

'Was it Dad?'

'No.'

'Then who was it?'

She makes a futile attempt to play down the situation. 'I think it was someone coming to pick up some stuff from the offices for Dad. Nothing for you to worry about.'

Susie throws her a dirty look. 'Come on,' she says to Elliot. 'You need to get back to sleep, darling.' Susie takes him back to bed. She mouths to Ashley, 'Police. Now.'

'Stay with me,' Elliot says.

Susie tucks him in. 'Of course.'

'Pat his back. It's the best way to help him get to sleep,' Ashley tells her sister. 'I'll make us a drink.'

She should call the police, but a nagging voice suggests

that's not a good idea. Not yet. A deep feeling of dread is telling her that whoever broke into their office knew what they'd come for. Was it the money?

She returns downstairs. Rufus follows her into the kitchen, his head nodding with the bone in his mouth. Checking the ceramic pot, she finds The Hub key still there. She definitely locked up earlier. She remembers now, throwing the keys in the pot and missing and her knees creaking as she bent to pick them up. The intruder must have broken into The Hub. But why didn't the alarm go off?

She makes two cups of cocoa, woozy from the sleeping pill she took earlier. Waiting for Susie, she logs into the iPad and brings up Danny's TE PRO email account. John Farnborough has sent an email to the rest of the group. A simple one line: *What do we do now?*

She drops her head in her hands, unable to believe how much, in just thirty-six hours, her life has degenerated to the depths of despair. And now someone has broken into her property. Her pulse is racing. They will be back, she's sure of it.

She wrings her hands. Where's Susie? Elliot must still be awake. She locates the torch on her phone and, with Rufus in tow, steps outside and leads the way to The Hub. She gasps loudly. A key is in the door. The spare key they keep in a lock safe at the side of the house. She pushes open the door and steps inside, turning on the light. Another loud gasp escapes her. The carpet tile above the safe has been tampered with, the edge pulled back.

Dropping to her knees, she opens the safe and examines the contents. The notebooks are still there, as are the piles of money. She gauges the thickness of each bundle, the plastic feel of each note slippery in her fingers. They all appear present. She quickly counts them. None have been taken. What the hell?

She scans the office. Nothing appears missing. Did she disturb the intruder before they could take anything?

She checks the alarm. It has been disabled. Her blood runs cold as the realisation dawns on her. The only person, other than her, who knows the code is Danny. And she knows it wasn't him.

Susie appears, tying a dressing gown around her waist. 'You've got to call the police.'

'I can't.'

'Whyever not, Ash?'

'Nothing's been taken. This is connected to whatever Danny has been up to. And to the woman he supposedly killed. I know it is. The intruder had no interest in the money. Only the iPad. That's what they came here for. And perhaps the phone. I'm certain of it. If I call the police, I could land him in it. He's my husband, Suz. I need to protect him.'

'You need to think of yourself, too.'

Ashley looks at her sister, her breaths coming short and sharp. 'Don't you see? If I go to the police now, I'd get grilled. They'll ask me about everything again and again. Sooner or later, I'd crack.' The tension in her voice is palpable. 'I know I would. I won't be able to keep up the pretence. It would all come out that I lied to them. I wouldn't be able to hide it.' Her breathing quickens. 'Then I'll be in big trouble as well.' The words are coming out faster and faster. 'Big, big trouble. I've perverted the course of justice, Suz. That carries a prison sentence.'

THIRTY-NINE

'You should've gone when you first found the safe. And you should've told the police about the iPad when they were here,' Susie says, draining her cup of cocoa.

After they've wrangled about Ashley's next move, Ashley takes her sister's cup and walks to the sink. She pours the remaining three-quarters of her drink down the plughole and washes the cups. She should have gone for tea. The rich chocolate has made her feel sick again.

She returns to the table. 'I'm sorry to involve you in all my mess.'

'Don't be stupid. I'm your sister. What're you going to do, then?'

'Find out who killed Lucy.'

'What do you mean?'

'The police get ninety-six hours to charge Danny or release him. So I have until Friday evening to find out who really killed Lucy.'

'And how are you going to do that?'

'Hell knows.'

After kissing her sister goodnight, they head their separate ways across the landing. Ashley chucks the iPad on her bed and goes to check on Elliot, only to find he is no longer in his bed. She runs out of the room, panicking. 'Elliot,' she screams.

Susie comes rushing out of her room. 'What's happened?'

'Elliot's not in his bed.'

They both turn to a noise from Ashley's art room. Ashley runs towards it and pushes open the door. Everything appears untouched, her paintings as she left them. But she knows he is in there. Gasps of breath, unmistakably his, give it away. She runs to the built-in wardrobe, a popular hiding place he often holes himself up in when they play hide-and-seek. Pulling open the door, she sees him curled into a ball, his body shaking. She hates her husband at this moment. Their son doesn't deserve this.

She pulls him out of the cupboard and lifts him into her arms, comforting him. Seeing the effect this is all having on him is crucifying her. 'Come on. Let's get you back to bed.'

'I want to sleep with you.' Another sob. 'Please, Mum.'

'Of course you can.'

'What if they come back?'

'They won't.'

'How do you know?'

'They'll be too scared of Rufus.'

What is she saying? Whoever came tonight will return. She's certain. Another lie. Her husband has turned her into a liar. This is not her. She hates herself for the lies she has told, especially to Elliot. But it seems, when you start, you can't stop.

When she was a child, despite her mother hammering her father for his deceit, she constantly fibbed to her daughters about their father, painting him as a saint. What a wonderful man he was. How he loved them all so much. It wasn't until she was about Elliot's age that she started to see what an ugly picture he made, that the colours were out of focus. He loved them all right. There was no doubt about that. But there's no way wonderful was an adjective to describe her father as a man.

Susie returns to bed. Ashley strokes Elliot's head, waiting for him to fall asleep yet again. Her mind is a tornado of thoughts. She considers Susie's insistence that she calls the police. They've had a break-in, after all. But she can't tell them about the safe, so what's the point?

Who came here tonight? It has to be someone Danny gave the code for The Hub to. But why? Lee enters her thoughts, but she dismisses that as quickly as it appears. He accused Danny of murdering his wife.

What about Tom? That doesn't make sense either. They don't have that kind of relationship.

John Farnborough? He was the one who emailed the group saying *What do we do now?* A policeman breaking into their property? Surely not. It doesn't make sense. The guy is a professional. But who could it have been?

Why has Danny kept so much from her? She's meant to be the person he tells everything to.

Unless that's the problem. Unless he doesn't want to tell her everything anymore because he doesn't want to be with her.

One more restless night paves the way for another morning waking up groggy and nauseous. As soon as she stirs, Ashley emails Danny's solicitor, asking for an update. Her mind continues to question who came to their house last night.

She quietly slips out of bed, leaving Elliot sleeping, and showers in the en suite of her art room. He can't go to school today. He's bound to spill the news about what has been happening at home. She doesn't want the village grapevine to grip onto the news of the break-in last night. They will find that juicy lump of gossip too irresistible not to spread, and she'll have the police knocking on the door again.

She perches on the arm of the bright green sofa, staring at a neon sign declaring *Party Until It Hurts* hanging on the wall among other abstract pictures and memorabilia. As she towel-dries her hair, she turns to her current work-in-progress of their London flat on an easel by the window. Six squares showcasing each room, including the unofficial roof terrace, as she remembers it. The early-morning sun shining through the blinds heightens the vibrancy of the painting as pangs for their last home continue to overwhelm her.

A knock at the front door draws her to the hallway. She peers out of the landing window, expecting to see the police, but Tom's van is parked on the pavement. She wants to ignore him. Ignore everyone until her husband comes home. But she's being selfish. She has avoided Tom enough. He must be struggling, too, and he is her brother-in-law.

She runs downstairs and opens the door. His eyes are red. Has he been crying? 'Tom,' she says.

'I've been trying to get hold of you.'

'I'm sorry.'

'Mum has been trying to get hold of you as well. They've managed to get a flight home today.'

'Good.' An inward groan: her mother-in-law is the last person she wants to see.

'I'm not going to work today, so I thought I'd offer to pick Elliot up after school and take him to the cinema or something.'

'Elliot's not in school.'

On cue, Elliot bounds down the stairs. 'Uncle Tom. Guess what happened last night? We had a—'

'Elliot.' She doesn't want Tom to know about their intruder last night.

'What happened?' Tom asks, raising his bushy eyebrows.

Elliot glances her way. She gives him the look. The one that tells him to be quiet. He gets it.

'We watched the new *Monster Family* movie,' Ashley says, cringing for lying in front of Elliot.

'You didn't wait for me, champ?' Tom opens his arms to scoop up Elliot. 'How about I take you to the cinema today? We could pick up a McDonald's if you're good.'

Elliot's face lights up like the morning sun shining behind his head. 'I'm always good.'

'I know.' Tom pinches Elliot's cheek. 'McDonald's it is.' He smiles at Ashley. 'What d'ya say, Mum?'

'Can I? Please?' begs Elliot.

Ashley succumbs. It will give her the chance to get her head straight before she meets Lee. 'What time's the film?'

'I haven't checked. If he's not going to school, we could catch a lunchtime one. I'll take you to Great Burton Park first if you want. Run off some of that energy. Go and get some clothes on.'

Elliot wriggles himself free from Tom's arms. 'Be right back.' He bolts off up the stairs.

Ashley rolls her eyes. If only he moved that fast when *she* asked him to get dressed. 'Thanks, Tom. I've got some things I need to get on with, so this will help me.'

Tom catches her arm. It feels odd for him to touch her. He's not the touchy type. 'If there's anything I can do to help you while you're going through all this, please let me know. I'm here for you.'

'Tom, are you all right? You're kind of hurting me.' He is still holding onto her. She looks down at his hand clutching her arm tightly.

'Fine. Sorry.' His clipped words suggest he is anything but fine. But then who would be given the current circumstances? He releases her arm.

Ashley runs up the stairs after Elliot, looking over her shoulder to see Tom fall to his knees and greet Rufus like a fan meeting a celebrity. She finds Elliot wiggling into his Spurs tracksuit. She squats down until she's at his level.

'Elliot, listen to me. This is serious.'

He pulls at the elastic of his waistband. 'What?'

'You mustn't say anything to anyone about the break-in last night.'

'Why? Haven't you called the police?'

She doesn't know how to answer him. How do you tell your son you think their dad has got himself involved in something he shouldn't have? 'I will. But I want to speak to Dad first. Please don't say anything until he's home.' She cringes for asking her son to withhold the truth. But what choice does she have? She points at his tracksuit bottoms. 'Take those off,' she says. 'It's boiling outside. I'll find you some shorts.'

In the chaos of the overflowing laundry basket, she locates a pair of Elliot's shorts. She hasn't put a wash on since before the weekend, and it has started to smell. She pulls out a pair of Danny's jeans. The expensive pair he often wears to client meetings. Paired with his linen blend blazer, they make a great smart-casual outfit.

She recalls Danny wore them to the meeting with Hayley Williams from Clampitt Homes last week. Exhaling heavily, she checks the pockets. Only once before has she checked her husband's pockets. That time after Elliot was born, and he didn't come home until the early hours. But their relationship has shifted to another level. Every corner of his life needs inspecting now.

Her hands skim the rear pockets. Nothing. She tries the front pockets. They're empty as well. She pokes her finger into the small coin pocket behind the main front pocket but finds nothing. Desperately she wants to believe her husband's innocence, but it's getting harder and harder.

What has her marriage come to?

FORTY

'Mum, I'm waiting. What're you doing?'

Ashley spins around to see Elliot at his bedroom door in his underpants. He looks like a mini Danny, standing there with his fisted hands on his hips. She swallows the lump in the back of her throat. 'Sorry, darling. Here, catch.' She tosses the pair of shorts at him. 'Go and choose a T-shirt, and I'll be there.'

'I'm not wearing dirty shorts.'

'It's all I've got, I'm afraid.'

'No way, Mum. That's disgusting.' He starts yelling. It's so unlike him. He's usually the calmest of kids. He typically takes life in his stride, but now he is screaming and shouting like a child possessed. Where did he learn to behave like that? The shock of the past few days is taking hold.

She drops Danny's jeans on the floor. 'Calm down, darling.' She's out of her depth here, swimming in murky waters new to her.

Tom's heavy footsteps pound up the stairs as Susie's bedroom door opens. She rushes out in her nightie, only to rush back in when she sees Tom.

'I want my daddy.'

Tom stands across the landing at the top of the stairs. He mouths across the hallway to Ashley, 'You want some help?'

Elliot's sobs grow louder. They make Ashley want to sob too. Her heart is breaking. Piece by piece, Danny is destroying her. She wants this to end. Right now.

She looks at Tom. He is probably the best person for Elliot at the moment. Some boys' time is just what he needs. She is too attached to the situation. Not that Tom isn't, but the last thing Elliot needs is to see her stressed and upset, too. She solemnly nods at Tom.

Tom strides into the room and sweeps Elliot in his arms. 'Hey, champ. Don't cry. You'll make Uncle Tom cry, and that's not a pretty sight. Come on. McDonald's is waiting for us. What's it going to be? Big Mac and fries? Or McNuggets?'

'Big Mac,' Elliot says between sobs.

'Big Macs all round, then. But listen, you mustn't tell your Aunty Ren.' Tom pats his belly. 'She says I'm getting fat. What do you think?'

Elliot laughs, spluttering through his tears, 'That's mean.'

'Exactly what I said. Now come on. Get dressed. Burgers and fries await us.'

Tom steers Ashley out of the room with an arm around her shoulders and leads her downstairs into the kitchen. 'I can keep him overnight if you want. I'll keep him entertained and Renee will cook his favourite spag bol.'

The offer is tempting. She needs to find a way to help Danny. And she needs to catch up with some work. They're going to lose clients if not. That reminds her. She needs to cancel Danny's commitments for the rest of the week.

But she's not sure she wants Elliot to stay away the night. It doesn't feel right. She needs to protect him in these troubling times. He might wake up in the night and need her. 'Maybe best he stays with me.'

'Let's see how it goes.'

. . .

Ashley leans her head on the glass door, staring into The Hub as she mentally calculates how little she can get away with doing workwise today. There's so much on her to-do list, but she is too distracted to concentrate. Her heart misses a beat. Who was here last night? Was it the same person who she thought she heard at the gate yesterday morning?

'What is going on, Danny?' she says, fogging the glass with her breath. She glances towards the patch of earth where Danny said the builders dumped all their cast-off rubble. 'What have you got involved with?' She grasps the door frame to steady herself as Lucy's face stares back at her. Danny said he wanted to grow laurels or cypress trees in that space. What were his exact words? 'The cypress signifies the end of a major stage in our life and the shift into a world of new choices.' What did he mean by that? With everything she has found since the weekend, is it a sign of her paranoia, or was he absently referring to the end of their marriage?

Work seems like another world now. One she was always at home in but now finds a struggle to get comfortable in. There's too much around her reminding her of Danny. His chair where he would be sitting if he hadn't been arrested... for murder. Murder. The word keeps spinning around in her head. The empty space where his iMac should be. Without it, the heart and soul has been ripped out the place. His briefcase. It's open. The police must have gone through it. His smart jacket hanging up on a peg next to the door.

She swallows hard, placing the iPad and phone that hold secrets he has kept from her beside her mousepad. Files are missing from the shelves lining the far wall. She approaches them, detecting the officers have taken four box files relating to the finances and admin of the business. What's that got to do with Lucy?

Her phone beeps. It's Lee. He can't make their catch-up today. He still needs to see her, though. Could they postpone until tomorrow?

Frustrated, she texts him back. Tomorrow will be fine.

Ashley switches on her computer and checks for an email from Krzysztof. There's still nothing. She logs into Danny's email, locates the latest correspondence between him and Krzysztof, and copies Krzysztof's address. Returning to her email account, she composes an email to him, asking him if he has sent the file as she hasn't received it. And yes, she has checked her spam folder. Numerous times. She gives him her phone number, asking him to call her.

She cancels the first of Danny's meetings planned for the next day, asking if they can rearrange for the same time next week. But after pressing send, she wonders if this is the best approach. What if Danny isn't back next week? What if the police get it all wrong and actually charge him for Lucy's murder? The thought of him never coming home is inconceivable, as is the notion of running their business alone. She parks the thoughts. They've come too far to throw away what they've achieved. Like it or not, she has to get through this. She sends another four emails, telling the clients Danny was due to meet that he needs to postpone. She leaves it at that. He could well be home today. Then, they can make a call on whether to cancel the rest of the week's commitments.

Now for Guy Roberts, the local planning officer. She has been thinking about him ever since she saw he was one of Lucy's group. Clicking on the search bar, she finds the number for the council's planning and building control division. A chat with him might shed some light on this dim situation. But she's out of luck.

'Guy's on annual leave,' his monotone-sounding colleague informs her.

'When will he be back?' Ashley asks.

'He's off for two weeks. Today's the first day. Can someone else assist you?'

'No, that's fine.'

Damn. That's unhelpful. Perhaps he's at home. Not everyone goes away during their annual leave.

He takes on private work, so she finds his number easily online. But when she calls, she gets his voicemail. Damn. She leaves a message asking him to call her at his earliest convenience. It's worth a try.

She considers calling Patricia Cartwright and John Farnborough but decides Oriana is the best person to speak to. She finds her number. 'Can I come and see you, Oriana? I need to ask you something.'

'Ask away.'

'Not over the phone.'

'Aaron is going out at three o'clock. How does that suit you?'

'Perfect.'

Oriana coughs. 'I'm sorry to hear about Danny. It's not good. Not good at all. How are you bearing up?'

There's no hiding anything from anyone around Thyme End.

'I'll tell you more when I see you.'

Ashley works through her inbox, unable to fully concentrate. How can she? A client is not happy with an aspect of the landscaping on his set of CGIs. He wants to see the line of trees to the north-west of the development extended. Can she adjust the image and get back to him by the end of the day? Not even a please. She grits her teeth and ignores the email.

An order for three exterior and interior CGIs has come in from a new client Danny has been messaging since the new year. He will be thrilled. But attached is an unrealistic deadline. As there frequently is. Next Friday at the latest. Danny would agree to it. She can hear what he would say without him even being in the room. 'You've got to grab every opportunity in this game.' She doesn't want to. But the threat of Danny never coming home is now hanging over her like a lead balloon. She replies to the email to say yes, they can do this. She has to keep going.

She googles *Murder in Thyme End*. It sounds like a cosy mystery, not the chilling murder of her husband's childhood friend. Pictures of Lucy flood the screen. A vivid display of her through the years. A chill runs down Ashley's spine as she views Lucy's life in haunting snapshots. An old school photograph with her hair, as long and blonde as the day she was murdered, tied in two plaits; her standing in front of Victoria Falls; her wearing a large backpack, winking at the camera, outside Bali airport; Lee and her on their wedding day. And one of her holding up a framed certificate, sitting at her desk above the garage where she would meet her vicious end. There's no denying it. Lucy's stunning beauty was present throughout her life.

Ashley starts to read one of the articles, but stops after a couple of sentences. It's too much. Lucy's smiling face seems to stare back at her from the dead, an eerie reminder of a life that violently ended far too soon.

She returns to Danny's emails, sifting through each one, looking for clues to help her piece together this complex puzzle that is baffling her hour by hour. This must be what the police are doing – scrutinising every email. But she finds nothing to explain what she found on the iPad, or anything else to cast suspicion over her husband. And certainly nothing that could explain who would want to harm Lucy.

Her phone rings.

Finally. It's Krzysztof.

FORTY-ONE

'I received your message. I'm sorry. I got your email address wrong; I left the e out of your name. I've sent the file now.'

'I'll take a look and get back to you.'

Ashley ends the call and opens his email, finding the plans for the fifteen hundred houses being built in Surrey she had never heard about until all this trouble kicked off. The same question comes to mind. Why has Danny outsourced the work without discussing it with her first? She finds the answer to Krzysztof's query – a simple misunderstanding on his behalf – and emails him back.

Her stomach rumbles for the first time since Sunday. She thinks of Lucy. Not a minute passes when her pretty face splashed with blood doesn't flash through Ashley's mind. It's haunting her day and night.

She goes to the house to find something to eat. Mumbles of Susie's authoritative voice sound through the ceiling. She flicks the kettle switch and paces up and down the kitchen. This is unbearable. She doesn't know what to do with herself. She can't even take Rufus out; it's too hot. A long walk is usually her go-to for relaxation. One of the only benefits she can see of living in the country is the plenitude of options for an enjoyable dog walk. What more could a dog lover ask for than a back gate that leads to open farmland?

Rufus is sitting by the patio doors, his face forlorn. He's not stupid. He can sense all is not well in their abode. She strides over to him and strokes his fur. 'It's too hot out there for a walk, buddy. I'll have to take you later.'

Her stomach rumbles again. She walks to the fridge, and apart from the pizza left over from last night, she finds it as empty as her stomach. Tesco delivers a weekly shop on Tuesday mornings, but she never submitted an order yesterday as she usually does. She picks up the carton of milk from the bottom shelf and swears. There's only a splash sloshing around in the bottom. She tries the cupboards. There's not even any bread.

The thought of popping to the shops fills her with dread. News of Danny's arrest will be common knowledge. Her chat with Oriana proves that. She can just imagine the busybodies eager to speak to her. Any piece of news will do. It will only get twisted as it is whispered around, taking full hold and morphing into juicy macabre stories villagers get off on. But she has no choice. She needs to feed everyone.

She grabs her bag and car keys. She could walk, but it's too hot. Besides, she wants to get this over and done with as soon as possible. She doesn't enjoy food shopping at the best of times. Perhaps she'd be better off driving into the neighbouring town. But it's a forty-minute round trip, and she wants to read through the emails on the iPad again before she sees Oriana.

As she walks out of her front door, a figure bounces out of nowhere. 'Mrs Morgan, can we talk? It won't take long.'

It takes a few seconds before Ashley realises who the scruffy-looking bloke snapping her photo is. 'Go away. I have nothing to say to you.' She thought all the reporters had got fed up and left.

'If you give me your story, we could work on a deal.'

'Leave me alone.'

'I could really make it worth your while.'

'Didn't you hear me? I said, leave me alone.'

Jumping in her car, she races to the local store on Royal Oak Street, which sells the bare minimum at double the cost of supermarkets, but they can get away with it in the name of convenience. Locals will also pay the high prices because they want to preserve the store, which has existed since the early 1800s. Mr and Mrs White, the current owners, have worked there since leaving the local primary school over half a century ago. There was a celebratory party for them in the village hall earlier in the year that Danny took Elliot to while Ashley nipped to London to see her sister and cousin.

Ashley walks inside. An old-fashioned bell jingles above her. The air conditioning pumps coolness her way, a relief after the outside heat. Mrs White drops the bag of potatoes she is about to stack on the reduced items trolley. Her head tilts to the side, her forehead as wrinkled as a walnut.

'Mrs Morgan,' Mrs White says, addressing Ashley by her surname as she does with every customer. She's a lovely woman but hasn't moved with the times. She retrieves the bag of potatoes and places them in the trolley with the reduced loaves of bread and other items that have reached their sell-by date.

'Mrs White.'

The shopkeeper adjusts the collar of her short-sleeved linen shirt and crosses her arms over her chest. 'How are you, Mrs Morgan?'

'Bearing up. Thank you for asking,' Ashley says, her face pained. She's finding it impossible to find a smile.

'And Danny? How are things with Danny? I heard he's still at the station.'

The bell jingles again, and another customer enters the shop. Ashley grabs a basket and heads for the first aisle. Engaging with anyone is not on her agenda. It never is, but especially not today. Danny always says she should make more of an effort with the locals, but she finds it difficult. Growing up, her family, or rather her mother, always kept herself to herself. Mainly because her father's infidelity meant that her mother's ears were constantly burning worse than the fires of hell. So Ashley turned out to be more of a private person. Whereas Danny can spark a conversation with a stranger in any situation, she favours the company of her art and her books.

Cruising the short aisles, head down, Ashley chucks items in the basket to make a couple of easy meals: a bag of pasta, a jar of Bolognese sauce, and vegetables to throw together a basic salad. From the dairy counter, she grabs a block of butter, a carton of milk and a packet of cheese. That should last them until she can arrange a supermarket delivery. She tosses a packet of smoked bacon and an uncut loaf to make a sandwich into the basket, adding a packet of crusty rolls. Comfort food, that's what she needs right now. A bacon butty will do the trick. They are out of ketchup. Elliot complained there wasn't any for the fry-up Danny made on Sunday morning. She swallows hard. Sunday morning – the last few hours of normality their little family enjoyed together. She goes in search of a bottle.

'Ashley. How are you?'

She turns to see Sonia, the mum of a boy in Elliot's class. An individual she has zero desire to speak to. Sonia's son invited Elliot on a playdate after Elliot's first day at the village school. When Ashley arrived to pick up Elliot, the kids were still watching a movie, so Sonia invited Ashley to join her for a drink. Eager at first to make some new friends, Ashley accepted. She could spare the time for a cup of tea. But when she followed Sonia into the kitchen, Ashley quickly learnt that a brew was far from Sonia's mind.

'My wine o'clock has started already,' she said, winking at Ashley. Picking up a half-empty bottle of red, Sonia pulled a face suggesting she had no shame. 'Don't tell my husband if he comes home,' she giggled as she shared the remaining half of the bottle between her empty glass and another one she took from the cupboard. Ashley listened, astounded as the woman proceeded to tattle about every member of the local community, hardly pausing for breath. It was a one-sided conversation that lasted a long and painful twenty minutes as Ashley shifted uncomfortably on the breakfast bar stool, learning who was shagging who and the rise in the divorce rate in the village since the pandemic.

With no desire to befriend a woman who woke each day without a gossip hangover of shame, Ashley never returned the invitation for another playdate. She has only spoken to Sonia when the situation has forced them together at school events. She was at the party, but Ashley had artfully avoided speaking to her.

Sonia grabs Ashley's wrist and shakes her arm. 'Ashley. Are you OK?'

Ashley stares at the overweight woman in a black sleeveless T-shirt tucked into three-quarter-length leggings, her shoulders as sunburnt as her face.

'I went to the station late yesterday to give my fingerprints. They think they've nearly got everyone's now. They can't be sure, as Lee didn't even have a full list of who was there. Poor Lucy organised the invitation list. Hopefully something will come out of it. I hear they're carrying out a post-mortem on Lucy. Poor woman. Bludgeoned to death in your own home. It doesn't get worse than that, does it? And your poor Danny.' Sonia tuts, shaking her head. 'Have you managed to speak to him?'

Ashley shakes her head, afraid to open her mouth. Too scared for the words that might shoot out and attack this shameful woman.

'Too bad. Is there anything I can do for you? Elliot is welcome to come over and stay.'

'He's with his uncle today.' Ashley grabs a can of sweetcorn off the shelf and drops it in her basket. 'But thanks for asking.' She lifts her hand and waves. 'I must get a move on.'

Sonia grabs Ashley's shoulder as she tries to walk away. Ashley flinches. 'No one thinks he's guilty. You know that,' Sonia says with a pitying smile. She continues to follow Ashley past the refrigerator section.

'That's good to know,' Ashley replies.

Sonia's determined hand is still on her shoulder, hungry for more titbits to fuel her fire of gossip. She is dead set on not letting Ashley get off that lightly. She asks the burning question that is probably blazing in everyone's mind. 'Why was Danny in the garage with her?'

Ashley's jaw drops at the brazenness of the woman. She remembers the look in Danny's cold and unyielding eyes when she asked him the same question. It was as if he was someone else entirely. A stranger, not the man with whom she had shared nearly two decades of her life.

'I'll see you around, Sonia.'

'We all know he didn't do it, if that makes you feel better,' Sonia repeats, calling after her. 'Everyone's rooting for him around here.'

Danny the golden boy. Everyone who meets him adores him. Ladies gush over him. Men wish they were him. He is everything everyone strives to be: generous, kind, driven and successful, supportive and a joy to be around. One hundred per cent perfect.

But they don't know what Ashley now knows.

'Pop in any time if you need someone to talk to. Oh, and did you hear? The police have cautioned Charlie Mitchel's dad.'

Ashley stares at her absently.

'He was the person seen leaving the party by the gap in the fence. Blimmin' scoundrel had nicked a box of booze. Twelve bottles of that expensive champagne the waitresses were passing around. The posh pink stuff. Talk about getting caught red-handed.'

'I need to go.' Ashley picks up a bottle of ketchup and weaves her way through shoppers moseying along the aisles, hurrying to the till with her head down in the hope no one else tries to catch her attention.

Mrs White rambles about the weather. 'It's not good for the farmers, you know. They're concerned if this heatwave continues, it could ruin their harvest. And the poor duck pond on the green is almost parched dry.'

Despite the air conditioning, Ashley is sweating. She feels as if she is caught in a trap. The trap of Thyme End. The whole village is watching her, waiting to see what happens next. She needs to escape.

She haphazardly loads her purchases into her bag for life, not caring that the large bottle of ketchup is squashing the bread. She taps her card on the terminal, nodding but keeping quiet. All she wants is to get out of there. Everyone is staring at her, feeling sorry for her, or wondering if she is married to a murderer. Picking up the bag, she turns to see Sonia whispering in the ear of another school mum, both staring at her.

'Crops are failing,' Mrs White continues. 'It's already killed fruit and vegetables on the vine. A whole planting of onions died on Warner's farm.'

Ashley shudders.

Death.

It's all around the village.

FORTY-TWO

Thyme End Hall is a seven-bedroomed early-Georgian house that occupies a plot of land in excess of four hundred acres off the main country lane that leads into the village. Having travelled extensively with her first husband, Oriana Lewis makes for interesting company, and Ashley usually enjoys her visits there every Monday evening to help Oriana with her painting.

Ashley drives through the blue decorative gates that lead to a carriage-style drive with rutted tracks branching off in various directions.

One of Oriana's carers answers the door, a stocky woman about Ashley's age wearing a floral maxi dress. The woman nods down the high-ceilinged hallway. 'She's in her study. Can I get you a drink? Oriana has asked for a pot of tea.'

'I'll join her. Thank you. Milk, no sugar. I love your dress. It's beautiful, so summery.'

The woman blushes. 'I made it myself. Oriana loves it too. I have some leftover material, so I'm making her a new headscarf.'

'You're so talented.'

Ashley walks along the creaking floorboards of the long hallway to find Oriana sitting at her large oak desk in the study.

It's a substantial room with wood panelling covering all four walls. Two floor-to-ceiling bay windows provide much-needed light to what would otherwise be a dark space. The two canvases Ashley has been helping Oriana paint for the past couple of months sit on easels in front of the windows. They look good. Oriana has talent. Ashley hopes she gets to finish them before she gets too ill.

Oriana is wearing a bright patterned scarf on her head, but her face is far from cheery. Her features are gaunt and haunted as if she has seen a ghost walking the floors of her country estate. The photographs decorating the marble fireplace surround are a reminder that her illness has stripped her once youthful complexion and replaced it with a yellow tinge and sagging skin.

She slowly gets up and walks around her desk to greet Ashley. It looks as if it's an effort. Her back is hunched, her face ashen, and she appears the worst Ashley has ever seen her. They embrace. Oriana is a bag of bones in Ashley's arms.

'This is all too horrible. I have no words.' Oriana's eyes are glassy with heartfelt sadness.

Ashley could cry for her. Life can be so bloody cruel at times.

They talk about Lucy, and the effect the murder has had on both of them. 'I can't believe your Danny has been arrested. That's the most insane thing I've ever heard.' Oriana walks to the window and points outside. 'When they were children, Lucy and Danny spent their summers playing in the grounds of this estate. There's an old worker's hut in the wooded area by the entrance. They made it their camp. Even from a young age, they had such a tight bond. With Simon, too, until he changed.'

Ashley wants to talk about the present, not the past, but engages politely. 'What do you mean, changed?'

'It was when they were around nine or ten. Simon developed a crush on Lucy. Not that he would admit it, but mums know these things, don't they?'

Ashley nods her understanding. 'We sure do.'

'Lucy wasn't interested, and Simon grew jealous of her and Danny's friendship. The circle of three became two. Then Danny stopped coming here as much, but Lucy was like a daughter to me, and when her father remarried, she practically lived here. She loved this place as much as I do.'

Oriana has opened the door for Ashley to pose the question she came to ask. 'Then why are you selling your land?' She blurts it out, sounding more frantic than she means to.

Oriana frowns, the look of confusion adding to her gaunt appearance.

'I found an iPad Danny was hiding from me. Details of a development on your estate of three hundred houses. That's a lot of houses.' Ashley surprises herself, opening up to this dying woman she has known for such a short time.

'No! You've got it all wrong.' Oriana holds out her frail hand, gesturing to two worn upholstered armchairs by the easels at the window. 'We should sit.'

'No! I don't want to sit. I've been through hell since Sunday. I'm so confused. In forty-eight hours, I've discovered so much about Danny that I didn't know. It's like I'm married to a stranger.' Ashley raises her voice. She can't help herself. 'I want to help him. I want to believe he's a good man. But at every juncture, I discover something else that makes me question that.'

There's a knock at the door and the carer walks in with two cups, a pot of tea and a plate of biscuits on a wicker tray. She places the tray on the small table beside Oriana, digs into her pocket and produces a plastic box. 'Here are your afternoon meds.' She walks over to the desk, fetches Oriana's glass of water and gives it to her before pouring their tea and leaving the room.

'What exactly have you found? Tell me,' Oriana says.

Ashley relays what she found on the iPad. 'I'm going out of my mind.' She combs her hands through her hair. 'There appears to be a group involved in the purchase of your estate to develop it, under a company that was owned by Lucy. Three hundred homes. I don't understand why you and your husband would want to do that. I thought you loved Thyme End. And I don't understand why Danny has kept his involvement in all of this from me.'

Oriana shakes her head, the sagging skin of her jaw quivering. 'No, my dear. You're confused. I need to explain. Please.' Oriana gestures to the chair opposite her.

Ashley gives in. She picks up a cup of tea and sits down.

'However, before I start, I need to ensure your complete discretion. You'll understand when I tell you why.'

Ashley straightens her spine.

'I didn't want Lucy to tell anyone about it. Well, as few people as possible. I swore her to secrecy. Lucy was true to her word.' Oriana collects herself as if summoning the energy for the conversation she is about to have. 'As you're well aware, I'm dying.'

Ashley nods. Oriana has never concealed this fact.

'I can't remember how much I've told you about Thyme End Hall's history and my association with it. Please tell me if I'm repeating myself. My mind is not what it used to be.' She places a hand across her pencilled brows. 'It's all this dreadful medication. It messes with my head.' She adjusts her headscarf. 'My mother and father bought this property when they first got married. I was born and bred here. When my first husband died, I never thought I'd find love again. But I did. Or so I thought. I met Aaron. As you know, he is considerably younger than me. Nearly twenty years younger than me.' Oriana pauses to breathe, wheezing. It appears to be an effort for her.

'Do you want me to get you something?' Ashley asks.

'No. Please just give me a minute.'

'Take all the time you need.' While Oriana settles her breath, Ashley looks onto the mature garden singing the song of summer with its vibrant display of flowers and shrubs. She sips her tea. Her heart hurts for the woman sitting opposite her. How she must loathe the fate she has been dealt.

'Simon changed after his dad died. He became a very difficult child. I did what I thought was the right thing and sent him to boarding school. With hindsight, I should've kept him here. He was a grieving child, who needed me, but we all do what we think is best at the time for our children, don't we?'

Ashley nods. 'There are no set rules to parenting.'

'Simon hated Aaron from the word go. When Aaron asked me to marry him, Simon tried to persuade me to arrange a prenup agreement. I told him I'd ask for no such thing. What kind of way is that to start a marriage? Simon wasn't happy. He thought Aaron was a gold-digger – only with me for my money.' She pauses, coughing again. 'I didn't like the way Simon was behaving. So instead of a prenup, I made a new will stating that' – her gaze follows her arm, sweeping around the room in a semicircle – 'although Simon inherits this estate when I die, Aaron can live here until his death. I also left Aaron a generous amount of cash.'

'That sounds reasonable,' Ashley says.

Oriana nods. 'But, six months ago, only days after my cancer diagnosis, Lucy called and asked to take me out to lunch.' Oriana pinches the thin skin above her nose. 'I knew something was up by the tone of her voice. She had something important to tell me, she said. It broke my heart.'

FORTY-THREE

Ashley waits with bated breath, wondering how this all connects to Danny and what she discovered on the iPad.

'Lucy found out, through her line of work, that there was talk of a large development in Thyme End. And when she dug deeper, in a nutshell, she discovered that Simon had struck a deal with Aaron. Upon my death, Simon was going to pay Aaron a considerable sum to give up all rights to living in this house. And, in conjunction with a friend of his, my son also planned to carve up the estate and build three hundred executive houses on the land, despite knowing that would've been wholly against my wishes.'

'That's truly dreadful.' Ashley's words sound lame, but they are the only ones she can find. She's still confused.

'Lucy got hold of the preliminary plans of the development. The ones I think you must have seen. I was devastated. While I was having chemotherapy, fighting for my life, my husband and son were plotting to profit from my death. How could they do that to me? Lucy and I discussed in great depth the best course of action. At first, I was going to gift the whole estate and all my personal wealth to the Thyme End community on the condition that this house was to be converted into a hospice and the land and my wealth used to finance it. But apparently that was fraught with problems.'

'Why?'

'Legal reasons Lucy explained to me, but I never quite grasped the details. So, Lucy was arranging to buy the house and land from me, transfer it into a trust and develop it according to my wishes. The old worker's huts to the left of the property will be converted and the site around it developed for living accommodation for staff working in the hospice – thirty houses in total. That's where I think you've got confused. It was all intended to complement the community, not tear it apart. You see, Ashley, my wealth has afforded me all the medication and care possible since my diagnosis. Other less fortunate people dying of cancer don't have that luxury. People struggle every day living with this wretched disease. I want to give back. I've changed my will to donate everything I have to the trust to sustain the hospice.' Her voice falters. 'It will require charitable input too, but Lucy was taking care of that with the help of the group.'

'You're totally cutting off your husband and son?'

'Too right I am. And you know how well-connected Lucy was. I don't know the details, but she had arranged funds to secure the project.'

Ashley listens intently, twiddling the ring with an oversized mother-of-pearl stone that Danny bought for her last birthday around her middle finger. This is not what she expected to hear today. It sounds as if Danny is only trying to do right by people. But why didn't he tell her? 'And you trusted her?'

Oriana's jaw drops slightly as if Ashley's question has offended her. 'I trusted Lucy with my life. She was such a good woman. We were trying to tie up all the legal aspects before I died and get the plans moving, along with the help of the others.'

'Quite an influential bunch.'

'Correct. Roberta Splinter was a lifelong friend of mine. But then she had that terrible accident.' She shakes her head. Her tiny diamond drop earrings shine in the sunlight beaming through the window. 'Lucy knows the planning officer, Guy Roberts, from her business dealings. Then there's a solicitor Lucy knew, to help advise on legal matters. She only pulled in Danny...' She pauses as if to clarity her thoughts. '... A few weeks ago.'

'I guess that's why there's very little on his iPad, and that's where I've got confused. What was he doing?'

'Helping her with some of the technical side of things. Drawings. Site plans. I don't really understand that area of it at all.'

'Why all the secrecy?'

'The clock is ticking for me. Aaron and Simon don't know about my plans and that's the way I want it to stay. Nothing must get in the way. I fear they will try to stop me.' Oriana pauses to control her persistent cough. 'Lucy said it would be better for everything to go through the legal channels before they find out. And as much as I want to see the pair of them squirm, I don't need that hassle in my final days on this earth. Simon will be beyond angry with me. After all, he was up to make an awful lot of money from his shameful plans.'

Ashley pauses, going through all this new information in her head. 'So Lucy was doing the honourable thing.'

'Indeed she was. Lucy gave them all iPads to connect through to keep everything separate and private. She got them cheap. All the paperwork and plans for the hospice and houses have been circulated that way.'

'I never saw them on the iPad Danny has.' Ashley's heart misses a beat. The police will find Lucy's iPad, surely?

'They were emailed a while back, before he got involved. He's a good man, Ashley. I've known him a long, long time.'

He *is* a good man. That's why she married him.

'What about the phone?'

'What phone?'

'I found a phone with the iPad. Danny has used it to connect to a guy in Poland who does the same job as me.'

'I don't know about any phones.'

'Does Lee know about all of this?'

'No. Lucy didn't want him to know.'

'Why? It doesn't make sense.'

Oriana pauses, as if she's unsure how to answer that question. 'She thought he would try to stop her. It was a massive undertaking, and she was already a very busy woman. I questioned, too, whether it was too much for her to take on. But she was adamant she wanted to help me. She was going to tell Lee about it this weekend, but when I asked her on Sunday if she had, she said they'd had an argument before the party, and she hadn't had a chance.'

'What did they argue about?'

'She didn't say. And I didn't want to pry.'

Ashley goes to divulge Danny and Lucy's argument on Wednesday but stops herself. 'Do the police know about Lee and Lucy arguing?'

'I guess he has told them.'

Ashley wonders if there was an ulterior motive for Lucy wanting to take on this considerable chunk of work. A fleeting thought passes through her mind. Were Lucy and Danny using this project as a front for their own plans? But no, surely that wasn't Lucy's style. Besides, she loved Oriana and the Thyme Hall End estate. She was all about getting involved in anything to help the community. So was Danny, but to a lesser extent. And there's no doubting Lucy's devotion to the dying woman sitting in front of her.

'Who will run with this now that Lucy's no longer with us?'

'I don't know. Lucy took me to the solicitor's on Friday. My will has been changed, and the paperwork all signed. The remaining group will have to take over from here.'

FORTY-FOUR

'They were all doing the honourable thing, then,' Susie says to Ashley.

'I know. I feel terrible for doubting him.'

They're sitting in the garden eating the leftover pizza from last night with a salad Susie threw together. Susie unbuttons her silk shirt, a stark contrast to the figure-hugging white denim shorts she is wearing: perfect working-from-home attire. No one sees her from the waist down over Zoom.

Ashley plays with her food, the aroma of the pepperoni too much. 'It still doesn't explain the cash.'

'Just wait to ask him.' Susie's eyes widen, her pizza slice suspended mid-air. 'Do you know who I think broke in here last night?'

'Who?' Ashley stabs her fork into a tomato. It splits open like she imagines Lucy's head did in that garage on Sunday.

'Tom. I reckon Danny spoke to him on the way to the station and sent him around here to get the iPad out of the safe before the police found it.'

'Why?'

'Because he didn't want the police to link him to Lucy in

any way. That's how Tom knew how to get in. And he came prepared for Rufus.'

'Nah. It doesn't make sense. You're only saying that because you don't like Tom. Why didn't Danny just take the iPad to his house when Tom was taking him to the station?' Ashley places her knife and fork together. 'I need to pick up Elliot.'

'Maybe it only occurred to him when they were driving to the station?' Susie says, trying to defend her hypothesis.

'I guess you never truly know someone.'

'That's what Mum always used to say.' Susie imitates their mother's tired voice: '"You never truly know anyone. Your father is a prime example of that."'

Ashley walks along the close towards the road, the gentle breeze welcoming after the heat of the day. Is that a twitch of a curtain from the neighbour's lounge? She stares at the window but doesn't see anything. She glances at the house opposite, scanning the windows, certain she can see shadows. But is it her imagination? The past few days are driving her crazy. Or perhaps it's the hypocrisy of middle England? They all know everyone's business but choose to acknowledge they don't.

She turns around, deciding to walk along the footpath that leads to the fields. Taking the left-hand fork along the track to the village, she frees Rufus from his lead, thinking about everything Oriana told her today. Lucy and Danny's actions were commendable. But she still can't understand why they kept it all from her and Lee. She stumbles on a stray branch. Her legs are weak from a lack of food and the stress from the mess her life is in. She curses the day they moved to Thyme End. It's not what she wanted. Not really. She was swept along by the undercurrent of Danny's desires. The bland colour of the walls of the house she saw as a blank canvas to make her mark, and more space to enable them all to breathe a little easier, drew her in. But it hasn't made her happy.

Ashley completely understands the attraction for Danny. It's where he grew up. The country living, the community. But it's just not her. She will always be a city chick. If only she could rewind to the day she finally agreed to the move. Danny was so happy when he popped the cork on the Dom Pérignon Vintage his parents had bought him for his thirtieth birthday. He always said he was saving it for a special occasion. With hindsight, the nagging sensation in her belly she felt when he handed her a glass of the bubbly was telling her she was making a big mistake. 'Listen to your instincts,' her mum always said. 'Your gut instinct. It never lets you down.'

Charcoal clouds darken the evening sky, burying the descending sun. The promise of some rain is a relief after the intense heat of the past few days. A gust of wind carries the murmur of chatter from customers in the beer garden of the pub, growing louder as she approaches. There's a faint rumble of an aircraft taking off in the distance from the local airport about fifteen miles away. That's where Roberta Splinter was heading the morning she ran her car off the road. Ashley remembers hearing it on the radio.

Usually, Ashley loves her evening strolls with Rufus. It's a chance to clear her mind. But tonight, unanswered questions jam-pack her thoughts, and her internal anxiety defies the tranquil landscape. She's scared that whoever broke in last night will be back to get what they came for.

A sudden rustle wrenches her back to reality. Rufus barks. Whirling around, she sees a figure emerge with a dog into the fields, a stranger in her familiar world. It's making her edgy. Picking up the pace, she traverses the expanse of the field until she reaches the secluded footpath leading to the rear entrance of The Ugly Duckling. The pungent odour of grease from chips cooking in the deep-fat fryers wafts in the air.

Not a table is spare in the crowded pub gardens. Those who weren't lucky enough to secure one are sitting on the grass verge with their pints, glasses of wine and baskets of chips. Children are running around the outdoor play area. It's an unusual sight for a school night, but Ashley knows why. People have come out to play a game of tittle-tattle, dissecting the grim narrative of her reality.

As she sweeps past, the conversation dips to a hush. A ripple of shock spreads through the crowd. 'That's her. That's the wife,' a voice whispers, spurring Ashley to hurry along the side path. She passes the open door to the pub kitchen, where the chef is calling for a waitress, and a bartender is pulling glasses from a dishwasher. She quickens her step towards the road, getting away from the Thyme End gossip kings and queens as quickly as she can.

Arriving at Tom's terraced cottage, Ashley peers through the window into the small, dark room that doubles as a lounge and dining room. Tom and Elliot are sitting at the small, rectangular dining table at the far end, playing a board game. Elliot is drinking a can of Coca-Cola, and Tom has one hand around a half-full pint of beer. He rolls a pair of dice with the other. Elliot laughs as he moves a figure around the board, his face lit up like the moon in the darkness of the room. It's the first time Ashley has seen him properly laugh since he stood with Grace at the top of that inflatable slide on Sunday, waiting to launch himself off. Was that only two days ago? Her aching heart tells her she has lived a lifetime since Lucy's fate shattered their lives. Elliot looks so content. She doesn't want to disturb him. Conversely, she wants him to come home.

She knocks on the window. Their heads turn in unison.

Elliot waves and mouths, 'Mum,' and runs towards her. 'What're you doing here?' he asks as he opens the door.

She steps into the lounge. 'I've come to collect you.'

Rufus charges for Elliot, and Elliot hugs his hound. 'Can I stay here the night, Mum?'

'Ashley, dear.'

Ashley inwardly grimaces. The familiar voice and the sound of footsteps precedes Miriam's entrance from the kitchen. Derek follows in her shadow, like a faithful dog trailing its mistress.

'Miriam, Derek! You're back.' Ashley doesn't know if this is a good or bad thing. Miriam Morgan is the most domineering person she has ever met. Like a manager who breathes heavily down your neck eight hours a day, butting in every time you aren't doing your job the way they would. But on the flip side of that, she is organised and efficient, and she adores Elliot.

Ashley closes the front door.

Derek, his closed mouth stretched into a straight-lipped smile, lifts a hand in a tired attempt to wave.

Miriam seems to have left her need to look after her appearance on the cruise ship. Her silver bobbed hair is lank, as if she hasn't washed it in days, and it's the first time Ashley has ever seen her without make-up.

'It's been a nightmare trying to get home, but we finally made it. Trains, planes and automobiles. Cost us a fortune, didn't it, Derek?'

'It did.'

Looking at Derek makes Ashley yawn. It appears as if he hasn't slept in days, either. Ashley loves Derek. More than she loves Miriam, if she's honest. Actually, if she's brutally honest, she doesn't love Miriam at all. It's more of a grudging respect because she is her mother-in-law.

'We've been trying to get hold of you, Ashley. You carry on playing, boys,' Miriam says to Tom, patting him on the shoulder as if he is still a child. She takes Ashley's hand and instructs Derek on his next move with a flick of her head towards the kitchen door. She looks Ashley directly in the eye. 'We need to talk.'

'Stay with Elliot,' Ashley orders Rufus and succumbs to Miriam's hand, tugging her into the kitchen, where Renee is clattering around drying the dishes.

Ashley acknowledges Renee with a hello as Miriam pulls her out of the back door to a wooden love seat in the tiny rear garden. Two cups and saucers with the remnants of tea sit on the shelved table connecting the two chairs. Derek follows like a lost puppy dog.

'You two sit. You look exhausted, Ashley. But that's understandable,' Miriam says.

Renee appears with a spotted teapot. Silently, as if she knows her place in the dynamics of the family she is not officially a part of, she tops up the two cups. 'Give me a second, and I'll bring you a cup,' she says to Ashley as she leaves.

'I've arranged a solicitor.' Miriam is off. Taking control like a CEO who has walked into a shitshow and doesn't trust their subordinates to sort out the mess. She paces the small space in front of the seated two. Her usually heavily made-up eyes appear as small as the buttons on her blouse without the lashings of mascara she typically applies. 'It'll cost us a fortune, but he came highly recommended.'

Ashley grits her teeth, saying little. She has learnt over the years that it's the best way to deal with her mother-in-law. Besides, it sounds like the solicitor she has appointed is at the top of his legal game. It's more than likely, knowing Miriam, the best hope for getting Danny out of the mess he has found himself in.

Miriam bangs on in a hushed tone about her shock at what has happened, and what, in her humble opinion, needs to be done to free her innocent son, stopping only when the neighbour opens their back door to let their dog into the garden. But she doesn't stop pacing. Pure heart attack material, that woman,

Susie has always said. Ashley is surprised she hasn't already had one. When the neighbour lets the dog back in and closes the door, Miriam turns to Ashley.

'Now tell us what has happened.'

Ashley is sketchy with the truth. She omits to disclose everything other than what happened on Sunday. And how vulnerable everything has made her feel. Miriam is the last person she needs involved in her personal life.

'That's all I know. I'm as stunned as you.'

'This is all ludicrous,' Miriam says, dismissively waving her hands. 'Our Daniel wouldn't hurt a soul, would he, Derek?'

Derek shakes his head, staring into his cup of tea.

'Let alone Lucy. Poor Lucy. I loved that woman like my own. We were devastated when Daniel broke her and Tom up, weren't we, Derek? Tom and she made such a great couple.'

The pit of sickness lurking in Ashley's stomach stirs. 'What do you mean Danny broke Lucy and Tom up?'

'Did he never tell you?' Miriam asks.

'Tell me what?'

'Daniel and Lucy had a brief relationship just before they went off to university.'

FORTY-FIVE

'It's what split Lucy and Tom up. Daniel was a liability at that age. Although, if you ask me, our Tom and Lucy were never destined to be together. Lucy was far too career-minded and ambitious for our Tom. Wasn't she, Derek?'

Ashley is stunned. Danny and Lucy had a fling? Why has he never told her?

Maybe because it was more than a fling.

'Elliot can stay with us tonight. It'll give you some space,' Miriam says.

Ashley considers her options. She wants to leave now and take Elliot with her, but she knows he is better off staying with Tom or going home with his grandparents. Whatever Miriam is, she is an excellent grandmother. She kept boxes upon boxes of books from Tom and Danny's youth and reads to Elliot all the time. If she's not reading to him, she potters in the garden with him, growing vegetables from scratch that she is currently teaching him to cook. The TV is always switched off and an iPad is never in sight. And if she is busy, Derek entertains Elliot with the model railway that has taken over their double garage since he retired. Not that Miriam minds about losing the garage. It keeps Derek occupied and out of her way, she says.

'We'll let them finish their game and take him home. We've got everything there. It looks like you could do with a good night's sleep. Although I guess it's impossible to sleep at the moment.' She glances at her gold wristwatch. 'It's gone nine o'clock. We can unpack in the morning, Derek. Then we can start to sort out this utter mess our son seems to have got himself into.'

Ashley's footsteps quicken across the village. It's as if her husband has stripped her bare, and tormenting news greets her at every corner. Danny and Lucy? A bitter taste of disbelief rises in her throat. She wants to think Miriam has got that wrong. But she knows she hasn't. If there's one thing you can be sure of with Miriam, she doesn't get things wrong. Never. Ashley thinks back to the two women in the school toilets. It appears gossiping Trisha was well informed after all.

Rufus pulls her along. She glances up at the menacing outline of the church in the distance, her eyes filled with tears as she imagines Danny and Lucy as teenage lovers. A chill runs through her, and it's not from the breeze. She lengthens her step as she strides past the medieval terraces heading towards the old guildhall. Was that movement she detected in the shadows?

She stops and stares into the darkness, listening closely. A passing car casts a shimmer of light across the face of the old double-fronted houses on the corner of the road leading to her close. The village is menacing in the dark.

She crosses the road and breaks into a jog, stopping suddenly as a pair of beady eyes appears from the shadows between a tiny alleyway where a medieval cottage meets a Georgian house. Rufus growls. Her heart pounds, thumping in her chest until a black cat with topaz eyes skulks into view. She jogs the rest of the way home, trying to rationalise how jumpy she feels. It's the bloody village. It's spooking her.

She wants to leave, pack a suitcase and take Elliot back to London.

Now.

Susie is sitting in the dark of the garden puffing on a cigarette when Ashley arrives home. Ashley switches on the outside lights and relays the latest chapter of the twisted tale of her husband's life.

'It happened years ago, Ash. You weren't even together. What does it matter?'

'It matters because he never told me about it.'

'Did you ever ask him?'

Ashley leans against the patio doors. 'Yes, and he denied it. I've also commented before that she was a flirt. She was always touching him.'

'I noticed that at the party.'

'He said she'd always been like that and she was like it with everyone. And it's true. She was.' She grimaces. 'Argh. I hate talking about her like this. The poor woman is dead, for heaven's sake.'

'He probably never told you about them because he didn't want to hurt you.'

'I guess so.' Sadness lowers Ashley's voice. 'Do you remember when we were young, and Mum used to cry all the time?'

'When she found out about Dad's latest floozy?' Susie puffs on her cigarette. 'How could I forget? Especially the time she discovered it was the neighbour's daughter. You'd have thought that would've been the deal-breaker.'

Ashley gives a pathetic half-laugh. 'The girl was barely eighteen.'

'What was he thinking? She wasn't even attractive.'

'I don't think he cared. That was the worst one, wasn't it?'

Susie shrugs. 'I'm not sure. His secretary was pretty bad. Mum cried for weeks over that one. Remember?'

Ashley nods. 'I do. Why didn't she just leave him?'

'I never understood it until Stuart had his affair.'

Ashley hesitates. 'You left him, though.'

Susie rolls her big brown eyes. 'It took me seven months.'

'Was it really that long?'

'It sure was. I knew I should've left him as soon as I found out.'

'Why didn't you? You've never really told me properly.'

'It's hard to explain. I was a mess. I hated him, but despite what he did, I couldn't imagine a future without him.'

Ashley nods. She understands. That's how she has always felt about Danny. But now a niggling doubt is eating away at her about their future.

'We'd mapped out our life together. The house we were going to buy. The kids we were going to have. The holidays we were going to take. According to Stuart, we were going to travel the world. He was my everything. And then one night...' She pauses and clicks her fingers. A sound so loud in the calmness of the evening. 'One night, and it was all over. I saw him a few weeks ago.'

'You never said,' Ashley remarks, her sister's words tugging on her vulnerable heartstrings. Within days of meeting each other, she and Danny had also mapped out their life together. An exciting and comforting plan, not too dissimilar to the one her sister made with her ex-husband. Has their plan now been wiped out too? The thought fills her with sadness.

Susie takes a long drag of her cigarette and slowly puffs it out. 'He has become that insignificant in my life that I forgot. He was with a woman.' She snorts. 'She had the same haircut as me.'

'That's creepy.'

'I just thought to myself, you poor bitch.'

'After Mum and Dad, I always said if I found out my husband was having an affair, I'd leave him.'

'But he hasn't had an affair. Everyone has a past, Ash. I'm more concerned about all that cash you found.'

Ashley sighs heavily. 'I'm going to bed. I'm beyond tired. Don't forget I'm meeting Lee in the morning.'

She is even more keen to meet him now, after all she has discovered today. There are so many questions that she hopes he can answer.

Ashley takes another of Danny's sleeping pills. It's the only way she'll get some sleep. But it doesn't work. She spends the night mostly awake, terrified that whoever came here last night will be back for what she believes they were after – the iPad and the phone.

Around 3 a.m., she manages to drop off, only to be woken soon after by a sound. She sits up, disorientated. Rubbing her eyes, she listens. But she hears nothing more. Was it her imagination? She kneads her knuckles into her temples. The situation is slowly driving her crazy.

She jumps. There was definitely a noise. She gets up and creeps over to the window, to see if she can spot movement in the garden. The Hub is in darkness.

Clank. There it is again.

There's someone in the house.

Are they here for Danny?

Or for her?

FORTY-SIX

Ashley's heart can't take it. It's ramming against her chest so fast, she's going to pass out. She leans against the wall, steadying herself before creeping to the door. Pulling it ajar, she listens. A noise is coming from the stairs. Someone is coming up. She stands back, looking around for something to strike them with, but she can't see properly.

A subtle shadow flitters across the landing, every creak of the floorboards loud in the tense quietness. As the shadow grows closer, Ashley prepares for a confrontation. She grabs a shoe, only to see the shadow creep into the spare room.

'Susie!' she cries out.

'What?' her sister replies.

Ashley opens the door. 'I thought you were a bloody burglar.'

'I'm sorry, I needed another glass of water. It's boiling tonight.'

'You scared the hell out of me.'

Susie apologises. 'You're too on edge. Chill out and get some sleep.'

Her sister is right. She's a bundle of nerves about to snap.

. . .

Susie is already working when Ashley stumbles out of bed the following morning. She quickly showers and, after saying her goodbyes, jumps into the car. She's going to be late meeting Lee.

The journey to Brewer's Farm is mainly along bendy country lanes, so Ashley tries to stay focused as she drives. Miriam's revelation about Danny and Lucy's fling when they were younger played on her mind all night. A news report on the radio repeats yesterday's headline, stealing her thoughts. The police have arrested a local man under the suspicion of the murder of a local woman, Lucy Ellis, during her daughter's ninth birthday party. Their inquiries continue. Ashley switches the station. The image of Lucy's smashed-in head is consuming her enough already.

At the T-junction on the edge of the village, she turns right. Driving carefully, she adheres to the speed limit despite being late. Her hands are shaking so much, she doesn't trust herself to go any faster. She has no desire to join the drivers who have succumbed to the dangers of that stretch of road. She snarls at the arse in the white van driving far too close behind her. Why do some people do that? It's not going to make her go any faster. Aren't the small wooden crosses on the verge, cluttered with fresh flowers from the recent addition to the casualties who have lost their lives, enough of a reminder that this is not a road to muck about on?

Her phone rings. It's Elliot. Digging deep, she finds her happy voice. It's not easy. It's hiding out in the depths of her soul. 'Hey, buddy. How are you this morning?'

His voice fills the car through the speakers. 'Grandad's taking me fruit picking. Can Grace come?'

'Not today.'

'But I haven't seen her. She'll be sad.'

'We'll talk about this later.'

He rattles off what he has been up to this morning. Miriam has already read him a book, started and finished a one-hundred-piece jigsaw puzzle of sharks with him and walked him to the village bakery to buy croissants for breakfast. 'Granma wants a word.'

Ashley cringes at the crackling sound grating through the speakers as Elliot passes the phone to Miriam. 'All sorted. The new solicitor is visiting Danny today. This morning, hopefully. Hold tight. I'm confident they'll get him out of there.'

Although she wants to see her husband, Ashley wishes she shared her mother-in-law's conviction.

The van behind her is so close, if she brakes, it'll go right into the back of her. She slows down. It appears to get closer. Who is that fool? He's stripping her already frayed nerves right down to the core. She slows down to thirty miles per hour. The van driver pulls out. Speeding up, he revs past. He is wearing a baseball cap and turns his face away so she can't see him. He drives so close, she veers off the side of the road, hitting the grass verge. She beeps her horn. Not that it makes any difference. The driver is long gone. She stops the car, shaken. Why are there so many idiots on the road?

When she reaches Brewer's Farm, she parks the car. Lee has messaged, sending his apologies. He will be fifteen minutes late. As she climbs out of the car, nausea overcomes her. She usually enjoys the hot weather, but the heat has really got to her. It's insufferable. She gags. Leaning a bent arm on the roof of the car, she drops her head, clinging to the door with the other arm. Her legs feel empty, hollow, as if all her muscles have been sucked out of her. An instinctual part of her brain tells her to sit down. She's light-headed, disconnected from her surroundings, struggling to hold her weight. Getting back into the car, she rests her head on the steering wheel. Her loose sundress clings to her back. She mutters words of encouragement to herself. She can't pass out. Not there. Breathe, Ash. Breathe. That's what Danny would say to her if he were there.

She shuts the car door and restarts the engine, whipping the air-conditioning dial high. Food. She's got to eat. She hardly ate anything again yesterday. Every time she attempts it, all she can see is Lucy's body horizontal on that garage floor and her husband standing over her. She lays her head on the passenger seat, the cool air a relief against her face. After a couple of minutes, it passes. She sits up, wiping her forehead. Food is a must.

The farm shop is housed in a massive converted barn. She scans the shoppers moseying around the tables filled with unique gifts and unusual food: black truffle focaccia, port and brandy cheddar and sugar-free liquorice. Danny loves liquorice. He bought a packet when they came here with the Ellis family. And he bought her a ginger cake.

Ginger cake. An overwhelming desire for a sticky slice engulfs her. She snakes her way through tables filled with luxurious candles, china, scarves and photo frames, and heads to the café at the far end of the building. A large blackboard declaring, 'Brewer's Burger: a mouth-watering beef patty with all toppings – try if you dare', chalked in white, hangs over the counter. Ashley eyes the displays of flatbreads, quiches, salads and sandwiches while she waits in the queue. It all turns her stomach. Junk food, that's what she wants. Sweet, sticky carbs.

'What can I get you?' the teenage waitress with a mass of tight black curly hair asks. Her face is as fresh as the food on offer. She looks so young. Eighteen, Ashley reckons. She has probably just finished school. When Ashley was that age, Susie had just turned twenty-two. Their mother had been dead for three years. Susie was no longer her legal guardian. It was a scary time. But then she met Danny. Handsome, strong and caring Danny, who took over from where Susie left off. He was her first proper boyfriend. She'd had casual dates before with boys from school. But nothing that led to more than a slobbery kiss. From day one, Danny has always had her back, looking out for her and protecting her.

Damn you, Danny. Where are you now?

'Are you OK?' the waitress says.

Ashley grabs the edge of the counter with both hands as the realisation dawns on her.

This can't be happening. She thought it was the deceitful jumble of havoc Danny has involved her in making her feel so sick. But it's not that at all. She has felt like this before. Only once in her life, but it's the same feeling she had nine years ago. When she fell pregnant with Elliot.

FORTY-SEVEN

Ashley shakily takes the slice of ginger cake and cappuccino she managed to order to the wooden picnic tables dotted across a patio and grassed area outside. She finds the only free table, relieved to sit down, an umbrella providing welcoming shade. The grassed area runs alongside a pen housing two pot-bellied pigs with brushings of white on their snouts and lower legs. They weren't here when they last came. Elliot would love them. She must bring him back here.

It's loud with mothers and their babies, and toddlers in plastic highchairs making a mess of their food. A heavily pregnant woman at the table to her left is encouraging her daughter to eat a carrot stick. The woman's extended belly is as round as a medicine ball and looks as heavy. Ashley places the palm of her hand on her own belly, as flat as a board. Can she really be pregnant? The thought has shoved aside her fear of why she's here – to talk to the man who has accused her husband of murdering his wife.

She takes some deep breaths. The nausea hasn't subsided. If anything, it has worsened. If she is pregnant, and Elliot's beginning is anything to go by, she might as well get used to it. It's here to stay for a good few weeks.

Taking her phone out of her bag, she studies her diary, trying to remember the date of her last period. She used to mark the dates – PD: period due. But it got too depressing. And it made her anxious. Only serving as a reminder of the pending disappointment as the highlighted day approached each month. Danny kept out of her way on the day preceding PD day. He said she became unbearable.

She rubs her hand across her belly, swallowing the tears threatening to gush. She has wanted to be pregnant again for so long. To experience that seed of life grow within her. But it feels all wrong now.

'Hello, Ashley.'

Lee startles her.

'Would you like another drink?'

Ashley glances up from her phone.

Lee looks washed out. Stubble coats his chin, and his usual vibrant aura of confidence is lost in his bubble of grief.

She stands up. It's awkward. Usually when they meet, he kisses her cheek, but today he stands firm on the other side of the table.

'I haven't drunk this one yet,' she says. 'I was going to get you one, but I didn't know how long you'd be.' Pointing to her cappuccino, she misjudges how close it is. She knocks the side of the cup, spilling milky coffee onto the saucer. As she tries to steady it, her hand is shaking so much, more coffee spills.

Lee peers over his black-framed glasses. 'I'll get you another one.'

Ashley sits back down, watching Lee return inside to get the drinks, his shoulders slumped. What *has* he got to say to her?

With a trembling hand, she picks up her fork and picks a layer of cream cheese frosting from the cake.

'No, Mummy,' the girl with plaited hair on the table beside her screams at the woman. 'Don't want. Don't want.'

Ashley glances back at her phone, listening to the kid's objection. The day she and Danny took Elliot to the beach. That was when her last period started. She remembers now. It was a very warm morning and Danny insisted they make the most of it. She counts the days. Thirty-eight. She draws the forkful of cake to her mouth.

'Don't want. Don't want,' the kid screams again.

Ashley's stomach churns at the smell of ginger. Placing the forkful of cake onto the plate, she picks up her drink. Drops dribble from the bottom of the cup and fall onto the table. On the way home, she needs to stop at the pharmacy.

Lee reappears with a tray and sits opposite her.

'How are you?' Embarrassment colours her cheeks. 'Sorry, that's a bloody stupid question.'

Lee unloads the tray. His hands are trembling as much as hers are. 'Bearing up.' He slowly slides a cappuccino towards her.

'And the kids?'

'As you would expect, traumatised.' He doesn't say it horribly, but he doesn't need to. The impact of his words makes her shudder.

She offers the cake to him. 'I bought this but can't face it now.'

He shakes his head and pulls the tab on a can of Sprite. It hisses and pops as the seal opens.

She breaks the unbearable silence. 'Why did you ask me here?'

He clears his throat. 'I'm sorry, too, for what you're having to face. It must be hell.'

She hunches her shoulders. She didn't expect him to say that. 'Not as bad as what you're going through.' She exhales a large breath. 'Jeez, Lee. I'm so dreadfully sorry.'

His jawbones stiffen. 'I know.'

'Danny is still in police custody.'

'I know.'

'Is there any update? I don't get told a thing.'

His voice breaks. 'They had me in for questioning, you know.' He pauses, momentarily closing his eyes. When he opens them, they are glassed over. He bangs his fist on the table. The cappuccino he bought for her wobbles. 'They grilled me for a whole fucking day.' The pregnant woman at the table next to them glances over, frowning. 'And there's been a whole bunch of reporters camped out in the lane since Sunday. Every time I leave the house, they hound me like a pack of wolves.'

Ashley's hands fall to her belly as if she is protecting the seed she knows deep down is growing inside her. 'That must've been hell for you. Reporters have been hanging around my house as well.' After a brief silence, she continues. 'Listen, Lee. Whatever you think about Danny, you're mistaken.'

He leans forward, staring her in the eyes. 'You need to know something, Ashley.'

She leans backwards. Dread creeps through her heart, tightening its grip with a greater intensity than her hands clenching the table. She wants to leave, get in her car and drive ten thousand miles away.

'Do you know what Lucy said to me on the morning of the party?'

Ashley shakes her head, bracing herself.

'I was running around like a blue-arsed fly, frantically trying to make everything look perfect for her.' He scoffs. 'Perfect should've been my wife's middle name. She was insistent on having balloons over the entrance gates to the house. I thought they'd be better over the front door. We argued.' Another scoff, louder this time. 'The police didn't like that we argued. All couples argue for heaven's sake.'

'That's for sure.' She encourages him to continue: 'What do I need to know?'

'She argued with a lot of people recently.'

Ashley starts to say she knows. That Danny and Lucy argued last week. But she stops. Is that the right thing to say in the circumstances? Lee will more than likely tell the police if she does. Maybe she should come clean about everything. Danny and Lucy arguing. Danny saying, 'I could kill that woman.' Danny's involvement in Lucy's plans for Thyme End Hall estate. But Lee is not the person to come clean with.

'She argued with me in particular. A lot.' He sips his Sprite. 'I thought it was the pressure from work. She had a lot on. She was too bloody ambitious for her own good. And she was always doing something for someone. She seemed to have more time for everyone else than me. When we argued before the party, do you know what she said to me?'

Ashley stares at him. She wants him to stop. She doesn't want to know. Equally, she wants him to carry on. She shakes her head.

'She said she wanted a divorce.'

The news shatters her perception of him and Lucy as the perfect couple. They had always appeared so good together. But, then again, what does Danny always say – no one knows what goes on behind closed doors. As pieces of her husband's puzzling predicament rearrange themselves in her mind, she begins to question the facade Lucy and Lee presented to the world.

'A divorce?' she asks. 'Where did that come from?'

'She said she was in love with someone else.'

FORTY-EIGHT

Ashley lets go of the table and clenches her hands together as tight as a knot, trying to ground herself amid the chaos that has wrecked her life. Where is all this going to end?

'Who?'

Lee removes his glasses, staring her deep in the eyes. 'We didn't get to finish that conversation. Grace walked in on us arguing. Lucy ran out.'

Ashley is desperate to ask him if he suspects it was Danny. But why put that thought in his head if it's not already there?

Who is she trying to kid? Of course it's already bloody there.

'I did think something wasn't right with you on Sunday. But I'd never have known something was up with you and Lucy from the way you two were together.'

'The act you put on for your kids, hey?' He takes another sip of his drink. 'It was hell, but I didn't want to ruin things for Grace.'

Ashley tilts her head back. Not a cloud blemishes the midday sky. As perfect as her memories of Lee and Lucy. Of her and Danny. Perfection that, hour by hour, has morphed into disloyalty and mistrust over the past three days. She returns her gaze to him. 'Why did you bring me here to tell me this, Lee?'

'I think you already know why.'

She grabs an elbow with each hand, crossing her arms over her chest and arching her shoulders. 'Why?' she whispers.

'Oh, come on, Ashley. Do I need to spell it out for you?'

She grits her teeth, not knowing what to say.

'Because I think it was Danny who she was having an affair with.'

Ashley's hand shoots to cover her mouth. It's not enough for the force of the coffee spurting out. It escapes through her fingers and splatters her clothes. She gets up, coughing and retching as she absorbs his statement.

People turn to stare. Lee whips his legs over the bench and rushes around to her, guiding her towards the toilets at the side of the building.

'I'm sorry to put that on you, but I thought you deserved to know.'

She should have known nothing good could come from meeting him.

'Go home, Lee. Leave me alone.' Her body trembles as she rushes into the ladies', a cold sweat coating her skin despite the heat from the sun. She doesn't make it into a cubicle. Gripping the cold porcelain sink, she heaves, the retching sounds echoing around the small, windowless room. Closing her eyes, she wills the sickness to pass. But her body has other plans. Nausea overwhelms her senses. She vomits until there's nothing left inside of her, which isn't much, given what little she has consumed over the past few days.

She glances in the oval mirror. Her eyes are watering as if she has been crying. She washes her hands and cleans her face, the pain of Lee's revelation like a merciless knife slashing at her heart. Taking a paper towel from the dispenser, she runs it under the tap and dabs the splatters of vomit on her clothes.

The stains remain, but at least it won't smell as bad. She grips the edge of the sink, desperate for some semblance of control amidst the hell. As she gazes at her tear-streaked reflection, she grabs her belly. Her life will never be the same.

Leaving the toilet, she returns to the table with purpose in her stride. Lee is still sitting there, nursing his drink.

'I'm so sorry,' he says again. He looks as if he genuinely means it.

'I need to go.' She grabs her bag and rushes back to her car. Lee follows her, trying to stop her. 'Leave me alone, Lee. Whatever you think of Danny, he wouldn't do this.' She delves into her bag for her keys and clicks open her car. 'And he's not a murderer.' She climbs in, starts the engine and drives off, leaving him standing alone. A soul as lost as her.

The heaviness of his words lingers in the stifling air. She can't breathe. She opens the window, unable to wait for the air conditioning to blow cold. Doubt for her husband races through her mind. Could Lee be right? Could Danny and Lucy have been having an affair? She stifles a sob, torn between the evidence she has gathered and the loyalty she fiercely holds. A loyalty being chipped away at, piece by sordid piece.

FORTY-NINE

Ashley drives into the neighbouring town, not wanting to be seen in the village pharmacy. The Thyme End grapevine would have a field day if they picked up that she was pregnant.

Finding the section she's looking for, she grabs an over-the-counter pregnancy test kit and a bottle of Elliot's favourite bubble bath and heads to the till. On second thoughts, she darts to the women's health section and swipes a bottle of folic acid from the shelf as well.

On her way back to the car, Ashley passes the barber shop where Danny takes Elliot to get their hair cut. Next door is the coffee shop Danny's golfing buddy's wife owns. The guy Danny said left that Post-it note. Danny said his wife wanted new signage for the shop. It's not the type of work Blue Banana Studios usually takes on, but you never know where it might lead. That's what he told her.

She glances up at the signage. The bottle-green colour and the old-fashioned font could certainly do with an update.

Taking a deep breath, Ashley walks inside. The pungent smell of coffee hits her. It's a smell she usually adores, but today, her hormones tell her otherwise. She swallows the mixed feelings trapped inside of her. Fear and elation: panic that she is pregnant at a time like this, and pure exhilaration for the gift she has desired for so long.

The place is busy. Two women occupy the table by the door. One is peeling away the pith of a tangerine, the other eating a slice of cake. A young man with a curved back, wearing a black leather jacket, is bent over his phone at another table. Retired couples enjoying brunch take up most of the other tables.

'Can I speak to Larry's wife?' Ashley asks the middle-aged woman serving behind the counter.

'That'll be me,' she says, her voice as cheery as her yellow dress printed with red cherries on green stalks. 'I'm Paulina. What can I do for you?' She smells floral, like lavender, and is wearing rose-red lipstick, impeccably applied.

'I'm Danny's wife, Ashley. He and Larry sometimes play golf together.'

The broadness of Paulina's smile reduces. Only a fraction, but it's noticeable. 'I'm sorry to hear about your husband. Larry is dreadfully upset. How is he?'

The village grapevine has spread its ugly vines into the next town.

Anger rips through Ashley. She wants to scream, tell this stranger she doesn't know. No one seems to be telling her a thing. But she's hoping the new solicitor Danny's mum has assigned will be able to change that.

'He's doing OK. He mentioned before all this started that you were looking for new signage for the shop.'

How does she sound? Talking about business when her husband is in a police cell being questioned for murder. But she has to know if Danny was telling her the truth. Did Larry really write that Post-it note?

'I was passing and thought I'd introduce myself.'

'That's right,' Paulina says. 'I want to liven up the outside.

It's looking pretty shabby and old-fashioned out there, isn't it? Larry mentioned you.'

Ashley inwardly sighs with relief. Danny was telling the truth.

On that singular matter, at least.

'I could design something pretty special for you,' Ashley says, surprised at her apparent confidence. It's more Danny's style than hers. He's the salesman. If he never comes home, perhaps she has got it inside herself to venture into that side of the business.

What is she thinking?

Of course he's coming home.

A young woman walks into the café, pushing a toddler in a buggy.

'You're busy.' Ashley digs into her bag and produces a business card from the inside pocket. She hands it over. 'Here's my card. Call me when you have a moment, and we can discuss options.'

'What a cute card,' Paulina says. 'Did you design this?'

Ashley nods.

'I love your style. Just what I'm looking for. My assistant is on holiday, so it's a bit mad at the moment, but I'll call you next week, and we can arrange a meeting to discuss ideas.'

Susie is in the kitchen making a sandwich. 'I was preparing a quick lunch before my next call, then I've got to head back to London. Where've you been? I thought you'd be back ages ago.'

'I went to town for a few things.'

Susie waves a butter knife in the air. 'I popped down to the baker's to get some fresh bread. Crikey, everyone was talking about Danny and Lucy. Funny, they wouldn't have said half the things they did if they knew who I was. So! Come on. What did Lee have to say?'

Ashley comes straight out with it. 'He reckons Danny and Lucy were having an affair.'

Susie puts down the knife.

'She asked him for a divorce the morning of the party. They had a massive argument, and she claimed she was in love with someone else. He's convinced that someone is Danny. Digest that while I pop to the loo.'

Locked in her en suite, Ashley opens the plastic pharmacy bag. She collects a sample, still shaking like a frightened child lost in a dark place. A cold, pitch-black place.

Two and a half minutes later, she has the answer that inwardly she knew already.

Sitting on the bed, she tries to process the result. She clutches the pregnancy test tightly, as if holding onto it can somehow stop the confusion in her head. She should be elated. It's what she has wanted for so long. The chance to grow their little family. But not in these circumstances. It's not right.

Descending the stairs, she stifles a sob. Danny should be the first person she shares such news with. She enters the kitchen. The patio doors are open. Susie has taken lunch into the garden. Ashley walks outside, dodging the stream of cigarette smoke from Susie sitting in one of the striped deckchairs. Two plates of cheese and ham baguettes and two glasses of juice await on the small table Danny made from a piece of tree trunk.

Susie inhales a large puff of smoke. 'Do you believe him?'

'I'm pregnant.'

Surprise and disbelief clash as Susie's jaw drops. 'Heavens. When did you find out?'

Ashley holds up the pregnancy kit clearly showing two lines. 'Just now.'

Susie balances her cigarette on the ashtray and hoicks herself out of the deckchair. She springs over to Ashley with her arms open wide. 'Congratulations.'

Ashley stands rigid.

Susie steps backwards. 'You are pleased, aren't you?'

Ashley looks at her sister blankly.

'Oh, Ash! You've wanted this for so long. Don't let everything that has happened spoil this for you.'

'How can I not?'

Susie guides her to the other deckchair. 'Please, be happy. This is a special time for you.'

Ashley wipes away the two tears that spring out of her eyes. She was determined not to cry, but it's as if discovering she is pregnant has given her untamed hormones the go-ahead to create more disruption in her life. She picks up a glass and takes a sip of her drink.

'If it wasn't Danny who Lucy was having an affair with, then who was it?' Susie says.

Silence falls between them as Ashley ponders the answer to her sister's question. 'Lucy certainly wouldn't have been short of opportunity, what with how well connected she was. Danny always said she excelled at networking. She was known in so many circles.'

An uncanny intuition alerts Ashley to someone else in the house before the figure appears at the patio doors. She clanks her glass onto the table, her head telling her one thing, her heart another.

Susie turns her head to the patio doors. 'Danny!'

Ashley should feel the marked joy she hears in her sister's voice. So why doesn't she?

FIFTY

Ashley stands up. She should be rushing towards her husband, throwing her arms around him and telling him what a relief it is to see him. But she can't find it in herself. Her hand flies to hold her stomach, as if trying to protect her unborn child from this man she doesn't feel she knows anymore.

He walks towards her.

She steps backwards. 'You're home.'

Something has happened between them. For her, anyway. Every unearthing from the past few days has liberally watered the seed of nagging doubt inside, and it has grown into an ugly plant of distrust. Who is this stranger in her garden?

'Ashley?' he questions, deep concern embedded in his expression.

He can feel it as well. They've lost something.

Susie gets up. 'I need to be on a work call. Good to see you, Danny.' She holds her slender hand to her ear, her little finger and thumb sticking out – a gesture telling Ashley to call if she needs her – and disappears inside.

Ashley's heart is racing. She wasn't expecting to see him.

What was she expecting then? For him to be charged with Lucy's murder? 'This is a surprise.'

'Mum and Dad came up trumps with a new solicitor. He was as sharp as a blade.' He appears different somehow, worn out, drained of his usual healthy glow.

'How did you get home?'

'I've got my car back.' He tries to take hold of her. 'What happened to your face?'

Ashley pushes him away. She can't bear his touch. She strokes her cheek. With so much going on, she had forgotten about the fall. The swelling has gone, but she knows from looking at her reflection this morning, an ugly mark remains.

His head drops to the side. 'Ash,' he says gently, squinting.

She slips inside to get the key to The Hub. 'Come with me.' The coldness in her voice is chilling. 'You've got some explaining to do.'

He follows her, trying to grab her shoulder. 'Ash? What's happened?'

She unlocks the door, crouches on the floor and rips up the carpet tile to reveal the safe. She punches the code into the keypad and opens it. 'You tell me.'

Danny scratches his head, scrunching his eyes. 'I can explain.' He stands at the door, his dejected face the picture of a man defeated.

She holds up a wad of cash and chucks it at him. An action so out of character. Normally, she's more composed, but her life isn't running on normal anymore. Her normal has become a confused mass of lies and deceit, a knot she doubts she'll ever be able to untangle. She can't control herself, and her rampant hormones aren't helping. She grabs the notebooks and throws them his way, followed by another wad of cash.

'Where the hell did this lot come from?'

Danny scrambles around, picking up the cash. 'Calm down,

Ash.' His voice is gentle. It tears at her heart. 'And I'll explain it all.' He holds out a hand to her, an offering of peace.

She swipes it away and shifts her bottom along the floor until her back is against the wall. 'You've got a hell of a lot of explaining to do.' She draws her knees to her chest. 'And if you lie to me, I'll walk. And I'll take Elliot with me.'

Danny looks at her in horror. She knows why. She's behaving erratically. The same as when she accused him of having that affair after Elliot was born.

He coughs. 'The money isn't mine.' He hesitates, coughing again. 'It's Tom's.'

'Tom's?' She didn't expect that. He's lying, she's certain of it. It's the way he cleared his throat. As if his mouth needed room to expel the untruths he was about to tell. 'What're you doing with it, then?'

'He has done a lot of cash-in-hand work and wanted me to keep it safe for him.'

'This is a lot of money. A lot of jobs.'

'I know. He's saving up.'

'For what?'

Danny grimaces, rubbing his forehead. 'He's going to propose to Renee.'

Ashley looks at him in shock. 'Why didn't you tell me?'

'He asked me not to say a word to anyone.'

'Even me? Your wife. His sister-in-law. Let me get this right. You think I'm unable to keep a secret? Bloody hell, Tom of all people doesn't think I can keep a secret. That's rich coming from him!'

'He wasn't wholly sure he was going to go through with it.' He clears his throat again, a slight tinge of red creeping up his neck.

Does he think she was born yesterday?

'And what about the phone and iPad?'

Danny's lips twist to the side. He sits on his heels facing her.

'And before you think about lying, I got into the iPad. What the hell have you got involved in, Danny?'

'Calm down, Ash. It's not what it looks like.'

'Calm down? This is just the tip of the iceberg of shit I've found out since Sunday.' Three days of controlled emotions are exploding like a bomb. 'Start at the beginning and tell me what this is all about?'

He relays the plans for Thyme End Hall. It corresponds with what Oriana told her.

'Did you send someone here to get the iPad?'

He nods.

'Who?'

'Tom.'

'You trusted Tom over me?' Ashley places the flat of her hand across her forehead, staring at him incredulously. 'Elliot was scared out of his mind. So were Susie and I. What were you thinking?'

He holds out a hand, firmly indicating for her to let him finish. 'Before you say anything, I swore him to secrecy. When he was driving me back to the station on Monday morning, he told me he was scared I was going to get arrested. That was the word going around the pub Sunday evening. It made me think. I was scared he was right. That I was going to get arrested, and that the police would come here and search the house. I told him to come around here and take the iPad out of the safe.'

'Why the iPad?'

'I didn't want them to know I'd been involved with Lucy on something Lee didn't know about. I wasn't thinking straight. I just thought it'd cause more problems than it was worth.'

'You're deluded, Danny. They'll find that out when they go through Lucy's things.'

He kneads his forehead with his fist. 'You've got to keep this to yourself, Ash. Oriana is trying to get everything wrapped up before she dies. She doesn't want Simon or Aaron to get wind of her plans.' He unbends his legs and sits on the floor. He pulls his heels to his bottom, resting his forearms on his knees. 'Lucy swore us all to secrecy. To protect Oriana.'

'And she was more important than me? Tom was more important than me?'

'No! No way. How can you say that? I was going to tell you at some point. I just didn't want to stress you out. You've more than enough on your plate with work. And we want you to get pregnant again. You don't need the stress.'

He isn't telling her the whole truth. It's as if he's trying to convince her that two plus two equals four, but she can only make three. Which makes her question what else he is keeping from her.

FIFTY-ONE

Ashley folds her arms across her chest. 'So what part were you playing in Lucy's plan with Oriana?'

'I was providing all the marketing materials to get the new application through the process. Lucy only involved me a few weeks ago. I was going to tell you all about it. I promise.'

'And that's where Krzysztof Adamski comes into the picture.'

'How do you know about him?' Danny asks, sounding taken aback.

'I found emails between the two of you. And I've spoken to him on your *other phone*. It looks to me like you were using him for more than just this project.'

Darkness shadows his face. 'You've really been snooping on me, haven't you?'

'Do you blame me?'

The vein in his forehead pumps. As if he's trying to disguise his frustration. 'I was going to tell you about all of this, Ash. Honestly, I was. But I've had so much going on. We've both been up to our eyeballs in work this past month. I was waiting for the right time.' He grinds his back teeth.

She eyes him questioningly. 'And what about the phone?'

'That thing! It's ancient. I came across it when we were packing up to move here. I didn't want to give Krzysztof my details when I first called him. I wanted to keep everything separate in case I decided not to use him. You've got too much work on, Ash. You know that. I know that.' He settles into his salesy cajoling patter. 'I've got so many plans for Blue Banana. I want to expand and employ more people. Give us a better life. But we can't afford to do that at the moment. There's a potential new development I've been going after in Surrey. It's huge. It will open so many doors for us. But it was too much for you to take on with all the other deadlines we have. So I was looking at ways to outsource some work.'

Give us a better life. His words disturb her. What was wrong with the life they had? They were happy.

But were they? Haven't the past few days clarified just how miserable she is living in the confines of the Thyme Hall grapevine?

'Without telling me?'

'I was going to tell you.' He runs his hands through his hair. 'Of course I was. Lucy put me in touch with Krzysztof to check out his CGI prices for her plans for Thyme End Hall. And while I was at it, I was getting a price for the Surrey development. Lucy said he was cheap, and he was good.'

'I'm your wife, Danny. Your business partner. Did it not occur to you to pass this by me?'

He lifts his arms and drops them by his side. 'Like I said, I didn't want to stress you out more than you are already. The whole point of moving here was for you to be less stressed with work so you could get pregnant.'

So why have you been piling the work on, she wants to ask but doesn't. 'Why didn't you call me after they arrested you?'

'I asked my solicitor to call you.'

'Who did you use your one call on?'

'Tom.'

'Why?'

'I wanted to make sure he did what I had asked him to do about coming around here.'

'How could you do that with the police listening?'

'I'd been arrested. Tom knew what he had to do.' He pauses, bowing his head. 'Look, Ash. I've fucked up. I'm sorry. I should've told you about all of this.'

Her heart is breaking. The man she has given her life to has betrayed her. 'Is this why Lucy hadn't paid us?'

'I lied to you.'

'What?'

'She was juggling her finances, trying to make her plans with Oriana work. That's why I said she could delay her payment to us.'

'But she's loaded... Was loaded.'

'It caused a short-term cash flow problem for her.'

'And what about us?'

'I agreed it with her before Pickstones went bust.'

Ashley bangs her fist on the floor. 'I should've come first. *We* should've come first.'

'I'm sorry.'

'How come she had two and a half thousand pounds to give to the school playground appeal?'

He looks at her questioningly.

'I've read all your emails, Danny.'

'That's her personal money. Her business accounts are separate.'

'What about the sleeping pills you never told me about?'

He grimaces. 'I was having trouble sleeping again, so I got some more from the GP.'

'Without telling me. Why? I don't understand why you've kept so much from me.'

He raises his voice. 'Because I love you so much. I was trying to protect you from all my worries.'

Ashley stares at him. She wants to hug him, but at the same time she wants to slap him so hard across the face, she'll leave a handprint on his skin. How are they going to overcome this mess?

'I can't believe you didn't tell me. And I still don't understand. Why all the secrecy over the Thyme End Hall estate? You could've shared all this with me.'

'Oriana didn't want Simon and Aaron to get wind of any of it. Simon was moving ahead with his plan to build three hundred houses on the estate when Oriana dies. Who would do such a thing? I told you he was a problem. Lucy was trying to get as far as possible through the process so they were good to go as soon as the sale went through.'

'So what do you take me for? One of the bloody village gossips?!'

They glare at each other. His dark eyes have blackened. He speaks in a monotone. 'It was a bad judgement call. I see that now.'

'And what about Lucy?'

'What about her?'

'Were you and her having an affair?'

'For fuck's sake, Ash.' Danny kicks his heel into the floor. Rolling onto his knees, he gets up, hands on his hips. 'What kind of question is that?'

Ashley stands up too. 'Were you?'

'Hell, no!'

'Lee told me you were.'

This stalls him momentarily. 'When did you speak to Lee?' he asks.

'We met at Brewer's Farm this morning.'

'Ash! You met the man who accused me of murdering his wife. Are you insane?'

'He told me Lucy asked him for a divorce on Sunday. She told him she was in love with someone else.'

He looks genuinely surprised. Or have the past few days forced him to brush up on his acting skills?

'Grace walked in on the argument, and guests started to arrive, so Lee never got to find out who it was.'

'Well, it certainly wasn't me.'

'Why didn't you tell me you and Lucy had a fling when you were younger? That you were the reason she and Tom split up?'

He glares at her. 'How did you find that out?'

'Never mind. Why didn't you tell me?'

He raises his voice. He's close to yelling. 'Because it was in my past. A mistake I made that I deeply regret.'

'And what about the bank overdraft? That was news to me.'

Storming towards the door, he kicks the frame hard. The whole building vibrates. 'It was only temporary until Lucy paid us.' He punches the wall several times and turns to her, a look of the devil alight in his eyes.

Ashley stares at him, aghast. Where is the pleading husband begging for forgiveness from moments earlier? This is not the man she knows – the calm, controlled Danny. But he has been through hell these past few days. His pent-up anger needs to be dispelled somehow.

'Where's Elliot?' he asks.

'At your parents'.'

'What's he doing there?'

'What do you think, Danny? I've been a bit tied up.'

'What? Sitting drinking with your sister?'

She's speechless, her words lost in the shock of his sarcasm. She feels as if she's been shoved out of a plane and doesn't know where her parachute is going to land.

'I'm going to get Elliot.' He leaves The Hub, slamming the door with such force, the whole building shakes again.

Irrepressible rage rushes through her. But it's not from the way he just spoke to her. It's because she can't decipher the branch of truth from his tree of lies. She stands with her head against the glass door. Her breaths are coming thick and fast. Danny is in the dining area of the kitchen, speaking on their landline.

He catches her gaze. Who is he talking to?

Leaving the house, he runs along the path and pulls open the door to The Hub.

'That was the solicitor. They've arrested Lee for Lucy's murder.'

FIFTY-TWO

'Lee!' Ashley says, incredulous. 'What?'

Earlier today, she was drinking coffee with a murderer.

Furthermore, she listened to him try to pin his wife's brutal murder on her husband. She has always been a good judge of character. How could she have got Lee so wrong?

Danny snarls at her. 'That's right. Lee. Her husband is guilty. Not yours. That's what you thought all along, isn't it? Are you happy now?'

The way he looks at her unsettles her. He is hunching over venomously, and his head seems to be dropping into his shoulders. He has been put through the wringer, and now it's showing.

Shame washes through her. All this time, she has tried to push away the nagging doubts about her husband messing with her head. Her husband is innocent. He didn't kill Lucy. How could she have thought that about him? He is devoted to her and Elliot, her rock. What kind of wife is she?

The weight of suspicion and dread she has carried on her shoulders since the party disappears, replaced by an overwhelming rush of love for her husband. The relief is all-consuming. She wants to reach out and hug him, feel his loving arms around her.

'Danny, I'm so sorry.'

But anger follows. He might not be guilty, but he has still kept stuff from her. Lied to her. Deceived her. She starts shouting at him, a rage she didn't know she possessed. 'What was I meant to think? This shroud of mystery, all this deceit. You've pushed me to the absolute limit.'

He doesn't stay to listen. The door slams.

Ashley steps into the garden to get some air. The tyres of Danny's car screech as it roars to life, its engine's angry growl reflecting its driver's wrath. Tears fall down her face. She holds her belly, clutching the life they have made together. Despite him lying to her, she should never have thought him capable of murder.

How do they come back from this?

Shaking her head, she walks into the kitchen and switches on the radio. An Adele song drowns out the voices over Zoom filtering through the floor from the bedroom above. Danny loves Adele. She changes the station.

She leans against the worktop, trying to control her anger. This isn't how it was meant to be. This should be one of the best days of their lives. She is pregnant. Another child is joining their little family. They should be celebrating. But you don't share the same bed with someone for seventeen years without knowing when something is amiss. Things still don't add up, but she doesn't know where to direct the finger of blame. He is still hiding something from her.

She runs the kitchen tap, fills a glass with water and takes one of the folic acid tablets she bought at the pharmacy. Her hands are trembling. This isn't the way to start a pregnancy. She needs to calm down.

Sitting at the kitchen table, she takes deep breaths. Although a new life is growing inside her, there's a sense of emptiness, too. The same she felt when her mother died. Is it grief? Has she lost something?

The voices above stop. The bedroom door opens, and Susie rushes down the stairs. 'I'm sorry, but I couldn't help overhearing the shouting and his car roaring off. What the hell has happened?'

Ashley relays their argument and Lee's arrest.

'That's good news, isn't it? I mean, not good news as such, but at least you have some answers. Where's Danny gone?'

'To pick up Elliot.' Ashley takes a sip of water.

'Did you tell him about the baby?'

Ashley shakes her head.

'Why not? It's the best thing for you two right now.'

'I couldn't bring myself to. I'll tell him when the time is right. Heavens, he's been keeping enough from me. He still is. I know he is. What's so frustrating is that every time I challenge him, he either admits he has lied and has plausible excuses for his lies – to protect me – or there's a perfectly rational explanation. But I can't get out of my head there's more being left unsaid than answered.' Ashley thumps her elbows on the table. 'I'm so confused. And there's something else.'

'Go on.'

'He lost his temper badly in there.' Ashley nods towards The Hub. 'He scared me.'

'You need to keep calm, Ash. For the baby's sake. What did Mum always say to do when you're faced with a dilemma?'

They answer the question in unison. 'Make a list.'

Ashley clenches her teeth. 'I feel like I'm losing my mind.'

Her phone beeps. It's a text from Danny.

I'm sorry we argued. It's been a hell of a few days for me. I'm going to have a shower and have something to eat here and then bring Elliot back. I don't blame you for snooping. Let's talk some more when I get back. I love you so much. Danny X

She can't find it in her to reply.

Susie glances at her watch. 'Listen, I must get going. I need to get back to London before the rush hour starts. I feel bad for leaving you. Are you sure you're going to be OK?'

'You go. I'll be fine.'

'I can come back tomorrow night after work. I just need to be in London for the meeting in the morning, and I need to join a call to the US this evening.'

'Go, Susie.'

'It's probably the right time with Danny now back. You guys need time together as a family.'

'Shh... did you hear that?' Ashley gets up and dashes to the radio. She turns it up loud. They stare at each other, open-mouthed. The police are questioning a forty-year-old property developer from Coventry in connection with the murder of local woman Lucy Ellis.

Grabbing her phone, Ashley pulls up the local news. 'I don't believe it.'

'Believe what?'

Ashley sums up her findings for her sister. 'Get this. This guy from Coventry has been away on holiday, so he definitely didn't kill Lucy, but he has admitted to having an affair with her.'

'Wow! The plot thickens,' Susie says. 'Lee was telling the truth. She was in love with someone else. That answers one of your questions then. Danny and Lucy were not having an affair.'

Ashley should feel relief, but it doesn't come. Instead, the same emptiness and vulnerability persist.

'Talk through everything with him rationally when he comes home. Are you sure you don't want me to stay?'

Ashley fakes a smile. 'Just go. I'll be fine.'

But she's not fine.

She's scared.

Very scared.

FIFTY-THREE

Ashley doesn't know what to do with herself when Susie leaves. Work is calling, her mind a blur of unanswered emails, unfinished mood boards, CGI amendments and deadlines that now can't be met. She tidies the kitchen, although it doesn't need tidying – just a few plates and glasses from lunch that need washing up. She stares out of the window into the garden, the sun casting a radiant glow across the parched grass. Susie has left her cigarettes and lighter there.

The news comes on the radio.

'The police are appealing for the driver of a red car who was seen speeding on Plough Lane leading out of Thyme End on the tenth of June around 6 a.m., where local MP Roberta Splinter lost her life, to come forward. They believe the driver could have information relating to the fatal accident.'

Red car?

The radio summarises the other news headlines before reverting to 80s music. The tenth of June. Ashley drops the tea towel and grabs her phone. Finding Danny's diary, she searches for 10 June.

'Oh, hell.'

Danny left early that morning. He was going to a meeting in Winchester and wanted to beat the morning mayhem on the M25. How early, she doesn't know. She was still asleep, but it was before six o'clock. She remembers waking up, and he had already gone.

A red car. Her blood runs cold.

She grabs her laptop, rapping her knuckles on the worktop while it fires up. A colouring book and pens on the side catch her attention. It's so quiet in the house without Elliot. A sudden desire to have him home overcomes her.

She finds the details of the client. It was Mike Booker. The guy who rudely demanded she send those files on Sunday. She switches to Danny's emails and reads through the correspondence between Mike and Danny. They definitely met that day. Danny sent follow-up notes from their meeting to Mike the next day. Ashley studies the email. Danny opened the exchange, making small talk and apologising again for being late to the meeting. He joked about the state of Britain's overcrowded roads, and the bedlam of traffic around Heathrow. It's a good job his parents didn't miss their flight. The cruise ship wouldn't have waited. Ashley frowns. That was a lie. He never took his parents to the airport that day. Tom had dropped them off at Heathrow the day before.

She scrolls to the BBC website, locating reports about the accident involving Roberta Splinter and an update emulating the news from the radio. She presses play on a video. A reporter is at the scene, standing by the small wooden crosses marking the previous victims of that stretch of road. When it finishes, she presses play again to relisten. And she can't help herself pressing play for a third time.

A loud knock at the door startles her. She's not expecting anyone. Fear seeps through her. Could it be the police again? Gingerly, she goes and answers it, relieved to find Tom standing on the doorstep in his work clothes, a pair of tattered cargo shorts and an over-washed Levi's T-shirt.

'I heard Danny was back. I need to see him.'

Ashley is about to tell him Danny is at his parents', but, on second thought, she opens the door wide. 'Come in.'

His work boots clump along the floor as Tom follows her into the kitchen. 'What a relief he's home.'

She swings around, holding onto the worktop. 'Tom, I need to ask you something.'

He folds his arms across his chest, his whole body language defensive. 'Go ahead.'

'I need you to answer me truthfully. Why is Danny holding twenty grand for you?'

'Sorry?' The lines on his forehead deepen. 'Twenty grand?'

'The twenty thousand pounds Danny is holding for you in his safe.'

'I know nothing about it.' He shrugs. 'It's nothing to do with me.'

Is he telling her the truth? She can't tell.

His eyes avert to Ashley's laptop on the kitchen worktop, still playing the news bulletin. 'What's that?'

'Remember the MP who had that accident a few weeks ago? She drove her car off the road and into that tree.' Danny has always told her to mind what she says to Tom, but she is past caring. 'Apparently, a car was seen driving along the same stretch of road. A red car.' Her voice breaks. 'And Danny was out on the road around that time.'

The colour drains from Tom's face. 'Wh-wh... where's Danny? He... he ... He's been trying to get hold of me.'

'He's gone to pick up Elliot from your parents'.'

He stares from her to the laptop.

'What aren't you telling me, Tom?'

His cheeks puff out, tiny breaths escaping his mouth as if he's trying his utmost to stop words coming out. He releases a large breath. 'It's what Danny and Lucy were arguing about when I saw them in her office. I didn't catch it all, but Lucy said something about him driving too fast, and if he didn't go to the police, then she would. Look, I've got to go.'

'No, Tom. You've got to help me.'

He clamps his hand over his mouth, shaking his head. He looks from the laptop to Ashley. His hand slides down his chin and grabs his neck. 'I... I... I should...' His words stutter with panic. He dashes to the door with Ashley on his tail. 'I need to see Danny.'

She grabs his T-shirt. It rips. The sound tears through the silence. 'Tom. Don't go. He'll be back soon. Stay here.'

He ignores her, his large frame lunging for the front door. He swings it open and runs along the path.

It's as if he is scared of his own brother, of Danny. This heightens her fear. She stands staring as Tom's van rumbles down the road.

Her hand covers her mouth, her eyes wide. She's sure her husband killed at least one person... and maybe another.

She needs to get away from here, too.

FIFTY-FOUR

Running upstairs, Ashley grabs a backpack from the cupboard in her art room. She stares around the room, her room. The one she has kept true to herself with its vivid colours and the assortment of knick-knacks she has collected over the years.

It's never going to be the same.

She dashes to her bedroom and chucks a change of clothes inside the backpack before darting to Elliot's room and doing the same. She pauses at the top of the stairs, her hand clinging to the banister. Maybe she should stay and have it out with Danny – talk about it all rationally with him. But she can't. Her thoughts are all over the place. She needs to get Elliot and herself away for a few days to gather them and find a way forward. They can stay with Susie. The thought of being in London lightens her dark mood. On second thought, Susie's flat will be the first place Danny will look for them. She'll book a hotel somewhere for tonight. She'll leave when he's asleep.

This is what her life has come to. She doesn't know her husband anymore. But she does know something bad has happened... and she has to get away from here.

She needs her laptop. Leaving the bag, she runs downstairs to the kitchen. The folic acid. She needs to pack that as well. She grabs the packet from the cupboard and shoves it in her pocket as the front door opens. 'Mum, we're home. Dad's home. Can we have pizza?'

Pizza. If only life were that simple.

Elliot runs into the kitchen and throws his arms around her. 'Missed you, Mum.'

Danny appears in the doorway. The news report of the appeal for the driver in the red car on her laptop catches his attention. He squints from her to the laptop, his black eyes piercing. She needs to get away.

She bends down to kiss Elliot. 'I've missed you too, darling. So very much.'

Danny peels him away from her. 'Go and find a DVD you'd like to watch.'

'I don't want to watch a DVD,' Elliot protests.

'Now!' Danny barks.

Elliot looks at Ashley. She nods at him. 'Mum and Dad need to talk for a moment, darling. We won't be long.'

Sensing the discord between his parents, Elliot skulks off to the lounge.

Ashley looks from the news report to Danny, who is now staring at her intently. Her heart is beating so fast, she feels sick. 'Tom was here before you got back. He knew nothing about the twenty grand you said was his. So tell me, Danny. Where did it come from?' Ashley points to the laptop. 'Was it bribe money to shut Lucy up?'

'No!' His menacing eyes fix on her, unnerving her even more.

The TV sounds from the lounge. Elliot has found a cartoon to watch. She needs to get him away from here.

'You have to tell me everything, Danny. Otherwise, I'm leaving you.'

'Don't be so melodramatic,' he says, flippantly. 'You aren't leaving me. I can't live without you. And you can't live without me.'

Once upon a time, she would have agreed with that. But she's not so sure anymore.

'Then tell me.'

'The twenty grand isn't Tom's.'

'Then whose is it?'

'It was Lucy's.'

'Another lie you told me.' Ashley glances at the laptop and back at him. 'What were you doing with it?'

He drops his head.

She braces herself. How well has she ever known him, this stranger standing before her?

His voice lowers. 'I was looking after it for her.'

'Why?'

'She didn't want Lee to know about it.'

'And what about the red car?' She nods her head towards the news report paused on her screen. 'Was that your car?'

He doesn't reply. He doesn't need to. The sullen, regretful look on his face confirms that what she has known deep down is the truth.

'For fuck's sake, Danny. What happened?' Ashley asks, stony-faced.

'I was going to meet Mike Booker that day. The new client. You knew about that. Lucy and I were also going to a meeting early that morning in town about Thyme End Hall. It was the first time I'd been at one of their meetings. I was going to drive to Mike Booker's offices afterwards.'

'Lucy was in the car with you.'

He nods.

'Why didn't she drive herself?'

'She had meetings lined up in town afterwards and had arranged a lift back. I don't know. It isn't important.'

He is dancing around issues like a prize fighter. Any ounce of trust she had left for him has now evaporated in the continuous lies.

'I think everything is important, Danny. I need to hear it from you. Did you kill Roberta Splinter?'

FIFTY-FIVE

Danny clenches his jaw, raising a hand in submission. 'I didn't murder her,' he insists. 'It was an accident.' His lips curl downwards in shame.

Her stomach turns. 'What happened?'

He fidgets from one foot to another. 'Lucy and I were arguing. I wasn't concentrating properly.'

'What about?'

Sweat beads along the creases of his forehead. 'It's so bloody complicated, Ash.'

'Then uncomplicate it.'

'She was having an affair and was planning to leave Lee. He was possessive, and she had fallen out of love with him. I was telling her to give her head a shake. She didn't know how good she had it.'

'Who with?'

He closes his eyes, his face pained as if he wants to go back in time to correct the road his life, their lives, have gone down.

'Who with, Danny? Who was Lucy having an affair with?'

He opens his eyes. 'Some property developer from Coventry. I don't know him. That's what the twenty grand was for.

She was going to use it to start a new life. It was to tide her over when she left Lee.'

'What about the kids?'

'She was planning to take them with her.'

'And then what happened?'

'I veered onto the wrong side of the road momentarily.' He laces his fingers and holds his hands behind his head. He sounds as if he is about to cry. 'Roberta came towards us. She swerved off the road and hit the tree.'

'And you kept going?' Ashley is incredulous. This isn't the man she married. That man was kind and gentle, caring and compassionate.

He shakes his head. 'I don't know what came over me. I was scared.'

'You abandoned a person in need? Someone you knew. Someone you could've saved?'

'The car burst into flames. We could never have saved her.'

Ashley is stunned. Such selfishness takes a special kind of evilness. A deep sense of depravity she never knew her husband possessed. 'Why didn't you call the police? Or an ambulance?'

Danny covers his face with his hands, hiding the shame he must be feeling in spades. 'We passed a car. I told Lucy they'd see it and call it in. I think it must've been the people who've come forward.'

'I can't believe what I'm hearing. Lucy was right. You need to go to the police. You can't live with this... neither can I.'

'Ash, steady on. What good would it do admitting to it now? I'd be up for all sorts of charges. Causing death by dangerous driving and failing to stop at the scene of an accident, for a start. They'd lock me straight up. Is that what you want? Think of Elliot.'

'The poor woman could've burned alive for all you know, Danny.' Who is this monster standing in front of her? The tone in his voice has changed, a grating rumble as he makes a pathetic argument for his defence. 'Did you kill Lucy to shut her up because she was going to go to the police?'

His mouth opens wide. 'How can you even think such a thing, Ash?'

Because you did, she wants to say. She feels it in her bones. She stares him out, hating what she is seeing. The colour of his eyes has changed, a threatening evil that unnerves her even more. He is repulsing her.

'Look, you're tired, Ash. We're all tired. We've been working so hard these past few months... years, even... and now all this. Let's take a break. Go away for a while. It was Mum's suggestion. We can stay at their place in Sheringham. They're not going up there for a few weeks. You love the sea air, don't you?'

At any other time, the suggestion would be comforting music to Ashley's ears. Heaven knows she needs a break. But how can he possibly think she'd go with him now? The pieces of the jigsaw are coming together, and the picture is utterly terrifying. There's only one place she should be thinking about going, and that is to the police station.

Every fibre in her being tells her she needs to get herself and Elliot away from there as soon as possible. How can she create an opportunity for escape? Think, Ash, think.

'When?' she asks casually, forcing a hint of enthusiasm into her voice.

'Why not now?' Danny looks at his watch. 'We could be there by seven. Go to the pub for dinner. Walk Rufus along the beach. Have a nightcap in the garden. Do all the things you love doing. We love doing.' His voice has changed again. It is more upbeat. Is that a sliver of hope that he thinks she'll go along with his wishes? Just like she has gone along with his wishes for so long. She was lost when they met. Her mother had just died, her father long gone. Susie was busy getting her career off the ground. She was alone. And along came Danny. A knight in shining armour who scooped her up and promised her the world. She adored him for so long.

But this has all made her see him in a different light. And he isn't shining brightly anymore.

'What about the police? Don't you need to stay around?'

'It's not as if we're going abroad. I can give them the Sheringham address. It'll be fine. Come on, darling. Let's do this for us. For Elliot. In any case, Lee is in custody now. They would've lost interest in me.'

He is deluded.

'I have some deadlines I need to meet. You know that. I'll have to work while I'm there. We can't let business slip,' she says, knowing he'll like hearing those words.

'Leave it.' The tone of his voice changes again, irritated now. It's not her Danny. He'd never say that. What is he planning? Or is she being paranoid?

'I can't do that. *We* can't do that. You need to move your meetings. I've only rearranged tomorrow.'

'I'll go and take care of them. And I'll call the solicitor and tell him my plans. You go and pack.'

Ashley plays her next card. One to stall him. 'Once you've finished with my iMac, can you pack it up for me? I'll need it to work while I'm up there.'

'Take your laptop.' He is sweating profusely now as if he has taken a drug that doesn't agree with him.

'You know that thing's dog slow. Besides, it hasn't got the graphics I need.' That's a lie, but she knows she can get away with it. 'Go and get everything sorted. I'll pack, and we'll get going. And book a table at The Two Lifeboats for seven-thirty.'

With a sharp intake of breath, he says, 'Good idea. I could kill for one of their burgers.'

Her stomach turns at the thought.

He embraces her. Sweat bleeds through his shirt. Her skin

crawls. She can't bear his touch. A fleeting thought washes over her. Is this hormonal? Is she going mad?

He squeezes her shoulders, their noses touching. 'We'll get through this, darling. I love you so much.'

No, it's not hormonal. And she's not crazy.

Her husband was responsible for Roberta Splinter's accident. And he left her for dead. He repulses her. Instinct is telling her to get away from him.

Ashley rushes to the kitchen window, watching as he saunters along the path to The Hub with Rufus. Her heart is pounding. She needs to be quick. When he turns on her computer and sits down, she sparks into action.

Taking the stairs two at a time, she grabs the backpack. As she sprints back down, she stumbles into the wall at the bottom, hurting her arm. No time to stop. Dashing into the kitchen, she grabs her laptop and slides it into the backpack. She takes a quick peek at The Hub. Danny is staring closely at the computer screen, Rufus, their trusting companion, by his feet.

Rufus.

She stalls. She doesn't want to leave her beautiful dog. But she has to. Danny would never do anything to harm Rufus. She'll have to come back for him.

Rushing into the lounge, she speaks to her son as calmly as her anxiety allows. 'You need to come with me, darling.'

'I'm watching TV,' Elliot objects.

'Sometimes, you just need to do what Mum says.' She picks up the remote and goes to switch the TV off. On second thought, she leaves it on. She grabs Elliot's arm and pulls him off the sofa. 'Go and get in the car, please. Straight away.'

He looks at her backpack. 'What about Dad?'

'He's working. Come on, we're going on an adventure.'

'But, Mum.'

'Now!'

Elliot remains quiet as she hurries him to the car.

'There's a good boy.' She throws her backpack next to him.

'Where are we going? I've just got home. I don't want to go out.'

Ashley buckles him in before climbing into the driver's seat.

'Have you got Champ?' he calls from the back seat.

She knew she'd forgotten something. 'We haven't got time.'

'I want Champ.' He crosses his arms defiantly. 'I won't go.'

Ashley momentarily places her hands and forehead on the steering wheel, the cold sensation briefly grounding her. Danny killed Roberta Splinter. He didn't stop to help her. But Elliot won't settle without Champ. She'll never get him to sleep tonight and she's utterly exhausted.

Taking a deep breath, she gets out of the car, the weight of dread heavy in her chest. She sprints back to the house. Breathless, she fumbles with the door, her heart pounding painfully. It can't be good for the baby. She dashes up the stairs once more, but Champ isn't in his usual spot on Elliot's bed. Panic rises as she whirls around, the room balefully silent, before realising he took Champ when he went to Tom's house. He must've come home with him and be in the lounge where Elliot was watching TV.

Halfway down the stairs, she stops suddenly, locking eyes with Danny. His expression oozes contempt, a chilling threat in his gaze.

'What do you think you're doing?'

FIFTY-SIX

Ashley descends the stairs, guarded. Her husband is standing between her, Elliot and her getaway. 'Danny, I love you, but I think we should spend a few days apart. Give you some space to get things sorted.'

His eyes are as dark as her heart, having learned how much he has lied to her.

'You're leaving me. Taking Elliot.' His voice is deep, flat and low, like Rufus' growls when the postman approaches the house.

'No. It's not like that.' Ashley continues down the stairs towards the stranger she has spent nearly half her life with.

She tries to pass him, but he blocks her escape, grabbing her shoulders.

'Then how is it, Ashley?'

'You're hurting me. Let me go.'

He draws her towards him, her arms locked by her side, until their foreheads touch. Her heartbeat thrums in her ears.

'Don't even think about leaving me.' Spittle from his mouth hits her face.

He thrusts her forward. She stumbles into the banister.

Crumbling onto the stairs, she cowers. Her hands guard her head, expecting a rain of punches to fall. But nothing. She looks up. Danny has gone. The door opens and slams shut.

Elliot!

She runs out of the house. Danny is climbing into the driver's seat of her car. She runs to him. He sits bolt upright, his hands on the steering wheel, staring ahead. Elliot is directly behind him, his eyes fixed on Ashley.

Ashley runs to Elliot's door and tries to open it. The child lock is on. 'Danny, open the door.' She bangs on the driver's window. 'Please. Open the door.'

Danny lowers the window a few inches. 'Get in.'

Elliot looks pleadingly at her. 'Mum, I'm scared. Dad is acting weird.'

'Danny, open the door. Can't you see you're upsetting Elliot?'

'Get the fuck in the car. Now!'

She has no option. Circling around to the passenger door, she gets in. That maniac can't drive off with their son.

'Where's Champ?' Elliot asks.

'Forget Champ.' Ashley doesn't mean to sound harsh, but her words are a little too forceful. She places her hand on Danny's arm. It's cold and clammy, even though the weather is sweltering. 'Danny, turn off the engine. Let's discuss this.'

He revs the engine alarmingly loud, cowering over the steering wheel. Engaging the clutch, he slams his foot on the pedal and accelerates away. She pushes her hands onto the dashboard to steady herself. The wheels spin. Elliot starts crying. She tugs the seat belt and pulls it across her body. Turning to their son, she tells him everything will be OK. She looks around the close. Where are all the nosy buggers when you need them?

Danny pulls onto the country lane without looking.

'What the hell are you playing at?' A passing car could easily have taken them out. 'You're going to get us killed.'

But he isn't listening. It's as if he's in a different world. He hurtles down the road, his knuckles white with the force with which he is holding the steering wheel, his elbows splayed.

'Danny, you're driving too fast.'

He turns to her. 'That's what Lucy said.' An insipid smile appears on his face.

'Where are you taking us?'

His eyes fix on the road, his mouth silent.

'Please, Danny. You're scaring Elliot. And me. Stop the car and let us both out.'

Danny rambles, barely coherent. 'I hate being late,' he says. 'You know that. I said I'd pick you up at quarter to six, and you were late. Always late. It's your fault it happened. I wouldn't have been driving so fast if you'd been on time. And we wouldn't have been on that stretch of road at that time. And you come to me with all your marital problems.'

'Mum, what is Dad talking about?'

'Always the same. Late for everything. Ever since we were kids. Now look at what you've done.'

Ashley's heart is beating double time. Danny appears to be having some kind of breakdown, replaying his conversation with Lucy after the accident with Roberta Splinter.

'Danny, you're scaring us.'

He seems oblivious to her words.

Ashley reaches for her phone in her back pocket. He slaps her hand out of the way.

'I don't like this,' Elliot wails. 'I want to go home.'

Ashley contemplates opening the car door as they pass through Thyme End, but the baby won't survive the fall, and what would happen to Elliot with that monster behind the wheel? She looks around for someone to attract their attention. Anyone. Someone needs to save them. A young guy is walking his dog across the green, but he has his head down, nodding to the beat of whatever music is playing through his earphones.

Danny laughs, an evil cackle. 'I'm done for. It's over. I know you, Ash.' He appears to have returned to the present momentarily. Steering onto the road, he turns out of Thyme End. 'You won't let this rest, will you?'

As they approach Thyme End Hall, he slows the car, passing through the open blue gates. He veers off the main drive and down a narrow track bisecting dense woodland.

Ashley checks on Elliot. He is looking on, wide-eyed, his usual rosy cheeks ghostly pale.

The track stops abruptly. The car skids to a stop a few metres from a derelict, single-storey stone building with a tiled roof tucked away among the trees.

'Out,' Danny shouts, making it clear he is not making a request.

'Hang on, Danny. Let's talk about this.'

His eyes are bulging out of his head. 'Get out of the car now!' He scrambles out and opens the passenger door. Unbuckling Elliot, he roughly drags their son out of his seat. Elliot lands on his feet, but his legs give way. Danny yanks his arm and pulls him upright.

Quickly skirting around the bonnet, Ashley grabs Elliot.

'You get off him.' She shoves Danny away, but he is too quick for her, too strong.

He grabs her forearm and pushes the pair along the dirt track towards the building, the smell of dampness and decay overwhelming. Every instinct tells her to run, but she can't leave Elliot. Besides, there's no way she could outrun Danny. The shadows from the branches seem to claw at them as he herds them closer to the building. She contemplates screaming for help. But who is going to hear her out there? It's worth a try.

'Help. Somebody...'

'Help!' Elliot echoes her cries.

But Danny quickly silences them with vicious kicks to their shins. He growls like the devil himself. 'Shut the fuck up.'

He shoves them forward until they reach the hut, every thrust in the back a reminder of the grave danger they are in. Why didn't she take note of the way he had changed recently? Since they moved to Thyme End, but more so the last few weeks since Roberta Splinter's death.

The front door of the building hangs off its hinges. Danny kicks it aside. 'Get in.'

FIFTY-SEVEN

'No,' Ashley protests, trying to free her arm, knowing her efforts are in vain. 'We won't.'

Danny glares at her with venom. 'I said, get in.'

She considers fighting back again, but there's a baby growing inside her. She can't chance it.

The building is some kind of old gamekeeper's hut, its interior worse than the exterior. Ashley peers around. A small old table with three chairs occupies the centre of the room. On top of it sit books, boxed board games and old candles dripping with wax. From the age of them, they should be covered in dust, but they're not. It's as if the whole table and its contents have been cleaned. Is this where Danny and Lucy used to come with Simon when they were kids?

A broken window allows in shards of light, offering precious little illumination, other than to cast a menacing glow over Danny's face. He points to the corner of the room. 'Sit over there,' he orders Elliot.

Elliot obeys his father's instructions. Curling up into a ball on the floor, he clenches his knees to his chest as if his life depends on it. Ashley follows him, but Danny restrains her.

His mood turns delirious, psychotic almost, switching in an instant.

'What're you planning, Danny?' Ashley asks, attempting to draw him back to the present.

'If you hadn't been late, it wouldn't have happened. Can't you see it was all your fault? All the years when we were kids, I just followed. Because I loved you. I put up with all your little idiosyncrasies. Waiting, always waiting, for you to understand what I felt.'

'Danny, you need help. This has all got out of hand. Please let me call someone to help you.'

'And now you have the audacity to tell me to go to the police. Really? You can't live with yourself, nor should I be able to.' His breaths are laboured. From fear, or anticipation, Ashley can't work it out. 'Don't you understand? The police will throw the book at me. I'd go down for years. I can't do that to Ashley, or my son. We might as well all be dead. Ashley?' He looks as if she has suddenly appeared. 'What have I done?'

'What happened, Danny?'

Elliot sobs. Ashley mouths at him, telling him it's going to be OK.

Danny's words spill quickly, unhinged, his gesticulating arms flailing uncontrollably. 'I lost my temper. I grabbed the nearest thing to me, and I swung. All the blood, so much blood.' Tears flow down his face.

He murdered Lucy.

Her husband murdered his childhood friend.

Until this point, she has been hanging onto the thread of hope that she was wrong, bolstered by the hammer and Lee's arrest. But now she knows he did it, and she is terrified beyond words.

She needs to placate him, persuade him to let Elliot and her go. 'I understand, darling. And so will the police. You must speak to them, tell them what happened. We can get you help. I'll make sure of it.'

Danny glances from side to side, seemingly unsure of his surroundings, as if looking for something. He makes for a small bureau near the door, hurriedly opening each rickety drawer. Ramming each one closed, he swears profusely. He stumbles over to the window. Its frayed curtains hang listlessly. Reaching behind one of the drapes, he grabs a bundle of thick rope.

Ashley looks on in horror. Surely he's not going to tie them up. Who is this madman? She panics.

He holds the rope in his hands, staring at it intensely. A calmness seems to descend upon him. He nods his head vigorously, and his shoulders slump as if he has decided his next course of action.

He grabs Ashley by the upper arm. His strength has her rushing across the small room. Forcibly, he pushes her down on the cold, quarry-tiled floor beside a heavy, old-fashioned radiator on the far wall.

'Danny, please. Let's talk about this rationally. You don't want to do this.'

He isn't listening. He has returned to his trance-like state. Binding her hands together, he ties them to the radiator, her protests met with a sharp slap across the cheek. She winces with the pain. He turns to Elliot whimpering in the corner.

'Daddy, please don't,' he cries as Danny drags him to the opposite side of the room to a vacant cast-iron pipe forming part of the dated heating system.

'Danny, you can't do this. Elliot is just a child. Let him go.'

Her monster of a husband ties their son to the pipe and stands back, checking his handiwork, before, suddenly, inexplicably, he purposefully strides out of the building.

Abject terror widens Elliot's eyes. 'What is Dad going to do?' he whispers, as if he fears Danny is listening from outside.

How do you reply to such a question from a petrified child

when you have no answer? 'Dad isn't feeling very well, darling. Let him calm down, and he'll be back.' She considers screaming for help again now that Danny isn't here. But they are tucked away in the depths of the estate. No one will hear. And it will only fuel the fire of Elliot's fear even more.

'I hate Thyme End. I want to go back to our old house.' He is sobbing now, as if he has been bottling up nine months of misery, and the shock has released all his pent-up feelings at once. 'I wished we'd never moved here.'

Her heart aches that she can't reach out to comfort him. The musty scent of old earth and stone, a cave-like smell, catches in her throat. 'Let's talk about nice things.' The rope is biting into her wrists, preventing her from getting to their son and giving him the hug he so badly needs. She needs. Has she been so ignorant, so selfish? She should've seen that Elliot was unhappy, miserable, in fact. And her husband, why didn't she see this before – the gradual decline that has culminated in a total breakdown, and the murder of his childhood friend. Where were the signs? Were they in plain sight, and she chose to ignore them?

She looks to the ceiling, praying for help. Cobwebs hang above her, traipsing along the ceiling. She needs to find a way out of this mess.

'I want Champ. I'm scared.'

'We'll be OK, darling. I'm here. How about a story?' She feels as helpless as a kitten stuck up a tree.

'No. I want to go home,' he sobs.

She makes up a story. A calming one about a boy and his dog. They go on an adventure. A pleasant one in a fictitious world where there is no bad. It passes the time. She feels as if they've been trapped all night. She looks towards the window. Dusk is drawing in. Darkness will soon be upon them. Surely Danny won't leave them there all night. She struggles at the rope again. But he has done too good a job. The more she struggles, the more the rope tightens, biting into her skin.

Where has he gone? He didn't take the car. She would have heard the engine start. So he couldn't have gone far. 'What are you up to, Danny?' she whispers to herself. She focuses on the baby, silently vowing to direct her profound moments of fear to find a way out of there. She can't let Danny's insanity define their fate. She won't.

FIFTY-EIGHT

'Mum. I heard something outside.'

'Is someone there? We need help,' Ashley screams. 'Danny, is that you?'

Nothing.

It must've been an animal or Elliot's imagination. But no, footsteps pass outside. They are close by. They stop.

'Help,' she screams. 'Please help us.'

There's a slushing sound as liquid liberally douses the ground. Her heart contracts as she recognises the sweet smell of benzene. Fear engulfs her.

They're going to die.

Calm, Ashley. You've got to remain calm.

'Danny. Come inside and talk to me. Please, darling, come and talk to me.' It pains her to speak so nicely to him. But she's at a significant disadvantage here. Her desperate voice appeals for any mercy he has left inside of his tormented mind.

Danny's broad figure fills the entrance of the doorway, standing silent. A metal, flat-based container dangles from his hand. How she has loved that body, that man, for so many years.

'Danny. Please. Think about what you're doing.'

He sploshes petrol over the quarry tiles. The cloying smell is overwhelming, thick and sickeningly sweet. Ashley gags. He slings the empty can across the room.

'You're not thinking straight. What if I told you that you'd be killing four people.'

He stops and approaches her. The last of the daylight allows her to see him look at her inquisitively. His face is close to hers. Too close. His head is bending from side to side, as if he can't process his thoughts.

Ashley drops her head to her stomach and looks back at him. 'I'm pregnant, Danny. You're going to be a father again. Elliot is going to have a little sister or brother. You can't ruin what we've wanted for so long.'

'Mummy, is that true?'

'It is, my darling. You're going to be a big brother. I only found out this morning.'

Danny snorts as he turns and walks across to the table. Lifting a book into the air, he shakes his head. Ashley can't begin to fathom the thoughts going through his mind. He drops the book from a height and pulls out one of the wooden chairs.

'All that blood, so much blood.' He repeats the sentence over and over before producing Susie's silver lighter from his jeans pocket.

Ashley's voice trembles. 'We're going to have another baby, Danny. Listen to me.'

He taps the lighter on the edge of the table.

'We're going to be a family of four.'

He glares at Ashley's stomach.

Panic changes her tack. 'You won't get away with this, Danny. You do realise that.'

Elliot dips his head. Her heart burns for him.

Danny speaks dispassionately. 'I have no intention of getting away with anything. Life is over. For all of us.'

He takes a moment before standing and exiting the hut.

Could there be a reprieve?

She tugs at the ropes. Her wrists, raw and swollen against the coarse fibre, throb. Keep calm. If they're going to get out of here alive, she has to keep it together. She lowers her head to her hands, biting into the rope like an apple. The acrid taste of the cord makes her retch, but she perseveres, biting at any strand she can.

As each second passes, hope fades. Desperation kicks in. Her breaths come in spasms as she twists her wrists. It's no good. It's not going to happen. She tries again. Another gnaw at the rope as she continuously sinks her teeth into it until the faint smell of smoke hits her nostrils.

Danny re-enters the hut. She screams at him. He sits on the floor crossed-legged as if he is about to start a yoga class, not deliver his family to a horrific end. He rocks back and forth.

'Danny, no, come on. Please. Don't do this to us. Let us go. Or Elliot. Let him go. He's just an innocent child.'

But he is not listening. He appears in a trance, as if he is physically there but his mind is thousands of miles away.

Elliot coughs. 'Mummy.'

Danny remains sitting upright, ignoring his surroundings. He stares intently at Ashley.

The smoke intensifies, wafting into the room. Its pungent, acrid smell claws at her throat.

'You bastard!' Ashley screams at the man who no longer resembles the person she married.

She coughs. How could this happen? You think you know someone, and bam, a monster appears out of left field. Dust mixes with dense smoke in the air. Her eyes stream, blurring her vision. Uncontrollable coughing takes hold.

'I'm scared,' Elliot whimpers.

'Darling,' she coughs, 'Mummy's here.' What more can she say?

Wait, is that a figure she can see through the smoky darkness?

Is someone else in the room?

Or is she imagining it?

No. A body moves towards Elliot. She blinks, trying to clear the tears from her eyes. Someone bends over him.

Where's Danny?

She can't see him. She blinks again. Nausea overcomes her. She retches, but nothing comes up. She is fading into unconsciousness. Keep awake, Ashley. You must keep awake.

The figure has disappeared. She slumps forward, succumbing to her fate. Pain tears through her wrists, reviving her numb hands as someone pulls at them.

'Help me.' Her voice is a faded croak.

It's a man. She can tell by the size of his hands encasing hers. Elliot screams her name. Her hands release. She topples over. Her shoulder rams into the floor with a thud. She is losing consciousness.

Strong arms unceremoniously lift her up. They definitely belong to a man, she can tell. He throws her over a shoulder like a fireman. She never heard any sirens. What's that smell? It's faint, but she knows it so well. The intoxicating blend of smoky sandalwood. He marches her towards the door.

She tries to protest, hitting his back. She can't leave Elliot. Their son screams her name again, but it's faint, in the distance. He's no longer in the hut. They're outside now. The air is clearer, but the smell of smoke still threatens. The man walks her a short distance before gently lowering her to the floor next to Elliot. They cling to each other, him crying, her stunned to silence.

A third person joins their embrace. Then she hears that oh-so-familiar, calm and collected voice: 'I'm so, so, sorry.'

Her husband. He's back. For a moment, she relishes them as

a four, but only for a split second. She knows it's all over for them.

The evening is still warm, but they're all shivering. Flames rise up the sides of the hut. The fire catches hold of the roof, sending a sheen of orange billowing flames mixed with smoke into the air.

Danny, weeping like a baby, rises from his crouched position, looking down on Elliot wrapped in Ashley's arms. 'I love you. Both of you. All three of you.' He turns and walks purposely towards the hut.

'Danny, NO!' Ashley turns Elliot's head into her chest as her husband enters the burning building. She wishes she could run after him. But she's not letting go of her son ever again.

Yet she can't take her eye off the flames as they climb higher, hoping that, despite everything he's put them through, she will see him. Hoping to watch the man she had fallen for walk towards them, to hold all three of them again. Even though she isn't sure how much of that man is left.

When the roof collapses, the fire leaps up, as if in triumph. It's only then, the broken hut engulfed, that Ashley can look away.

THREE MONTHS LATER

Ashley watches through the lounge window as a bald-headed man climbs out of his van. Opening the double doors at the rear, he retrieves a Sold sign, which he carries to the edge of her front garden, and exchanges it for the existing For Sale sign.

She removes her hands from the pockets of her denim dungarees and returns to the mound of cardboard boxes in the middle of the room, the last of her Thyme End life ready to take to the charity shops in town. Apart from some personal belongings and everything in her art room, and Elliot's belongings he has chosen to take, she doesn't want any of it. As she builds the business, she can slowly replace what she really needs. What's important. Her priority now is their son and the baby growing inside of her.

'You can stay with me as long as you like, you know. I'm not going to chuck you out when my three months in Frankfurt is up,' Susie says, slipping a hoodie over her head.

The summer sun has given way to a cool breeze. Autumn seems to have arrived overnight.

Ashley picks up a flat-packed box and assembles it ready for the tape dispenser. 'I know. That's very much appreciated, but I need to start thinking about my future.'

'Isn't it a bit soon? You don't want to be rushing anything. Baby steps.' She laughs. 'Excuse the pun.'

'Not at all.' Ashley can't wait to be rid of the hand she has been dealt. The bad cards she never wanted to play. 'As of yesterday, I have a new business. Ashley D Designs.'

'You've changed the name.'

'Blue Banana Studios is officially no more,' Ashley says. 'It's a more traditional name, but I prefer it. I never really liked Blue Banana Studios. Another case of Danny's insistence and me going along with it, thinking he knew best. It was a pretty simple process, all online.'

'Yay, sis! Good on you.'

'You've just got to get on with life. That's what Lee said, too. Your kids see you through the darkest of days.'

'There was me, all worried about leaving you for two weeks, and you've just got on with it.'

'It's early days. I've bought the domain name, and I'll get cracking on changing the website tomorrow. I've designed a few new logos.' Ashley removes her phone from her pocket. She finds the four new logo designs she has worked on the past few evenings and shares the screen with her sister. 'Tell me which one you like the best.' She scrolls through the images.

Susie examines them a second time before saying, 'Number three.'

'That was Lee's first choice as well.' Ashley takes the phone back, studying the third image. 'He said the purple and gold look striking.'

'You seem to be getting close to him?'

'I guess so. We've both been to hell and back. Exposed to our own horror shows. I guess we can relate to each other's inner turmoil. It helps to have a friend who understands.'

Lee was a mess after he got arrested and then learned about Danny's involvement in Lucy's death, but he's slowly coming to terms with the direction his life has taken.

Susie grabs the tape dispenser and seals the box Ashley has assembled. 'How was Oriana's funeral?'

'Sad. I'll miss her.'

'It's cool she's left such a legacy.'

'If plans come together, the hospice is due to open next autumn. Tom told me at the church yesterday.'

'How's he doing?'

Ashley raises her eyebrow. 'I'm surprised you ask.'

Susie shrugs. 'I guess I feel sorry for him. It's such a sad way to lose your brother.'

'He's doing OK. Slowly getting his head around what has happened.'

Susie helps Ashley stack Elliot's DVDs into the box. 'And how's my favourite nephew?'

'I don't know. The nightmares continue. But the therapist says they should diminish with time. I think that'll start to happen now we're finally moving out of this place. He's better than he was when it all happened, that's for sure.'

'It's all change.'

Ashley takes a deep breath and slowly releases it. 'It sure is.'

'And how are you doing, really?'

Ashley shrugs. 'I'm still coming to terms with it all, if I'm honest. Now I look back, the signs were there all along. Ever since we met, Danny tried to control me. I let him because it was subtle, and I loved him so much. And I didn't know any better.'

She tells her sister how she's continuing to ride the roller coaster of grief. The turbulence lives with her constantly. Some days she's up. Some days she's down. She's getting through it by keeping herself busy.

And there's a light, shining through Elliot and the joy and expectation of a new life. 'My guilty husband, all along, hey, who would've thought?'

Susie shakes her head. 'Mum was right, you know. Do you ever truly know anyone?'

A LETTER FROM AJ CAMPBELL

Dear reader,

I want to say a huge thank you for choosing to read *My Perfect Marriage*. I loved writing Ashley's story. If you enjoyed it and want to keep up-to-date with my latest releases, just sign up at the link below. Your email address will never be shared, and you can unsubscribe anytime.

www.bookouture.com/AJ-Campbell

As for all authors, reviews are the key to raising awareness of my work. If you have enjoyed this book, I would be very grateful if you could leave a short review on Amazon and Goodreads. I'd love to hear what you think, and it makes such a difference in helping new readers discover one of my books for the first time.

The question I most often get asked as an author is where I get the ideas for my books from. *My Perfect Marriage* began when I read an article concerning the overdevelopment thrust on village and small-town communities that remains a constant threat in the UK. In the village where I live, several planning applications have been successfully challenged over the past decade, but not without much discord. Villagers are passionate about preserving village life, and I've often asked myself how far people would go and to what end to stop these developments...

or, indeed, to ensure they go ahead. From there, I started plotting!

All my novels undergo a rigorous editing process, but sometimes mistakes happen. If you have spotted an error, please contact me so I can promptly correct it.

I love hearing from my readers – you can get in touch via social media or my website.

Best wishes,

Amanda X

www.ajcampbellauthor.com

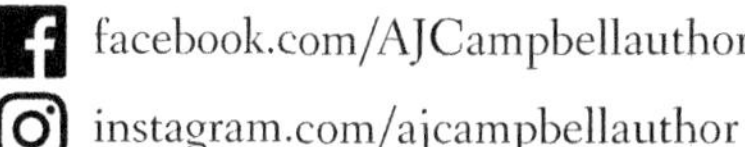
facebook.com/AJCampbellauthor
instagram.com/ajcampbellauthor

ACKNOWLEDGEMENTS

After self-publishing my first six books, I am thrilled to be part of the Bookouture team for the publication of *My Perfect Marriage*, my seventh novel.

Thank you to my brilliant editor, Natalie Edwards, for helping me to develop this story into the book it has become. It's been such a pleasure to work with you and gain your ideas and advice, which has helped me grow as a writer. Thank you to Lauren Finger and Jade Craddock, who did a cracking job with the copy editing. And thanks to the support team who help with all the other essential tasks that get books into the hands of readers.

To my shrewd beta readers – Mr C, Dawn H, Christine H, Maddie S, John B, Collie L and my sister Sally – thank you for helping me turn *My Perfect Marriage* into the finished version. The story is so much better because of your excellent observations. I'm blessed to have you.

To all the book bloggers who champion my work. Many of you have been by my side since I published my debut novel. Thank you for believing in me and continuing this crazy, thrilling ride. Your endless support means the world to me.

To my readers, thank you a million for choosing my books. Without you, I couldn't carry on writing. Your reviews, emails and comments on my social media pages keep me company and always make my day.

Thank you to my author buddy, AJ McDine. It's been exciting to share this new publishing experience with you and chat about plots and external deadlines new to us both. And Christine Henderson, thank you for everything you do for me.

Thank you to my boys, my world, for just being you. And last but always first, Mr C, thank you for all the endless cups of tea and tasty meals. Why did we wait so long to realise that you are a much better cook than me? Thanks a million for your ongoing encouragement while I write my books. And for making me kick the imposter syndrome on the days it shows up!

PUBLISHING TEAM

Turning a manuscript into a book requires the efforts of many people. The publishing team at Bookouture would like to acknowledge everyone who contributed to this publication.

Audio
Alba Proko
Sinead O'Connor
Melissa Tran

Commercial
Lauren Morrissette
Jil Thielen
Imogen Allport

Data and analysis
Mark Alder
Mohamed Bussuri

Editorial
Natalie Edwards
Sinead O'Connor

Copyeditor
Jade Craddock

Proofreader
Becca Allen

Marketing
Alex Crow
Melanie Price
Occy Carr
Cíara Rosney

Operations and distribution
Marina Valles
Stephanie Straub

Production
Hannah Snetsinger
Mandy Kullar
Jen Shannon

Publicity
Kim Nash
Noelle Holten
Myrto Kalavrezou
Jess Readett
Sarah Hardy

Rights and contracts
Peta Nightingale
Richard King
Saidah Graham